"You

The ra

Er. I blinked up at him, confused. What about threats, rantings, that kind of thing? I mean, really . . .

"She dies, you die."

We all looked to see Wan standing on the seat of the car, backlit by the dome light of the minivan. Wisps of fog were gathered around his feet. He had his sword out and pointed at the ninjas. "Move away from her if you value your lives."

It would have been very impressive had he been more than a few inches tall.

The rats chuckled, and even I smiled. Wan looked so earnest, standing there with his sword in his hand.

"She dies," the possum laughed. "And then we beat the information out of you, traitor."

Okay, not so funny now.

I leaped up, dodged one of the rats and hit the possum right on the snoot. Impressed?

The only problem is it didn't happen that way. My middle-aged fat body wouldn't leap up for nothing. So I did the best I could. I kicked one of the rats right on the shins. Smartly.

He dropped the knife and clutched his leg. Some ninja.

All eyes were focused back on me. "Kill her," the possum snarled.

—From "Ninja Rats on Harleys"
by Elizabeth A. Vaughn

ZOMBIE RACCOONS & KILLER BUNNIES

EDITED BY
MARTIN H. GREENBERG
AND KERRIE HUGHES

DAW BOOKS, INC.
DONALD A. WOLLHEIM, FOUNDER
375 Hudson Street, New York, NY 10014

ELIZABETH R. WOLLHEIM
SHEILA E. GILBERT
PUBLISHERS
http://www.dawbooks.com

First Printing, October 2009

1   2   3   4   5   6   7   8   9

DAW TRADEMARK REGISTERED
U.S. PAT. AND TM. OFF. AND FOREIGN COUNTRIES
—MARCA REGISTRADA
HECHO EN U.S.A.

PRINTED IN THE U.S.A.

ACKNOWLEDGMENTS

CONTENTS

Introduction
Kerrie Hughes   1

Death Mask
Jody Lynn Nye   4

BunRabs
Donald J. Bingle   29

for lizzie
Anton Strout   42

Faith in Our Fathers
Alexander B. Potter   59

Bone Whispers
Tim Waggoner   88

Watching
Carrie Vaughn   108

The Things That Crawl
Richard Lee Byers   119

The White Bull of Tara
  Fiona Patton   147

Dead Poets
  John A. Pitts   168

Super Squirrel to the Rescue
  P.R. Frost   179

Her Black Mood
  Brenda Cooper   195

Ninja Rats on Harleys
  Elizabeth A. Vaughan   216

Bats in Thebayou
  Steven H Silver   239

Twilight Animals
  Nina Kiriki Hoffman   260

The Ridges
  Larry D. Sweazy   276

About the Editors   307

INTRODUCTION

I used to live in Kansas, where blue laws at drive-in movies kept scenes of horror or sex from being shown on the outdoor screen. Instead, the moviegoers would hear the action but not see it, while children in neighboring houses could not see or hear anything that might warp their little minds. I know because I was one of those nearby children desperately trying to see the movies from my bedroom window a few blocks away.

Finally, at age 15, I was old enough to go to an R-rated, cut-apart horror film and saw a classic called *Dawn of the Dead*. Too much was removed for me to see the gory details, but the sounds of zombies munching on their screaming victims made me retch. I had to go home. I wasn't that scared when I saw *Jaws* in the theater, although I'm still not going to swim in the ocean. Or lakes for that matter—have you seen what happens to camp counselors? But I digress.

I'm still more terrified of zombies than I am of vampires, werewolves, and demons. I'm not scared of witches and ghosts because I know quite a few witches and have met at least two ghosts. Quite frankly, I am more afraid of psychopaths and corporate suits.

At any rate, for the last dozen years or so I've been making a very bad joke about zombie raccoons and killer bunnies being the cause of every unknown noise in the dark and my trash being knocked over and strewn around. It's probably neighborhood cats and dogs, but I'm not going outside to find out. I also must admit that the killer bunny thing is a Monty Python affectation, and I recently went to see *Spamalot* hoping to see some good old fashioned killer rabbit carnage. The show was good, but the bunny did not get nearly the stage time it deserved.

When soliciting authors for this anthology, I found that most of my invitees were quite fond of raccoons and would feed them on a regular basis. Jody Lynn Nye actually lets them eat inside her house. When I lived in a second-story apartment, a mother raccoon and her babies would climb up nightly to get a free dinner while my cat hissed and yowled from behind the safety of the patio door. My son and my cat made it very clear that wild animals should not be fed by humans, as it makes the population too large for the environment. I say better to feed the raccoons than be fed on by them!

As to the stories in this anthology . . .

I'd like to point out that Beth Vaughn has given me a story that is the second part of one that appears originally in *Furry Fantastic*. I'm hoping she will turn it into a book soon. Brenda Cooper has a story set in the same world as her stories in *Maiden Matron Crone, Children of Magic, Fellowship Fantastic,* and *The Dimension Next Door.* Alexander Potter also has a reoccurring character that appears in the same four anthologies. Clearly I am a fan of these folks.

The resulting anthology is an interesting mix of fairy tale, horror, and humor, and I would like to thank each and every author for their contributions and DAW for creating the opportunity for all of us to create these stories.

So sit back and enjoy the critters, but for the love of cats, don't go outside at night when you hear your trash cans fall over—it might just be those zombie raccoons!

Kerrie Hughes

DEATH MASK

By Jody Lynn Nye

Jody Lynn Nye lists her main career activity as "spoiling cats." She lives northwest of Chicago with two of the above and her husband, author and packager Bill Fawcett. She has published more than thirty-five books, including six contemporary fantasies, four SF novels, four novels in collaboration with Anne McCaffrey, including *The Ship Who Won*; edited a humorous anthology about mothers, *Don't Forget Your Spacesuit, Dear!*; and written over a hundred short stories. Her latest books are *An Unexpected Apprentice*, and *Myth-Chief*, cowritten with Robert Asprin. And, yes, she does believe in magic.

Uneasily, Ide Pilkington eyed the hollow end of the shotgun. Granny Morrow sighted along it, finger on the trigger, in no kind of hurry. He was a big, hefty, balding man, probably outweighed her two to one, but he couldn't outrun buckshot. He glanced guiltily at the injured raccoon on the ground between them, then up

at the one sharp blue eye regarding him over the gun
barrel. She had the one yellow light on the porch behind her and the light from the full moon overhead to
aim by.

"Now, you just move off my land as fast as your
miserable bandy legs can take you," Granny said, her
voice low with menace. "And don't you come back. If
I find out you've been botherin' one of my animals
again, you will wish that your parents had never met.
Git!"

Pilkington held up his hands in protest. "Now, just a
minute, Granny. I have a right to go after those varmints
been eating my tomatoes, and you know it!"

One bony thumb cocked back the trigger. Pilkington
backed up a few paces. He glanced toward the forest
just beyond the rail fence. He swore he could see glowing eyes. He bet the miserable furballs were laughing at
him. He put up his chin, hoping to stand his ground and
regain some of his dignity. Granny didn't raise her head
from the stock.

"They ain't varmints; they're my animals. Hurtin' one
of 'em hurts me just as bad as if I was the victim. You
been throwin' stones at 'em, and today you set a spiteful
trap. It was too much punishment for a coupla tomatoes,
and you know it. I told you, git. I'll give you to five, then
I'll pepper whatever part's facin' me with birdshot. Your
choice. One."

"Granny!"

"Two."

Pilkington didn't wait for three. It took him all the
way to five to get to the edge of the clearing that surrounded Granny's white painted farmhouse. The woman
was eighty-three if she was an hour old, but she was still
the best shot in the county. Even her sons didn't have

the aim she did. If she could pick it up, she could fire it. He raced across the sparse lawn and plunged into the bushes just as a shot rang out behind him. Twigs and bits of bark rained down on him. He sputtered and batted at his face, but he kept his thick legs threshing.

He emerged onto the gravel road that separated their properties and brushed off his shirt sleeves. Wouldn't do for anyone else to see him racing around like a scared rabbit. To his relief, no one was around.

"Curse that woman, she's a witch!" Pilkington said angrily. "Them raccoons told on me! I don't know how she knew about the stones, but she did! They hadda told her. Damn and curse them to the moon and back."

Any time he tried to put out snares or poison, he found the traps in a heap on his doorstep and the baited vegetables lined up like a display in a store. The only thing she couldn't control was what he did himself. It was pure frustration, that's what brought him to throwing stones and finally designing a deadfall full of stakes that he baited with ripe tomatoes. That raccoon never should have been able to get out of the pit. Not alive, anyhow. And it had gone and told on him before he could stop it.

It was an old feud between him and Granny, one that the neighbors up and down State Route 36 had advised him to forget about, but Pilkington just couldn't let it go. It wasn't like them raccoons made off with a tomato or two. The masked rodents bit into every half-ripe fruit they could reach until they found one worth eating. He had lost a quarter of the tomatoes on his vines. The lettuces had been double-decimated by the rabbits. The deer, against all common sense, had nibbled just about every jalapeno that was even close to ripe. He didn't even want to think about how much damage had been done to his corn by the ravens. He was going to go broke and lose the farm that had been in his family for generations, and it was all that crazy woman's fault.

Lennie Edgewater, his neighbor to the south, had advised him to leave out a pile of his best pickings near his back door every night as a bribe, and the critters wouldn't touch the rest.

"Your daddy was the one who told me to do it," Lennie had said, the brown eyes in his pouchy, coffee-toned face earnest. "Didn't he tell you the same? Granny made a pact between us and them animals. I can't believe you won't see sense. We get some good out of it, too. I haven't seen a single hornworm or caterpillar since I started, and there ain't no aphids on my wife's roses, either. Make friends with those critters, or it'll be the end of you. You're gonna have a heart attack."

Pilkington admitted he might be stubborn about it, but animals were stupid. How would they understand that meant to leave his crops in peace? What if they decided they had a taste for his prize squashes just before the county fair? How about if they ate down all his corn before the guy from the seed company came by to inspect? What if they didn't like what he put out, and destroyed his whole crop for the hell of it? How could Granny communicate with varmints anyhow?

He crept back toward Granny's place. What could she do for a dying raccoon? She came from a long line of witches, so the locals said, and her daughter Hazel was surely one, too. He couldn't stop himself—he had to see. He slipped as silently as he could through the stand of hickory saplings and peered up toward her house.

The moon lit up everything like a spotlight. Granny had left her shotgun on the porch. She knelt on the grass with a bundle of dark fur in her arms, her white head bent over it, keening quietly to herself. Pilkington's rational mind told him that she was just mourning over a critter as though it were a beloved pet. She might just be crazy. No harm in that. She farmed her land and pretty much minded her own business. But it was the sight of the other critters gathered in a circle around her that he couldn't rationalize in any way, shape or form. Deer, rabbits, a fox, a pair of coyotes, even a bobcat stood among a horde of raccoons. They looked sad, too.

No, he had to stop himself thinking that way! They were dumb animals! They must be standing there because they thought she was gonna feed them, or something like that.

She laid the critter down and passed her hands over it as if she were stroking it, but she didn't touch it. It lay still. Pilkington felt guilty for a moment that it was dead.

"Rest, pretty one, my pretty one," Granny said tenderly, her hands working back and forth. "Sleep safe. I won't call you 'less I need you. Dream of the moon and good harvests. That's right. Sleep in peace."

Pilkington blinked. It had to be a trick of the movement, but it seemed as if Granny wove a cocoon of moonlight around the body. He saw the ticked, fawn-colored fur and the ringed tail glow softly. There were marks on its belly where the stakes had pierced it. She turned the raccoon over and tucked its little hand-like paws under its chin as if it were asleep, but the eyes in the striped mask weren't closed. They glowed directly toward Pilkington. He flinched backward as if the eyes accused him. Then the light faded, and the glow disappeared into the black strip across its face.

Granny sat back on her skinny haunches and rested her hands on her blue-jean–covered knees. She nodded to the circle of animals. As if they were trained circus performers, a couple of badgers came forward and bowed to her. Pilkington was sure now that he was dreaming. They started digging beside the dead raccoon. In a moment they had heaved up a pile of earth that would fill a wheelbarrow. Granny picked up the body and laid it in the hole. The badgers turned around and began to scoop dirt on top of it. They rolled on the top of the mound like otters and smoothed it out. Granny gave them a pat on each of their flat, wedge-shaped heads as if they were dogs, a move that would cost an ordinary man his hand.

"Go on, git," she said, but it wasn't spoken in the same harsh tone she had used with him. She sounded like a mother telling her children to go and play. The wild animals melted off into the shadows. Pilkington felt something small brush past his pants leg as it went about its business. Granny stood alone in the moonlight with her head bowed. She looked up and glared into the trees. Pilkington felt as if she could see him. He started to back away slowly, taking care to set his feet down silently. After a moment, she turned and went back into the house.

That was nothing, he told himself. *There. Nothing.* Just like he'd thought. She was just a crazy old woman. The animals were easy to explain. Sometimes wild things knew that there was no harm in a person like that, like the old lady he once saw at a nature preserve who charmed a deer to come to her just by holding out her hand.

He went home, shaking his head. She wasn't no one to worry about. Them damned raccoons was, though.

Low in the bushes, dozens of pairs of glowing eyes watched him go.

Rolling the combine harvester over the yellow-green hayfields was pretty much mechanical: sweep up and down, keep the rows even, make sure the baler behind him was working smoothly. The roar of the engine was too loud for conversation, something Pilkington eschewed most of the time anyhow, and gave him time alone with his thoughts. Maybe *he* was the crazy one. If somehow the old lady could keep the wild critters from vandalizing his crops, maybe he should go along with it. How many other nutty things did he do for good luck? Cross his fingers? Throw salt over his shoulder?

"Mr. Pilkington?" Walter Sill ran out of the swaying hay ahead of him and shouted over the roar of the diesel engine. The lean farm worker waved his arms. "You got to see this!"

Pilkington threw the enormous machine into neutral and killed the engine. He swung down from the cab. Rain was forecast for later that day. He needed to get the hay harvested as soon as possible and get the covers on it, or it was going to rot. His other employees, mostly Mexican, were following the harvester, pulling bright blue pockets of plastic over the baled hay. He signed to them to keep working. A couple of them wiped their faces and nodded.

He followed Sill over the field until he came to the edge of the tomato field. Sill pointed. Pilkington stared at the place where the deadfall had lain until he had filled it in the other night.

"Practical joke by someone, huh?" Sill asked, with half a grin.

The mound of earth had been piled twice as high as it had been deep, but the new addition wasn't earth. It was dung, yards and yards of it, fresh enough to still be attracting flies. Pilkington felt his face get hot.

"That damned Granny Lawson!" he snarled. "I went over to talk to her the other evening. She must have told her grandsons what I ... I mean, about our discussion."

"I can just bet," Sill said, with a grin.

Pilkington fumed. He paced up and down, feeling fury rising in him like indigestion. "Dammit, I am not going to take that from anyone! Go get the front loader."

"What for?"

Pilkington jabbed a finger toward the pile. "I want you to pick that up, take it over the road, and dump it next to her driveway. If they think it's so damned funny over there, let them deal with it."

"Mr. Pilkington, I don't know if that's such a good idea ..." Sill's voice tapered off, and his lean face wore a sheepish look. Pilkington looked at him in astonishment.

"What's the matter? Come on, man. You went to Ag school. You're a college graduate in the twenty-first century. You got a MySpace page. You can't tell me you believe in her evil eye like some kind of ancient yokel. It was a prank. We're playing one back. Go do it."

Sill gave a sigh, but Pilkington could tell he liked the idea of a little mischief, especially if he could blame it on someone else if he got caught. While the hand was off getting the loader, Pilkington took a look around the heap of muck. There weren't any tread marks or footprints in the crumbly, gray soil to show how it had gotten there. If he didn't know any better, he might have said that animals had gone there one at a time to make their deposits. But that was ridiculous. That would suggest they were capable of spite. And organization. Too bad. If she was in charge of their behavior, then let her deal with the results. He went back to harvesting hay. Rain wouldn't hold off for anyone.

Early the next morning Pilkington remembered the

dung incident and felt a little guilty about it. He took the old jeep he used on the property and went for a little ride around the perimeter. Without seeming as though he was looking, he checked out what he could see of Granny's drive. Streaks of earth from his side to hers proved Sill obeyed orders, but the site where the front loader had stopped was empty. So her grandsons had gone and cleaned it up. Well, one prank deserved another. He was sure that'd be the end of it. He wouldn't do nothing else unless they did. He rolled back to office and started in on the day's paperwork. Seemed as though he had as many forms to fill out as plants in his fields.

"Señor Pay?" Pilkington glanced up. His Mexican foreman Esteban Ruiz was at his elbow. Most of his summer employees referred to him by his Spanish initial. Pilkington was too much of a mouthful.

"What's up, Ruiz?"

"*Los tomates,* Señor Pay. It is a curse!"

Pilkington headed for the old jeep. Ruiz jumped in beside him. Pilkington gunned it in the direction of the low hill covered with rows of lush green plants.

Pilkington couldn't remember a sunnier month. Rain fell just when it was needed, but most of the time the earth was bathed in hot golden light that was a farmer's godsend. The crops in his fields burgeoned. Thick masses of green leaves sheltered fat little fruits and vegetables. He was furious that so little of it could be harvested.

Ruiz didn't have to tell him what was wrong. He could see it. Every tenth plant—he could count it for himself—had been yanked up and left on its side. Most of them were already wilting in the heat. The rounded mounds of semiripened tomatoes poked up through the greenery.

He plucked one half-red, half-green fruit after another. There were fresh bite marks on every one of them. He dashed the last one to the ground. It was still so hard it bounced. He mashed it into the earth with his boot. Those goddamned raccoons!

"It's the devil, Señor Pay." Ruiz crossed himself.

"It is not a devil, dammit!" Pilkington roared. "It's a menace, and I am not gonna put up with it for one more second! To hell with Granny! I'm gonna take care of those damned critters!"

Bob Lerner leaned over the counter of the Club Hardware store and shook his head as Pilkington finished unspooling his litany of woes.

"Sounds like you have a big problem, Ide," he said. "Raccoons are tenacious little bastards. Once they get the idea you're feeding them, they come around forever, and they tell their friends."

"I've tried every damned thing I can think of," Pilkington said. "Nothing works. I've tried poison. They don't take the bait. I've tried snares. I've tried deadfalls. Got one, that was all. What I need are traps, leg traps."

Lerner shook his head. "Sorry, Ide. They don't make 'em any more. They're brutal as hell. The fish and wildlife people brought me a video on a laptop. It was pretty horrible. What they do to animals—and what animals do to themselves when they get caught in them . . ." He shuddered. "I wouldn't sell them even if I had them, and I'm a man who doesn't shrink at shooting deer or gaffing fish every year."

"But you had some a few seasons ago," Pilkington protested. He smacked a hand down on a shelf across from the counter. "They were right here."

"They're illegal everywhere. I couldn't sell them."

"So what did you do with them?"

Lerner shrugged. "Took 'em down to the dump. Good riddance."

Pilkington eyed him. "Where in the dump?"

Lerner shook his head. "Sorry, buddy, but you'll have to find another way. I'll ask around, see if anyone has any ideas. Say, have you thought of putting out a few apples or something? Like a gift to the little people?"

Pilkington felt his jaw drop. "Not you, too, Bob!"

Lerner looked sheepish. "Well, I've heard what some of the other guys say when they've had a few beers. Doesn't seem to hurt. Nature's a funny thing, Ide."

"I'm not going to let a few raccoons push me around, or one crazy old woman, either. Thanks anyhow."

Lerner gave him a nod. "Good luck, buddy."

It didn't take Pilkington long to figure out where in the "county recycling center" Lerner was accustomed to discarding unwanted merchandise. He drove along the winding passage between buried mounds of trash and sorting stations until he saw a heap of boxes with the Club Hardware logo still on them. Underneath bushels of rotten gaskets and rusty nails he found what he wanted. In spite of their months out in the elements, five of the six toothed, metal bows cranked open and snapped shut like sharks' jaws. Pilkington regarded them with grim satisfaction. He piled the traps into the back of his pickup under a tarp. He didn't want anyone to see what he was up to. Lerner was starting to sound like one of them PETA people. Even some of his hunting buddies cringed at anything but a clear kill-shot. What the hell was this county coming to? They weren't the ones staring bankruptcy in the face. They could mouth morals at him all they wanted, but would they pay his mortgage?

He'd have to wait until dark to put the traps out, then

find an excuse for keeping his workers out of the area where he'd planted them. A few nights of surprises, and the critters would be telling each other to stay away.

The sweet smell always drew the hungry ones. Wriggling meat there was in plenty beneath the soil, frogs in the ponds, fish in the streams, but the raccoons loved sugar. Their sensitive tastebuds, much more than humans', could appreciate even small amounts in ripening fruit and grain. It took too long to wait for full ripeness. A long winter had melted away the fat stored up under their molting pelts, and a long spring nursing young had left them with insatiable appetites.

Under the moonlight, the rounded shapes with the thick ringed tails held low looked like lines of fat beetles swarming toward their objective. Each female was accompanied by anywhere from one to seven offspring, usually no more than three or four. The baby raccoons, their snubbed ears and tails rounder and shorter than the adults', had to be reminded to stay within range of their mother. Still, like young of every species, their curiosity led them to sniff their way off the path. With their little black noses, they investigated the stalks of plants, or followed the trail of a slug that had crossed their path sometime earlier in the day. Their mothers summoned them back with snarls or nips. While the parents nosed carefully up and down the heady-smelling plants looking for tomatoes to eat, the litters of babies engaged in wrestling matches with their brothers and sisters, dug up grubs and roots, and tasted anything that came their way with alacrity. In their experience, nothing had ever happened that did more than surprise or momentarily frighten them. Nothing had ever hurt them. Not yet.

SNAP!

A shrill cry from one of the tumbling youngsters

brought one of the browsing females to a halt. She threw up her head, then went running toward the sound.

The rest of her babies were milling around, bleating near the body of one that hung upside down in midair from a metal hoop. It was limp as a hunk of moss. Blood ran down its belly onto the roiled earth beneath. The mother nosed the baby frantically, touching its ears, its nose, the side of its neck, refusing to believe her ears and eyes. It didn't move. Taking the scruff of its neck in her teeth, she backed away. The body did not come loose. She could not leave her child in this human-smelling thing. She pawed at the metal jaws of the trap. She could not budge them. Her heart pounded and she panted out her panic. What should she do? The rest of her children milled alongside her, fearful that the evil would befall them, too. There were no trees to climb, no burrows to race into. She was their only protection.

She was almost too upset to pay heed to them, but she did not want to lose any more. Where could they go that was safe? It was a long way back to the hollow log that was their home. Should she stay with the dead one or abandon it?

The other raccoons were upset and frightened by the baby's death. They ran around hysterically, hissing and growling at each other.

SNAP! SNAP! More of the metal teeth leaped out of the earth. One strong young male tried to leap as he felt the soil give beneath his feet, but the jaws closed on his neck. A young female lost part of her tail. An older female, too slow to get away, was crushed between the toothed hoops. Her lone kit ran around, crying, bewildered, and terrified.

At last, the dowager female of the pack took charge. She was the smallest of the adult raccoons, but she had seen more summers than any of them, being the mother, grandmother, or great-grandmother of all but a few newly arrived males. She chivvied them away from the terrible field. The mother of the dead baby didn't want to go, but her grandmother herded her away with bites and nips at her back. Her remaining youngsters followed. All the raccoons were shocked and frightened.

The elder female looked back, torn. One male was left alive and struggling in the last trap. He would follow later if he could chew his foot off and escape, but his strength was waning. The others must not stay in case the threat wasn't gone yet. The raccoons were still hungry, but hunger was not as strong an instinct as fear. They must go back to their safe place, the safest place they knew.

They streamed away over the field, until they could no longer hear the whimpers of the male they had to leave behind.

Pilkington was in the middle of the morning briefing to his employees when Granny, immaculately neat in a pressed pink denim shirt, blue jeans, and rubber boots, got out of her ancient station wagon and marched up to him. The top of her head only reached his breastbone, but he felt he was the one who had to crane his neck back to look at her.

"What do you want?" he growled.

"Give me the bodies," she said.

Pilkington glanced at the shocked looks on the faces of his men, then turned a stern face to her. "I don't know what you're talking about."

Her blue eyes glared at him like a lightning strike. "You ain't been able to lie to me since you were a child. I know what you're hidin'. Save me the bother of lookin' for 'em and makin' you a bigger fool than you are. Give me the bodies."

Pilkington felt like marching her back to her car and making her leave, but the farmhands were all looking at him with shocked curiosity on their faces.

He snarled, "Get to work! This is just a pile of crap."

Sill opened his mouth to say something but snapped it closed when Pilkington scowled at him. He signed to the others to follow him. The Mexicans closed ranks behind, whispering to one another in Spanish.

"Well?" Granny asked. "Perfidy don't get any better in waiting."

"You got a lot of nerve coming here and saying something like that in front of my people!"

"Better they know what kind of trash they're workin' for," Granny said. "Take me to the bodies. Right now."

There was no sense in arguing with her. He took her by the arm and steered her around the side of the hay barn to where the men dumped the organic trash like dead vines and branches they intended to burn. He kicked aside a canvas tarpaulin and stepped aside. He had gotten up before dawn and buried the dead raccoons, traps and all, figuring to set the whole thing on fire. No one would ever know what he had done.

But someone had told her. He refused to believe it could have been the raccoons. Someone must have seen him!

In the nest of rotting hay and leaves, the bodies looked pathetic, not dangerous. The black masks wore a tragicomic aspect. The largest of the trapped animals was a big male. Blood stained the sides of his jaws. His handlike paw was a mass of torn tissue and blood below the teeth of the snare. He must have tried to chew it off before he died. Guiltily, Pilkington recalled what Bob in the hardware store had said about the video the Fish and Wildlife people had made him watch.

Granny dropped to her knees beside the bodies and keened aloud. She looked up at Pilkington, tears in her eyes.

"O woe unto you, who have sinned against God! Weep for the children! That youngster isn't more than three months old. Poor little pup. This is the child of the one you killed before."

"You're a crazy old woman. You can't know about wild animals. They can't talk!"

Granny's voice was husky. "I know. I know them all. And her! It was her first season out! Your poor wife, may God keep her at his right hand, would have been so ashamed of you!"

Pilkington felt hot fury boiling enough to blind him.

"Now it's my time to tell you to get off my land, you crazy old bitch!" he roared. "Go on. You saw them. Now, go!"

Granny took her time prizing each trap open flat and easing each of the ragged bodies out. She rose to her feet and looked around. A wheelbarrow was propped against the wall of the barn next to the waste pile. She retrieved it and piled the small corpses in it. Pilkington watched her stonily.

"That was a crime against decency," Granny informed him, as she settled the last body. "Against Mother Nature herself. You can make amends."

"I ain't gonna make amends to a bunch of thieving varmints, and I sure ain't gonna make them to you."

"You're gonna pay for that, you idiotic Ide Pilkington. May God have the mercy on you that you didn't have on none of His natural creations."

Pilkington had had about enough of her preaching. "I

don't care what kind of delusion you have. I gotta make money to make a living, to keep this farm going. If this is what it takes, then I'd do it again."

Granny regarded him sadly. "We all have to live, unless we forfeit the privilege."

"Well, that's what your varmints did." Pilkington let righteous indignation overwhelm the chill he felt. "They uprooted my plants. I had to make them stop. Well, they stopped. Now, get out of here. We might be neighbors, but we ain't friends."

Granny shook her head sadly. "You could've lived in harmony, Ide Pilkington. Your pop would have been so ashamed of you. It's a good thing he's dead."

"Don't you dare talk about my father," he exclaimed. "He shot plenty of critters."

"No. He never laid a baby to rest that did no one harm. He never destroyed nothin' that wasn't mad or an outright danger. You're a disgrace, and I am sorry you set your own destruction in motion." She picked up the handles of the barrow and started back to her car.

Pilkington shook a hand at her. "You try anything, and I will sue you for every inch of land you have."

Granny didn't even look back. "You talk big about the land, but you don't understand what's important about it. I feel sorry for you. Goodbye, Ide. I think this is the last time we'll meet on this earth."

Granny had to dig the grave herself, as none of the night-walking animals would be out for hours. She made the hole big enough for all the critters, so they wouldn't get lonesome in the twilight, until they went back to nature. She picked up the baby. It fit in her two outspread hands like a puppy. Gently, she settled it into the hollow of the young female's body. They weren't mother and child, but they were kin. It would do.

The hardest one to soothe to sleep was the male with his mangled paw. His mask was twisted into a rictus of agony. Granny stroked his forehead before closing his eyes.

"Good night, children. You're safe here, I swear it."

She went to stand over the other grave and folded her hands together.

"I am sorry from my heart you don't get to sleep, but that youngster who died was one of yours. I figure I got to give you the chance. I'd prefer you rested in peace, but that's your decision to make. Do what you feel is right. If you leave it be, so will I." She opened her hands. A globe of milky light dropped from them and landed on the patch of earth. It began to sink in like oil. It would take some time until her question could find that wandering spirit, but vengeance was just. She had to lay the truth before God and let nature take its course.

Granny went inside, dusting dirt off her hands. Supper had to be gotten for her sons and her workers. Life for the living went on. That poor fool of an Ide Pilkington. She didn't want to think about him no more.

Pilkington was jubilant as he strode up and down the rows of tomatoes. The traps had worked. It had been over a week, and no more fruit turned up with bites taken out of them. No plants were uprooted. It looked like good common sense had won out over superstition. The critters wouldn't go where some of their kind had died. He had not seen a single raccoon on the property for more than a week. With any luck they'd start getting decent picking going pretty soon.

"You see what I told you, Ruiz?" he said. "No curse. No problem."

"Si, Señor Pay," the foreman said. "I get people here in one week, okay?"

"You do that," Pilkington said. Damn, it felt good to get things rolling the way they should be. Superstition be damned. Farming was a science. Combine the elements of the right weather, the right seeds, water, fertilizer, pesticides, weeding, and harvesting at the right time, and everything ought to come out okay.

Ruiz went back to supervise his men, who were hoeing the peppers, also untouched. Pilkington remembered he had to call the farm bureau. He headed for his old jeep to drive back to his office.

Just ahead of him, something crossed the open space between rows. Pilkington halted. Could be a snake. Fields were always full of mice, good hunting for corn snakes and black snakes, all harmless to humans. But that had been too bulky. An animal? It didn't scoot like a rabbit, and it wasn't big enough or the right color for a fox or a coyote. In fact, Pilkington could have sworn it was a raccoon. But they didn't come out in daylight unless they were starving or sick. He stepped over the row of plants, trying to catch up with it. Dammit, why couldn't they stay away from him?

He checked row after row. It was either too fast for him or it must have gone to ground. Well, if he found any more bitten tomatoes, he was going to reset those traps.

Pilkington hated office work. There were more forms to fill out than vegetables to sell, the guys used to joke. And even in this day of computers, most of them couldn't be done online. It was just a way for the government to keep the farmer from catching up and figuring out what a bad deal they were getting from everyone. He picked up a stack of papers for his accountant and smacked them on the desk to make them line up. Something sifted down onto his desktop. He looked at it. Dried soil. He brushed it away. Must have brought some in on his sleeve. It was hard to keep anything clean. Good thing he wasn't a dairy farmer.

He felt eyes on the back of his neck. "What do you want?" he asked.

No one answered. He spun the creaking chair around. The end of a tail disappeared around the door jamb. Pilkington shook his head. Probably his late wife's ancient pug dog. That animal was so arthritic it moved like a robot, but it just hung on. But that was too long and too furry to have been Dagwood's curly little tail. Could be a stray cat. Pilkington went out to see.

The pug was in his cardboard box in the hallway where he could see everyone coming and going. He looked up expectantly at Pilkington, who stooped to give him a quick pet on the head.

Dagwood always paid attention when something was in the office. He loved people and he barked at cats. Something had just walked through. So why didn't the dog make a fuss?

Hell with it. Pilkington went back to his paperwork. He sniffed the air. Something smelled foul, but he didn't think much about it. Everything stunk on a farm. No big deal. He picked up the stack of forms he had just been examining.

Right across the center of the first page was a line of muddy footprints. They looked like little hands, four fingers and a thumb. Raccoon prints.

Pilkington dropped the papers and looked under the desk. Those damned animals! They sometimes got into the vents or set up housekeeping in the ceiling. There had to be one in that room right that minute.

The footprints led off the back of the desk and ended at the closet where he kept his files. He opened the door.

A gray blur shot out of the cubicle. Pilkington let

out a yell as sharp teeth fixed in his shin. He kicked at the shape, which flew into the corner. It *was* a raccoon. Something about it looked wrong to him. Its fur was disheveled and dirty, and its head hung sideways. He also saw round, matted, dark marks on its belly. It rolled back onto its feet and leaped for him again. Pilkington fended it off and ran out, looking for a weapon. The animal came after him. He slammed the door on it. Dagwood stood up in his box and looked at him curiously.

Sill was coming toward the office, probably for a cup of coffee.

"There's a rabid raccoon in there!" Pilkington shouted.

"I'll get the shotgun," Sill volunteered. He ran back toward the barn. Pilkington found a shovel. His heart was still pounding heavily from the surprise. He gave a nod, and Sill threw open the door. They looked into the office.

"Nothing," Sill said.

"It's in there somewhere," Pilkington assured him.

The two men searched the room, pushing the desk and chairs out of the way.

"It's gone." Sill sounded relieved.

"There's no way it could have gotten out!" Pilkington said. He glanced into the hallway. Dagwood still didn't react. Could the old dog be getting deaf and blind as well as creaky?

"Granny Morrow might have had something to do with it," Sill said. "A ghost raccoon."

"Don't start with that again. No such thing as ghosts."

"Right," Sill said, uncertainly. "I'll just be getting some coffee, okay?"

"Yeah." Pilkington put down the shovel disgustedly. Sill poured coffee into one of the battered mugs on the stand and went back outside. Pilkington threw himself into the chair. He pulled up his pants leg to look at the bite on his leg. He wiped the blood off the puncture marks with his handkerchief. It wasn't too bad, but there was no rabies in raccoons this far west. He'd put something on it later.

Ghosts. He had never believed in them, but how else could a critter as big as a raccoon slip into a closed closet, or out of a room that had no other exits?

A wave of stink made his throat tighten, and he felt eyes on him again. He turned cautiously around.

The raccoon stood in the middle of the room. Its narrow jaws snarled at him. The eyes in the black mask were hollow. Pilkington scrambled up. It wasn't healthy. Nothing should look like that and still be moving. It lurched toward him, teeth bared. He felt behind him for the shovel. The raccoon snapped at him. He swept downward with the face of the shovel and smacked it right in the head. It rolled backwards. Before it could move again Pilkington went into a frenzy, battering the body over and over. He chopped off one paw with the blade of the shovel and pounded the head. He heard the skull let out a dull crack. He stood back, panting. It ought to be dead now.

To his horror, the creature stirred. How could it move? But it staggered up and resumed its march toward him. The foot he had chopped off remained on the floor, along with a chunk of furry belly. There were smears of dark slime but no blood. The critter didn't bleed!

The hollows in the dark mask regarded him balefully. He would have called anyone crazy who'd have suggested it to him, but that raccoon looked *familiar*. It looked like the one he had chased across the road to Granny Morrow's. But that was impossible. It was dead. She had buried it!

"What are you?" he asked, his voice hoarse with shock.

He should call someone. He ought to get Sill back here.

Granny had told him he had to make amends, or there would be consequences. Was that what it would take to get this specter to go away?

"What do you want?" he asked.

But raccoons, even those returned from the dead, couldn't talk. He backed away from it. The raccoon lowered its head. He'd seen that behavior among animals that were setting up for a dominance contest. He felt at a loss. He couldn't kill it. All he could do was get away from it or trap it so it couldn't follow him no more.

That was it! The traps! If he could get it stuck in one of those, he could bury it somewhere. It wouldn't be able to dig its way out of a grave with twenty pounds of metal clinging to it.

He backed out the door. Dagwood whined as he went, but he never made a sound as the raccoon went past. Didn't he see it?

He'd take the dog in for a checkup later. He had to take care of that damned raccoon first. Like a bad nightmare, it followed him around the side of the big barn toward the trash heap. Granny had been mighty obliging, opening all them traps up and leaving them set for him. That'd be just perfect. He looked over his shoulder to make sure it was following.

Was it grinning? No, that had to be its broken jaw. Pilkington ran. On three legs, his nemesis loped behind.

He reached the waste pile long before it did. He kicked all the rotted straw off the tarp that concealed the traps. He'd piled them up, not troubling to trigger them. It saved him time now. He set them in a line. All he had to do was lure the raccoon into one or more of them, and bang! Problem solved.

It looked so easy when the matadors on television did it, but bulls were straightforward animals. Raccoons were wilier. This one, dead or not, tracked him with its hollow eyes. Pilkington dodged back and forth, trying to draw it to leap at him again. It didn't take the hint. It followed his movements with its sunken eyes.

"Señor Pay!" Ruiz's voice distracted him. "You there, Señor?"

At that moment, the raccoon bounded toward him, mouth snarling. It hit him square in the stomach. Pilkington fell backwards onto the line of traps. SNAP! SNAP! SNAP! SNAP! The steel teeth banged shut on his arms and legs, crushing bone and tearing tissue. He lay spread-eagled, unable even to moan at the horrible pain. He felt hot blood pour out of torn arteries. His life was seeping into the soil he'd spent his whole life on.

The raccoon sat on top of the waste heap, looking down on him from the hollow sockets in its mask. It looked satisfied.

Ruiz came running toward the sound. He crossed himself as he knelt beside his employer.

"*Dios mio!*" he exclaimed. "I call the ambulance."

"Did you see that raccoon?" Pilkington gasped out, trying to lift his hand, but twenty pounds of steel held it down.

"No, Señor Pay," Ruiz said, his round face creased with pity. "I see only a curse. Lie still. I get help." The Mexican foreman got up and ran for the office.

Pilkington felt the pain in his limbs sift away, to be replaced by a numbness that left his mind clear at last. Granny was right, devil take the old witch. It had been stupid to start a blood feud over a couple of tomatoes or a few raccoons. He never realized how horrible and disproportionate the punishment he had inflicted on other living creatures was. He looked up at the raccoon and saw an instrument of justice. Pilkington swore that if God let him live, next time he had a problem with a critter, he would be more understanding. This raccoon could have been his death, but it showed him more mercy than he ever had.

The raccoon almost smiled at him. Then it turned and waddled out of sight.

BUNRABS

By Donald J. Bingle

Donald J. Bingle has had a wide variety of short fiction published, primarily in DAW-themed anthologies, but also in tie-in anthologies for the Dragonlance and Transformers universes and in popular role-playing gaming materials. Recently, he has had stories published in *Fellowship Fantastic, Front Lines, Imaginary Friends, If I Were an Evil Overlord,* and *Gamer Fantastic.* His first novel, *Forced Conversion,* is set in the near future, when anyone can have heaven, any heaven they want, but some people don't want to go. His most recent novel, *Greensword,* is a darkly comedic thriller about a group of environmentalists who decide to end global warming ... immediately. Now they're about to save the world; they just don't want to get caught doing it. Don can be reached at orphyte@aol.com, and his novels can be purchased through www.donaldjbingle.com.

"It's a myth," clucked Doris as she picked at her salad. "I don't believe it, not for one instant."

"You're just a spring chicken, dear," responded Doris' Aunt Clementine as she absentmindedly primped and groomed herself while they sat gossiping. "You don't understand how dangerous the world can be, how vicious." Clementine readjusted her sitting position, shifting forward and cocking her head to one side, bringing it closer to Doris. "Why do you think your mother treasured you oh so desperately before she was taken from us? You were the only child she raised but not the only child she might have raised. It's so sad, really."

Doris swiveled her head, looking about for someone else to greet or bring into a new conversation. She hated being cooped up with her old biddy aunt when she became melancholy like this. She acted quite addle-minded. Doris was convinced it was something in the old bird's diet; she'd heard there was something in commercial feed that can make your mind go when you get older. Dioxin, scrapie, or something. No doubt, that was what was happening to her aunt. Oh, she didn't mind that the dear old girl was consorting with a young stud less than half her aunt's age, but lately Clementine had begun to ramble constantly about danger and conspiracy theories. Really, she said the most outrageous things. It had gotten worse during the last part of winter, and now, well now she hardly shut up about it.

Doris looked out the open door toward the yard, but no one was approaching. She figured she might as well humor the old hen. Maybe if Clementine finished her story without too much aggravation, she would nap most of the afternoon.

Doris fixed Clementine with a steely gaze. "So, I would have had siblings, if they hadn't been taken from Mother. Is that what you're saying?'

Clementine bobbed her head and clicked her tongue. "Yes, taken they were."

Doris had heard this part before. "And you say they were taken by BunRabs."

"Just about this time of year, poor dear. Right around the time of the vernal equinox. They came, like they always come, from the east. Vicious, barbaric brutes, slaughtering anything and anyone who got in their way." A visible shiver went down the old dame's backbone, causing her to half-rise from her sitting position before settling back down.

"BunRabs," Doris said, fixing her aunt with an unblinking gaze of disbelief. "You're telling me that BunRabs are barbaric, vicious brutes." Doris turned her head back and forth, then refixed her gaze on Clementine.

"Yes, dear. Isn't that what I've been telling you?"

Doris had read somewhere, probably in some magazine she had found lying about, that you weren't supposed to shatter the delusions of the mentally deranged, and she imagined that the advice applied equally well to elderly old biddies with clear signs of dementia. But the whole concept of killer BunRabs was so ridiculous, she couldn't help herself.

"Aunt Clementine, I'm sorry, but that's just silly. I've seen BunRabs, I see them most days of my life. They're peaceful . . . even adorable. I can't imagine one of them attacking anybody."

Clementine clicked her tongue. "One attacked the President of the United States of America, one did, years before you were born. And he's protected by Secret Service men with machine pistols and helicopters and everything. It was all over the papers."

Doris shook her head. "The President's security personnel probably just overreacted. I'm sure it wasn't a conspiracy or even an intentional attack. More likely just a misunderstood instinctual reaction to sudden movement or something."

Clementine repositioned herself with an abrupt flounce. "You should really learn your history better. It swam out to attack the President while he was canoeing. The Secret Service guys never saw that coming! It swam out and hissed at him and attacked, nostrils flaring and teeth flashing, that's what the President said. He had to beat it off with his paddle."

"They swim?" Doris' eyes opened wide. "They hiss?" She shook her head. "They flare their nostrils?" Oh, yeah, she knew that last part already. It's practically the only thing they do.

"They surely do. The government's got pictures and everything. April 20, 1979. Like I said, BunRabs get mean around the time of the vernal equinox."

Clementine might be crazy, but she wouldn't make up stuff that could be checked with a quick Internet search, even if all Doris could do was hunt and peck on a laptop keyboard. But even if it was true, it was still incredible, unbelievable.

"BunRabs?" Doris asked in confirmation.

"I've heard tell," said Clementine softly, as if in confidence, "that even demons are afeared of 'em."

"Demons . . . afraid of BunRabs," murmured Doris in a daze of disbelief and confusion. "The cute little adorable furry things that hang out near the garden and do nothing but eat carrots and . . . flare their nostrils?"

Clementine bobbed her head. "Didn't you ever wonder why they do that?"

"Flare their nostrils?" Doris was growing more and more bewildered and, truth be told, a little scared.

"Eat carrots."

"I don't know," babbled Doris. "They're vegetarians? The beta-carotene makes them see better in the dark?"

Clementine gave a squawking, guttural laugh. "If they're vegetarians, what do they need to see so well in the dark for, anyway?"

That really ruffled Doris' feathers. "Carnivorous? You're telling me that BunRabs are carnivorous?" Her body shook involuntarily in irritation and fear, but she quickly tamped down her growing dread. "I've never seen them eat anything but carrots and leaves and berries . . . maybe a little grass."

Clementine shrugged her buffalo wings. "Most times they do, but when the season comes, the taste for flesh grows. Makes them omnivores, like humans, and you know how dangerous they can be. Yessirree, come spring, the BunRabs hunger for blood and meat. Nothing moves upon the face of the earth that they won't devour. No human, no bovine, no fat croaking toad, nor stampeding rhinoceros is safe from the BunRabs when the taste rises with the new spring moon. But it's us they crave, us they most seek out to devour. 'Tastes like chicken,' they say to each other wistfully when snacking down on a stranded motorist or a water buffalo cut out from the herd or even one of their own fallen in the fray. 'Tastes like chicken,' they say, their fur matted with blood and veins caught between their ungodly huge gnawing teeth. 'Tastes like chicken, but, boy, I wish I had me some real chicken instead. Ain't nothing like real country chicken, maybe with a side of . . .

"'. . . eggs!'"

Doris screamed and fainted straight away.

When she awoke, she knew her life would never be the same. She was a believer now.

"When did it start?" she asked.

"No one knows for sure," clucked Clementine. "The killer BunRabs, they've always had a taste for our ancestors, far back as anyone can count."

"At least that means that there is hope for us ... I mean for all of us collectively, as a species."

Clementine cawed sadly. "I wouldn't count on that, dearie. It's only when the promiscuous beasties are kept in check that we have reason to feel safe, as a species even if not individually." She pecked absentmindedly at a piece of straw clinging to her breast. "They hump anything that moves. I saw one mount a groundhog once—it did ugly, unspeakable things to that poor, fat rodent. All they do is eat and breed, like the virus that they are. Some say ..." Clementine trailed off, her eyes glistening with tears.

"What? What do they say, Aunt Clementine?" asked Doris in a quiet, trembling voice.

"They say ... they say that killer BunRabs are what drove the dinosaurs to extinction. BunRabs are a bigger threat than avian flu and fast-food restaurants combined," sniffed the old biddy.

Doris let that sink in. Once her distant ancestors had ruled the world, roaming the steppes and marshes, bellowing their dominance for millions and millions of years, until the BunRabs came. She had to know more.

"You say they always come from the east?" she asked. Suddenly it made sense why Aunt Clementine's young stud stood looking east in the darkest hours before the dawn and heralded each new day with a triumphant crow of survival and joy.

"In New England, they sometimes come from the east northeast—no doubt you've heard tell of the killing Noreasters up that way. But hereabout, they always come directly from the east . . . the dreaded easter Bun-Rabs, close to the new moon just before the vernal equinox, although the hare-y beasts can't be trusted any time or place."

She had to ask. "And what do they do? You say they come for the children?"

"They take the children, yes," sighed Clementine, "but they don't simply take them. Those rabid little Bun-Rabs are a damn sight more perverted than even that. They come into the coop and start chasing and terrorizing the youngest of the youngsters, herding the peeps until they run in circles in panic. Then they just snatch a poor defenseless peep up, biting off its head, and put it back down to run around in circles headless amongst its terrorized siblings, until it falls down. Then the Bun-Rabs will snatch it up again and drink its blood, before crunching down on the lifeless feathers and bones and spitting the beak at those still running. Those, those are the lucky ones . . ."

"The lucky ones?" peeped Doris, afraid to ask more.

"They pluck the hens alive, plunging metal rods into them and roasting them over an open fire of burning corncobs."

Doris' teeth would have been chattering, if she had had any, she was so afraid. "And the eggs?"

Clementine's old voice dropped to such a quiet whisper, Doris had to stretch out her neck to get closer to hear. "Some they eat, cracking them open, guzzling them down like the free drinks at a trailer-trash wedding reception. Some they stuff whole into their fat cheeks like crazed carnivorous chipmunks."

"To eat later?" It was sick, but Doris had to know.

"You'd think so, but no, those furry little monsters have crueler plans. They, well . . .they boil the eggs alive, then decorate them with their gang colors and garish graffiti. Then in the dead of night the weekend after the next full moon, they hide them all around the yard, atop fenceposts, under flower pots, in rain spouts, and in the mailbox, anyplace where they can be found and terrorize the survivors. Then, somehow ... no one knows how ... they make the little human children go hunt for the desecrated, dead eggs, crack them open, peel away the shell from the boiled unborn and eat them while surrounded by chocolate idols of the easter BunRab's leering visage."

"How ghastly," mumbled Doris, suddenly afraid to look at her own eggs nestled under her, lest she find they had been tagged with some hideous gang sign while she had dozed the night before.

Clementine nodded vigorously. "Those BunRabs are mean, sick mother ..." She blushed beneath her wings. "Well, they hump anything that moves, relatives included, the carnivorous little pervs."

Doris was quiet for a while as she pondered the sick, cruel world. She was nesting eggs right now in an attempt to bring innocent chicks into that world, but she had no idea how to protect her eggs or her chicks from the bloodthirsty butchery of the BunRabs. She thought so long and hard about the bleak fate that awaited her and her flock that Clementine fell asleep beside her. Finally, Doris woke her wise old aunt up.

"What can we do?" she asked.

"About what, dear?" came her aunt's reply.

"About the killer BunRabs," said Doris. "How can we stop them?"

"Squawk and peck," replied Clementine as her head nodded down and she fell back asleep. "All you can do is squawk and peck."

On the night of the new moon before the vernal equinox, the night on which the carrot-crazed fiends would have their greatest night-vision advantage, the killer BunRabs came from the east. Multiplying in number as only BunRabs can, they peeked out of culverts, crawled out of holes, scurried out of groundcover, and hopped out of woodpiles.

Doris was the first to know they were coming. While the rest of the henhouse slept the sleep of the soon-to-be-rotisseried, while the cock still doodled the night away roosting on a fence post where he could avoid the dewy damp of the alfalfa sprouts of the field below, Doris was awake. She had been awake since the cock had last crowed, waiting in trepidation for the night of the lepus to begin. The rest of the flock slept, but this was no time to be chicken.

Doris wasn't sure exactly what slight alteration of the night's gestalt heralded the BunRabs' evil presence. It could have been the subsonic, rhythmic thrum of the padded, furry rabbits' feet as the fearsome critters hopped silently in time through the cornfield east of the farmyard. It could have been the gentle breeze stirred by a thousand, nay a million, tiny BunRab noses wiggling and flaring in unison to suck in the breath of life to power their unholy quest for death and destruction. It could have been that the hypersonic background wail of the carrots and other root vegetables ceased as the omnivorous varmints forsook their vegetative delights for a maniacal dark night of carnivorous revelry. But most likely it was that a mother hen, once it has identified a threat to her offspring, has a sixth sense that no science experiment can detect and no fairy tale can explain—a sixth sense that squeezes the adrenal gland that makes all mothers sit bolt upright and spring up to the defense of their babies no matter the time of night.

Doris covered her somewhat sparsely strawed nest with a piece of corrugated cardboard she had pecked loose from an old feed box, then assembled a second—fake—nest atop it, leaving what would appear to be an empty nest in the keen eyesight of her beta-carotene addicted adversaries and leaving her eggs snuggled safe and warm below the false-bottomed nest. Then she woke up Clementine and Gertrude and Sadie and Mrs. Sanders and all the other mothers in the hen house and warned them of the coming battle. While the others scurried about blocking entrances and securing defenses, Doris strutted out into the night and flapped up awkwardly to a fence post to watch the coming slaughter.

Even though Doris' depth perception was not great (eyes on either side of the head will do that), her eyesight was keen. She could see the fuzzy, furry horde of death coming through the field. An advance scouting party led the way. Though disguised in fox-pelt clothing, there could be no mistaking the rabbity movement of the alleged fox as first the front BunRab, then the back BunRab hopped forward. If that wasn't scary enough, it quickly became clear that the pack behind the disguised and disquieting scout had already seen battle that night. The BunRabs were smeared with blood and—she shuddered—dried egg yolk. The oversized bicuspids of the sinister hares gleamed in contrast to their dark butcher's garb. Worse, the sharp relief of light and dark revealed to Doris that some of the twitch-nosed murderers had sharpened their pearlies into fangs of annihilation.

But, ultimately, none of that mattered to Doris. They could carry knives and brass knuckles for all she cared; guns and bandoliers of ammo, grenades, javelins, even suitcase nukes, it wouldn't matter.

She waited for it, waited until the horde was fully

committed to the field, 'til the stupid-looking undead
fox scout was at the ditch on the far side of the road
before she gave the signal.

Then the cock crowed and the cornfield blazed with
light.

Not sunlight. It was still two o'clock in the morning.
No, the cornfield blazed with the light of gunfire as a
bizarre collective of farmhands, hunters, and survival-
ist militia members enjoyed the benefits of their NRA
memberships. Shotguns pumped lead furiously, until the
shots churned up the roots of the fledgling corn stalks
and they toppled over. Rifles cracked sharp and fast,
followed by the clackety-clack of the bolt being thrown
and another round being chambered. Automatic weapons thundered as scoped spotlights snapped on, directly
into the beta-carotene–soaked eyes of the BunRabs,
blinding them, making even more sure than usual that
they would not see the bullets that whined forward at
supersonic speed to crash into to their big, dumb fore-
heads and explode out the back of their skulls, leaving
a hole the size of an entrance to the warrens, dens, and
hidey-holes the little buggers frequented and not much
brain matter behind. The barely controlled bursts of fire
simultaneously riddled the brainless bodies of the dying
BunRabs until they twitched faster than their little Bun-
Rab noses ever could, ripping flesh from bone, rending
limb from limb and creating the largest collection of un-
lucky rabbit's feet this side of the dollar store near the
interstate highway.

As the carnage continued, some big, dumb jerk with a
box of M-80s started lobbing the quarter-sticks of dyna-
mite from an oak tree blind into the middle of the field.
Between the bullets and the explosions and the blood
and entrails and the screams of the maimed and dying

BunRabs—yes, BunRabs scream a high-pitched scream like a little girl who has found a spider crawling into her blouse—the battlefield just east of County Road 14 rivaled Borodino, Gettysburg, and Omaha Beach.

Even after the initial barrage guaranteed that no easter BunRab would emerge from the cornfield of death to terrorize chicken or egg, whichever came first, again, the gunfire continued, first in a steady stream, then intermittently, as if those firing were unsure whether the BunRabs might be firing back or somehow dangerous to the conglomeration of good ol' boys armed with guns and fortified by copious amounts of corn liquor.

Finally, there was silence, both in the field across the road and in the henhouse behind. No BunRab had encroached one lucky foot or twitchy little nose into the farmyard. And as the second dawn of the morning came, Doris didn't wait for the Clementine's stud to crow the morning's welcome. She crowed herself, a crow of victory and joy and survival.

The final count: 862 BunRabs perished that night on what is now known as Easter Cornfield. Doris knew the deadly sum 'cause the good ol' boys, they collected up all the rabbit's feet, counted 'em up, and divided by four. Three squirrels, seventeen field mice, one thrush, and a fox were also caught in the crossfire and tallied as collateral damage, although Doris knew that the fox was already dead long before its pelt was aerated on that fateful field. Four hunters also managed to get themselves shot or wounded by flying debris during the skirmish, though none seriously. The night would have been a complete success from Doris' perspective if not for the fact that the good ol' boys decided to go chow down on bacon and eggs at the Sit-A-Spell Diner, down where there is an exit from the interstate onto County Road 14.

There was one additional death that evening, but Doris refused to give any credence to the notion that the frightful noise of the barrage is what caused old Aunt Clementine to die of heart failure back in the coop. Clementine was simply an old hen, though not as addle-minded as Doris had once thought, whose time had come.

The important thing was that not one chicken, peep, or egg was taken by the BunRabs that night. The chicks, they grew up without the fear of the easter BunRabs coming for them in the night. And that's real chicken goodness (unless you, gentle reader, are one of those barbarians who likes your chickens extra-crispy fried).

And, oh, by the way, in case anyone ever asks you: "Why did the chicken cross the road?" you can tell them it was so she could get to the other side, fly into the window of the farmer's daughter's bedroom, ignore the traveling salesman, flutter to the glowing screen of the laptop, access the World Wide Web, and post the following advertisement in the *Lincoln County Herald Tribune*:

TEN THOUSAND DOLLAR PRIZE
for most rabbits killed
Saturday, April 12
in the cornfield east of Jenkin's Farm
along County Road 14.
Cock will crow to signal beginning of tournament.
Lincoln County Animal Control Board.
Eat more rabbit and save your crops!
"Tastes like chicken."

Even if you can only peck at the keyboard, the Internet is a powerful tool for good . . . or evil.

Heaven help us if the BunRabs learn to use it.

FOR LIZZIE

By Anton Strout

Fantasy author Anton Strout was born in the Berkshire Hills mere miles from writing heavy-weights Nathaniel Hawthorne and Herman Melville and currently lives in historic Jackson Heights, New York (where nothing paranormal ever really happens, he assures you). He is the author of *Dead to Me* and *Deader Still*, the first two books of the Simon Canderous urban fantasy series. His short stories have appeared in *Pandora's Closet*, *The Dimension Next Door*, and *City Fantastic*. He is also the co-creator of the faux folk musical *Sneezin' Jeff & Blue Raccoon: The Loose Gravel Tour* (winner of the Best Storytelling Award at the First Annual New York International Fringe Festival). In his scant spare time, he is a writer, a sometime actor, sometime musician, occasional RPGer, and the worlds most casual and controller-smashing video gamer. He currently works in the exciting world of publishing, and, yes, it is as glamorous as it sounds.

Godfrey heard the sound of a voice calling his name before noticing someone standing next to his giant oaken desk, but as usual his brain didn't register it or the fact that it was female until the sound of it became more stern.

"Godfrey!"

Before looking up, the senior most archivist finished scribbling down the last of his thoughts into the moleskine notebook in front of him. One of the newer assistants in The Gauntlet stood there. She was an Asian girl with dark brown almond-shaped eyes and long black hair pulled back into a ponytail. *Probably to keep it out of her face or to keep it from falling against the pages on some of the older books,* Godfrey thought. He was pleased to see that she had taken the precaution, given the stack of books she was carrying. It didn't take much to set off rapid deterioration down in these caverns beneath the Department of Extraordinary Affairs, and the oil in hair could be just as destructive as fire.

The girl was definitely attractive, maybe only a few years younger than him, but right now, she looked a bit perturbed.

"Yes . . . ?" he started, fishing around for a name in his head. Godfrey thought it might be Clarice.

"Chloe," she offered.

So close, he thought. "Of course," he nodded, causing his straight black hair to fall across the top of his black horn-rims. He pushed the hair away from his face. "Can I help you?"

She hoisted up the stack of books in her hands. Against her tiny frame, they looked as if she had stolen them from a giant's library. "These are for you. From those two guys up in Other Division. You know . . . the one with the stripe in his hair and that other guy who's always in the leather jacket? He looks like one of the Village People."

Godfrey smiled. "That would be Connor and Simon."

Chloe stared at him blankly.

"They're two of the few people around here who treat us as something more than glorified librarians," he said. "They're okay. They were my personal saviors during that whole zombie debacle during Fashion Week, one of the few times I ever saw any action around here." He stood up and took the books from her. "Thank you."

Pushing piles of notebooks, file folders, and other tomes out of the way, Godfrey placed the new pile on top of his desk. He arranged them carefully, making sure his view of the small glass terrarium wasn't obstructed. Once Godfrey had sat back down, Chloe pulled the top book off the pile.

"I've been meaning to ask you," she said, holding it up. "Fairy tales? Since when does the Department of Extraordinary Affairs keep fiction on hand? Especially down here with all the serious research?"

Godfrey pulled it away from her and placed it back on top of the pile. "Who says it's fiction?"

Chloe smiled at him.

"Great," she said. "When I get back to the coffee shop, I can't wait to see what fairy tale creatures start chatting me up."

Godfrey laughed. "Don't be ridiculous. The actual creatures from those books don't *really* exist . . . that I know of, anyway. But the object lessons inside those stories . . . well, that's a different matter. Some of our field agents could learn a thing or two about leaving a trail of breadcrumbs . . ."

"With my luck, I'd end up getting the Three Little

Pigs instead of Prince Charming," Chloe said, giving Godfrey a look of bemused frustration. An awkward energy passed between them, one that Godfrey couldn't quite put his finger on. All he noticed was how long and painful the sudden lull in the conversation was becoming and also how red Chloe's face had become.

Thankfully, Chloe's eyes shifted to the terrarium as if noticing it for the first time, and Godfrey felt the sensation ease. She knelt down in front of it, searching for whatever was inside. Godfrey felt a swell of pride when she finally spied the tiny golden creature curled up in one corner.

"Is that . . . a snake?"

"Yes and no. More of a serpent, actually. If it can even truly be called that . . ."

Chloe raised her hand to the glass and put it against the part where the creature was sleeping.

"Do you remember that Glo-Worm toy from when you were a kid?" she asked.

Godfrey had to stop and think a moment before a faint memory came to him.

"Vaguely," Godfrey said. "I had more books than toys as a child. Big surprise, I know."

"It looks like one of those, only tinier," she said, her eyes wide with excitement and, if Godfrey was reading her right, nostalgia. "Not to mention the fact that it's also not wearing one of those little sleeping bag outfits they used to come in."

The creature's eyes fluttered open and it gave a sleepy look around. Chloe smiled and started making cooing noises at it. She turned her knuckles towards the terrarium and rapped at the glass.

"Don't tap on the glass, please," Godfrey said. "Lizzie hates it."

Chloe paused, her fingers inches from the terrarium. "Sorry. Just what is it? What is she, I mean?"

Godfrey perked up.

"No one's really sure," he said with excitement in his voice. How could it not be? Here he was talking shop with one of the cutest archivists to come along in the past few years. "The earliest evidence of their kind that I could find in the archives was from 1756. An agent named Thaniel Graydon documented a sighting of one of them."

Chloe whistled. "The Department of Extraordinary Affairs is that old?"

Godfrey shook his head. "Oh, no. The Fraternal Order of Goodness predates the underfunded bureaucracy of the Department by several hundred years, but Graydon spent years trying to track these little paper lovers hiding in the archives ... with little success."

"Paper lovers?"

Godfrey pulled a blank sheet from the moleskin notebook, crumpled it up, and dropped it into the terrarium. Immediately the creature slithered over to it, opened its tiny jaws, and happily began munching on it.

"The perfect recycling program," Godfrey said. "Works in nicely with the mandate from upstairs to 'go green,' but you can see why they would want to catch them before they could consume the whole archives. Graydon called them book wyrms in his notes, and so do I. Who knows what records have been lost to them?"

Chloe stood back up, stretching. "Why not just get rid of them then?"

Godfrey looked appalled at the idea. "For doing what they were made to do? Never. And what would we do with them? Release them into the city? Destroy them? They're perfectly controllable and harmless when you know how to handle them." He reached into the terrarium and extended one finger, and the tiny gold serpent wrapped its tail around it all the while continuing to munch on the paper. "Besides, Lizzie is a good companion."

Chloe put a hand on his shoulder and patted him. "Not much of a people person, huh?"

Godfrey smiled up at her. "I'm somewhat particular about who I like to spend time with, I suppose."

Chloe blushed, her hand lingering on his shoulder, and even being as thick as he was, Godfrey put two and two together. Unsure of how to handle the situation, he twisted away from her hand back toward his open notebook. "A creature like this is better than people in some respects. She's unconditional love. All she expects is to be fed, and with the amount of paper I go through in a day around here, food is in no short supply. And for that, she gives back so much more."

"That's great, Godfrey, but isn't there something more you want than that?" Chloe asked, a distinct tone of frustration in her voice. "I mean, look at this book of fairy tales. Do you see the prince hanging out all the time with the dragon, even if it's just a miniature one? Don't you think he should get out and check out some princesses?"

"Married to the manuscripts," he said, thumping his hand down on top of the newest pile of books. He paused, and his face grew somber. "You know, Emerson once wrote, 'Art is a jealous mistress, and, if a man have a genius for painting, poetry, music, architecture, or philosophy, he makes a bad husband, and an ill provider.' I suppose that applies to archivists as well."

Chloe's frustration seemed to grow. "What we do is most certainly an art," Chloe said, "extrapolating data, reworking it so it makes narrative sense for future generations of The Gauntlet. Okay, well, it sounds more technical than artistic when I put it that way, but you get what I mean . . ."

Godfrey nodded.

Godfrey felt Chloe lay her hand over his on top of the stack of books, felt the gentleness of it, and found a little shock of surprise rush through him. He looked up.

When he did, Chloe looked away, flustered. Her hand drifted off his and came to rest next to his on the pile of books. She slid the top one out from under his hand.

"Do you mind if I borrow this?" she asked, holding up the book of fairy tales.

"I thought they weren't really your thing?" Godfrey asked.

"I'll admit it's nothing as chipper or uplifting as your Emerson," she said, "but maybe I've had enough reality for one day and I just want to read up on what it's like to be treated like a princess."

Chloe spun around, headed back past several of the other archivists and further off into the depths of The Gauntlet. Godfrey watched her as she went, confused and frustrated, and not quite sure exactly what had just happened there.

Godfrey's nose was so deep in transcribing an account of a living gargoyle sighting that he didn't hear the echo of footfalls until they were upon him. He looked up with a start.

"Chloe!" he said. He checked his watch. "It's late. What are you doing here at this time of night?"

"I know. Weird, right?" she said. She was holding the book of fairy tales. "I got kind of lost back in the archives when I stormed off . . . I mean, when I *left* earlier. This place goes on forever!"

"So you've been lost this whole time?"

Chloe shook her head. "Actually, I sat down and started reading some of the fairy tales. It's fairly gruesome stuff."

Godfrey shrugged. "Did you think there was no price to be paid for happily ever after?"

She returned the book to the top of the pile she had taken it from earlier, then picked up the entire stack and moved it out of the way on top of the back half of the open-topped terrarium. She leaned against the edge of Godfrey's desk and shuddered. "Stepsisters slicing off toes to fit into glass slippers, little girls cutting their way out of wolves' bellies . . . Happily ever after doesn't come cheap, that's for sure."

Godfrey nodded and turned back to his transcription, not really sure what to say after their awkward exchange earlier in the day. He tried to push out of his mind the fact that the two of them were alone in the Gauntlet right now, but it wasn't working, and the best he could manage was to simply sit there keeping his mouth shut before he blew it again.

"Godfrey?" Chloe said, finally breaking the silence in a whisper.

Godfrey hrhmed in response without looking up from the moleskine notebook he was writing in. *Here it comes,* he thought, not sure how he'd handle her continued overture. Women were more mysterious to him than anything. What she said next, however, took him completely by surprise.

"Where's Lizzie?" she said.

Godfrey looked up. The terrarium was full of torn and discarded pages from his day, but from where he sat, he saw no sign of the tiny gold serpent. He stood and walked to the corner of his desk, making sure to check the terrarium from all angles.

Gingerly he picked up the arcane tomes lying over the back half of it, placing them back on the desk. Inside the terrarium, the paper had fallen in a perfect cascade that formed a path that reached to the very top of the terrarium's lip, only the wyrm was nowhere to be found.

"Maybe she's underneath . . . ?" Chloe offered and started shifting the papers around.

"Shh," Godfrey said, grabbing her hands to silence her.

A little charge of excitement ran up his arms.

Then both of them heard it and dropped their eyes toward the recently moved pile of books.

"Is that . . . chewing?" Chloe said.

"I hope not. That bottom book is the *Diobolica Arcanium.*"

"Is that bad?"

"It's not *not* bad," Godfrey offered and scooped the book off of the table, knocking the others over. He flipped it over, revealing a half-dollar–sized hole.

"She *chewed* through it," he said fascinated. He went to poke his fingers into the hole, then paused. "You might want to step back. I'm not sure what to expect here."

When Chloe didn't answer, he turned to look at her, but she wasn't looking at him. Chloe was staring at the spot on the desk where the book had been.

Godfrey spun around and looked also. A hole, this one slightly larger than the one in the book, was eaten through the top of the desk.

"Oh no no no," Godfrey said, heading for the corresponding drawer on the left side of the desk. He pulled open the drawer, yanking it completely free of the desk, scattering folders and books to the floor. All of them had soda-can–sized holes through them. This time, the edges of the holes were smoldering with tiny tendrils of smoke. Godfrey reached down to the bottom one and pulled it free. No creature, but an even larger hole was visible, the edges of it hot with tiny tendrils of flame. He pulled the drawer free from the desk, stomping at the flames, all the while examining the remaining hole in the desk bottom.

As Godfrey leaned in, a traffic-coned–shaped blast of fire shot from the hole. He felt his eyelashes singe off, the smell of burned hair filling his nostrils. Thankfully, Chloe pulled him back away from it in the last second before Godfrey could find out what burned flesh smelled like.

A skittering sound came from under the desk, heading off in the direction of the rest of the rows of endless archives.

"What the hell is going on?" Chloe asked. Godfrey was impressed at how well she was holding her composure in check.

"I think Lizzie is having a little indigestion." Godfrey started off. "Stay behind me. We've got to stop her before she lights up the whole archive."

"Ummm, maybe we should start with your desk?" Chloe suggested.

Godfrey stopped and turned back around. Flames licked higher and higher up the sides of the desk. He ran for one of the many extinguishers throughout the Gauntlet, but Chloe already had one in hand.

"This rescue's on me," she said and hit the nozzle. White chemical foam shot out and coated the entirety of Godfrey's desk. Some of the records might be damaged, but the fire was out. Godfrey could have kissed her and suddenly found that he actually *wanted* to. The realization was a little slow in coming. Before he could act, Chloe dashed past him into the archives, still brandishing the extinguisher. "You make a lousy damsel in distress," she added.

Chloe's words slapped him out of his daze. He shook off the shock of the situation and raced off after her.

When Godfrey caught up to her, she turned and said, "What the heck did you do, Godfrey? Feed it after midnight?"

Godfrey stated at her blankly.

"*Gremlins?* Hello?"

The sounds continued off to the left, and as they hit the end of the row, they turned to follow it.

"Sorry," he said. "Don't get out much. Archivist, remember?"

"Right. Well, once we deal with this, maybe I'll let you take me to one. You'd be surprised what you can learn from movies about surviving, as well as from fairy tale books, too."

Godfrey wasn't sure, but it seemed as though Chloe was asking him on a date. He decided to stay quiet. The situation was already complex enough without having to contend with his awkward social skills at the same time.

Chloe stopped and Godfrey did too. Off in the shadows, the sound of the fleeing creature changed. The slithering was replaced by the sound of feet. *No,* Godfrey thought, *not feet. Claws.*

From out of the darkness, the creature half slithered, half crawled out from behind the bookcase, adjusting quickly to its newly formed feet.

"Is that . . . ?"

"Lizzie," Godfrey finished. "Yes."

The gold of her body was deeper, her scales far more pronounced now that she was two hundred times her original size, but there was no mistaking the creature that had been Godfrey's pet. Besides the feet, there was another new addition—a long, muscular tail that flicked books off the shelves as it flashed back and forth. Gone was the kind face he had known these past few years, replaced by deep-seated venom in its eyes.

"Let's go," Chloe said, but Godfrey stood transfixed, looking for a hint of recognition in the creature's eyes. Chloe grabbed him by the arm and started to drag him off to the safety of another aisle to her right.

"No, wait . . ."

Chloe ignored him and continued pulling at him until they were safely out of the creature's sight. "Haven't you ever heard about curiosity and the cat?"

Godfrey peeked around the corner. Lizzie was still there, watching him.

"I think we have more of a St. George and the Dragon situation here, actually. Maybe if we could make it to the stairs . . ."

Godfrey ran off across the aisle, or tried to. Before he was even halfway across, Lizzie let out a burst of flame, and Godfrey was forced back to the same side, but down a different aisle. He stopped, dropped, and rolled to make sure nothing was on fire but other than the wave of heat that had hit him, he seemed unharmed.

"Dammit," he shouted, then remembered Chloe was standing just on the other side of the bookshelf between them. He composed himself and shouted over to her, "This isn't my forte! We're researchers, librarians. We try to leave the extraordinary affairs to the people upstairs."

The half-walk, half-slither of the creature started up the aisle toward them. A shiver of fear ran up his spine. While he tried to shake it off, Godfrey heard Chloe straining herself in the next aisle over, and then saw the upper part of one of the book cases move ever so slightly.

"Godfrey, get over here!" Chloe called out. "We've got to stop it before it sets the whole place ablaze. I can't do this by myself. I can't get enough strength behind this to topple it over onto her. You have to help me."

Godfrey checked the aisle. Lizzie was closing on them slowly but surely. He dashed out into the aisle and down the one Chloe was in before Lizzie could react.

"Help me with this," Chloe said.

Godfrey shook his head, leaning it back against the bookcase. "I can't. None of this is Lizzie's fault. She's not malicious. It's the book she ate. The *Diobolica Arcanium* is making her do this . . ."

Chloe grabbed him by the shoulders. "That may be, but you have to let go. Whatever that . . . thing is now, it's not your pet anymore. We have to stop it. I'm not sure about you, but I know I don't want to die!"

Godfrey nodded. Chloe was right. He had known it all along, but hearing her say it gave the idea substance.

He edged toward the main aisle. Lizzie was in a pocket of shadow, little flickers of flame showing where the corners of her mouth were.

"Heeeeere, Lizzie, Lizzie, Lizzie," he clucked out.

"For heaven's sake, Godfrey, it's not a cat." Chloe stepped to the nearest shelf and pulled two books from it, clapping them together over and over. "The thing wants paper, paper and magic."

She stepped out into the aisle, putting the bookcase between herself and the creature, baiting it.

"Don't let her roast me," Chloe said. "I'm trusting you on this one, God. It'll put a real damper on that date of ours."

Godfrey pressed himself to the bookcase, testing his

strength against it. He felt that it would topple at his shove. At least, he hoped so.

"I see that the modern day damsel in distress is no slacker," Godfrey said. "She's proactive."

Chloe gave him a look that burned more that he thought the flames would. "Oh, I see . . . so being bait is somehow a feminist statement?"

Godfrey shrugged. "Let's just concentrate on taking the gruesome out of this fairy tale, okay? Keep clapping the books together, please."

With a sudden burst of speed, the creature galloped forward. Godfrey guessed it had finally gotten used to its legs, and the sound of the books drew its attention; but now Godfrey wondered if he would have enough time to unbalance the bookcase. He threw his weight into it as hard as he could and dug his legs into the stone floor. The bookcase rocked forward, but it didn't topple. In fact, it swung back toward him like a pendulum.

"Godfrey . . . ?" Chloe's voice was full of doubt and panic. The creature was almost upon her.

The idea that she was an actual damsel in distress caused something deep inside to snap, and he dug his feet back in and met the sway of the bookcase with all of his strength. This time it pitched forward and hung at the precipice of balance. Not hesitating to see if it was enough, Godfrey stepped back a few steps and took a running leap at it. He scrambled up the side of it as if he were climbing a ladder and rode the bookcase down as it collapsed on the creature, crushing it under its weight.

Godfrey felt it squirm underneath the heavy wooden bookcase. The wyrm drew in a breath as if it were going to let out another blast of flame, but instead it let out a sort of whimper, its breath starting to hitch. Godfrey crawled gently off the bookcase and scrambled across the floor toward the head.

He turned to look at Chloe. "Get me the notebooks on the right side of my desk." She ran off immediately to get them.

Alone, Godfrey stared into the creature's face. The venom that had been there earlier was gone. Godfrey thought he saw a flicker of recognition in those eyes and began to pet the creature.

"I'm sorry," he said quietly to himself, over and over.

When Chloe returned, she handed him the notebooks. Godfrey opened one of them, tore out a handful of blank pages, and lowered them to the creature's mouth. Its lips parted, a blast of breath rising from them, and Godfrey pressed them forward until the creature's tongue flicked gently out and took them from him. The gesture was so like Lizzie he could have cried. It didn't surprise him when moments later he realized he was crying. Chloe kneeled down next to him, tearing apart notebooks and handing the pages to Godfrey, and the two of them fed Lizzie until she breathed her last.

Days later, Godfrey's arms still ached from the adrenaline rush that had allowed him to climb the side of the bookcase, but most of his pain came from within. He had just popped two aspirin when Chloe knocked on his office door.

"Hi," Godfrey said, glad to see her, but unable to muster a smile after everything that had happened.

"Hey," she said. "Has anybody said anything?"

Godfrey shook his head. "A couple of people asked what happened to my desk, but other than that, I think we did a good job of cleaning up."

"Good," she said, standing in silence for a moment.

"Listen, I just wanted to thank you for coming though for me. I know it must not have been easy."

Godfrey gave a sad smile. "Forget about it. Besides, I was just returning the favor . . ."

Chloe looked at him quizzically. "What favor?"

"When you pulled my face away from my desk, when she . . . when *it* blew that initial puff of flame at me?" he reminded. "So let's just call it Damsel: 1, Prince: 1, okay?"

"Fair enough," she said with a smile. "You know, that's the funny thing about fairy tales. Rarely is there just one version of the story." Her other hand had been hidden by the door, and she pulled it out from behind her. A tiny red and gold wyrm was wrapped around her hand, blissfully sleeping with a shred of half-eaten notebook paper wrapped in its tiny claws.

"My God," Godfrey said. He sat up and put down his notebook. "Where did you find her, err, him . . . ?"

Chloe shrugged. "Damned if I can tell what sex it is."

"Well, whatever it is, it's beautiful," he said, then paused. "I don't think I should keep it, though. Not after what happened."

"You did everything right that you could," she said. "I was wrong when I asked you about getting rid of them all together."

"How can you say that?" Godfrey said, shaking his head. "We almost died."

"But the reward you got out of knowing her, of knowing Lizzie for the time you did, that was worth it. Life is about risk. It's the only way you get any reward out of it. Take her, him, whatever it is . . . please."

Godfrey reached for Chloe's hand and the wyrm wrapped around it. Chloe opened her hand, and he took her fingers into his palm, lowering her slowly toward the empty terrarium.

"Careful," he said, "watch the sides."

Only when Godfrey looked up, Chloe wasn't watching the terrarium at all. She was staring at him and smiling.

"What?" he said.

"See? I suppose even princes can be trained," she said, and leaned in to kiss him. The warmth of her lips was comforting.

FAITH IN OUR FATHERS

By Alexander B. Potter

Alexander B. Potter resides in the wilds of Vermont, editing and writing both fiction and nonfiction. His short stories have appeared in a wide variety of anthologies, including the award-winning *Bending the Landscape: Horror* volume and a number of DAW anthologies. He edited *Assassin Fantastic* and the award-winning *Sirius: The Dog Star*, and coedited *Women of War* with Tanya Huff, all for DAW Books.

The Game of Life takes over the kitchen table one little stack of colored money at a time. The tiny writing in the squares jumps around when I try to read it, so I look at the pictures instead. I spin the dial hard enough to pop it loose from its lumpy green plastic dish, the one that's supposed to look like a clump of trees.

I think it looks more like green goo erupting in a volcano from the cardboard, but no one asked me.

I spin a seven, push my little pink car along the road, and park at the mandatory wedding chapel. I've already been condemned to a career as a teacher, which irks me.

Nothing against teachers, but the salary is $12,000, an awkward number to me. Not nice and round like the $25,000 doctor salary. After that disappointment, I'm in no mood to do the pink and blue peg dance.

"What if I don't want to get married?"

Laura shrugs. "Don't think it matters. You can still get kids. You just miss out on the money at the end when you trade in your family."

"I just want a friend in my car." I pluck another blue peg from the box and pop him in next to me. Laura gives me a pondering look, but I'm used to that and ignore it. With the marriage issue resolved, my mind wanders back to the elephant in the room.

Our father is out back with my kitten, Bernie, who seems to be sick. He just up and started hiccupping. After I got upset, Daddy suggested he sit with Bernie. That suited me. Daddy can fix anything.

I'm still worried, though. My mother suggested playing a game. I know it's a distraction. It works and doesn't work by turns. They know how attached I am to Bernie. I only stopped being allergic to cats last year. He's my first kitty.

The heavy tread of my dad's boots carries from the next room, and I forget the game. He walks into the kitchen, and he and Mom must have some signal because she ushers Laura out, and they're off down the hall. I look up at my dad, hoping so hard but already feeling a little sick.

"I'm sorry, Evan. Your kitty died."

The rumble of that deep, gentle voice tosses me over the edge, and I burst into tears. He catches me up in a hug, settling at the table with me on his lap. "I'm sorry, punkin'. I don't know what to tell you." He hugs me close, and I can feel his chest tremble as his voice catches. "Sometimes these things just . . . happen. It's not fair." I can't say anything because I'm crying too hard.

His voice picks up again with a slight shake. "I remember when I had this little dog, back when I lived up on the hill. He went everywhere with me, to work, to the barn. Then one day he broke his leg. I think a car must have hit him. I took him to the vet, who fixed him up with a splint and said he was fine. I thought he was going to be okay. He stayed home while he was getting better, and when I got home later in the week, he was dead. I didn't know why. The vet said maybe it was a blood clot. But I just didn't understand why. He was fine when I left."

I hug him tight. It hurts to see him cry and makes me cry harder, but at the same time I'm somehow glad he's crying too. It makes me feel less alone, even though the despair still sits like a rock in my stomach. He's a quiet guy, and I don't know that I've ever seen him cry. That he's crying with me over this, over a little black and white cat I've had less than two months . . . it makes me warm, somehow.

After Bernie, it's a small procession of gray tabbies and black cats, but my luck doesn't improve. Once I figured out my healing thing—that I can heal with my hands if the conditions are right—you'd think I'd have been all set. Unfortunately, car strikes or simple disappearances don't respond to hands-on healing. I can't raise the dead, I can't heal long distance, and healing ability doesn't help find something lost.

It sounds strange, but people don't have *house* cats in our neck of the woods. Every cat I know is an outdoor cat. A lot of them are barn cats. It never even occurred to me to keep a cat inside. So it goes over the next couple years . . . Gherkin, Picky, Inky Pool, Felicity, Periwinkle. It gets downright depressing.

Not to mention? Unfair. I honestly don't get why schools and adults make such a big deal about kids acting fair, when nothing else is fair.

Nothing.

The disappearances are the worst, because I just don't *know*. Don't know whether to hope or give up. Sometimes a cat will be gone two days and show up. So every time I watch for days. Walking up and down the dirt road in front of our place, shaking a box of Meow Mix and trilling, "Here, kitty kitty," until my throat aches. Waiting.

My dad knows how to handle these things. He grew up a farmer and spent a lot of time farming before he married my mom and went to work at the lumberyard. He developed that practical approach to animals that farmers get. When you spend your life with a lot of animals, some of which are headed for the table, things happen. You get used to saying goodbye.

The funny thing is, as practical as he is? He hates it.

He's good about my cats. Never tells me not to cry, always hugs me and helps. Builds little wooden boxes to bury the cat if we have a body, encourages me and helps me look if they're missing.

So when he finds me sitting on the back steps, staring down over the steep bank in back of the house because that's where Periwinkle appeared last time, he sits down beside me. We sit silently for a few minutes, before he puts an arm around me.

"She'd come home if she could."

He knows I worry that the cats just don't want to stay with me for some weird reason, that they desert. I can't help thinking it. It's second only to the fear that they're hurt and unable to come home.

"Probably a fisher cat got her."

It's the logical conclusion in Vermont, especially when you live in the woods. Which most of Vermont does. I've certainly heard it suggested, about my cats and when neighbor cats go AWOL. Just as before, my mind buzzes at the thought of these mysterious beasts. There's a taste of the weird about them, like stories about wood nymphs or haunted hunting shacks. I've never seen a fisher cat, and I'm not entirely sure what one looks like, but the idea of these *things* lurking out there, invisible to us, lying in wait for our pets, blazed itself into my brain long ago.

I think . . . maybe I'd like to get a look.

"I'm sorry," he adds, softer.

I lean my head on his shoulder. I never feel quite so safe as when I'm with him. He's not afraid of the dark, which is the coolest thing ever. I'm not afraid of the dark either, if he's outside with me. But it still amazes me that he'll just walk down over the bank toward the brook in full dark. I'd *never* go over the bank after dark. Ever since I read that Bigfoot book from the school library, I keep expecting to see Bigfoot just walking out of our trees, which freaks me out. Only at night though. For some reason I never expect to see Bigfoot during the day, which is strange since I've never heard that Bigfoot is nocturnal.

Daddy stands up, ready to start the backyard fireplace to grill hamburgers. I follow him across the yard and watch him set up the fire and start it with old newspaper and kindling. I love watching fire, and this means toasted marshmallows later. He lays the old metal grill over the cement block sides. "Get the burgers from your mother?"

"Sure." I run inside and wait while Mom finishes pressing the meat into burgers, with baggies on her hands. She hates to touch raw hamburger. Balancing the plate of meat and a beer for him, I walk back outside and settle in a little way off on the moss to watch him cook. It takes my mind off things, even though we don't talk.

The fire pops and sparks. I think about Bigfoot fighting off fisher cats, protecting my kittens.

Over the next week I continue to think about fishers, Bigfoot, and our back bank. Something has me hooked. I just need to wait for my brain to figure out how to tell me what. Finally, I'm sitting in my swing, listening to the faraway rumble of the brook, when my brain decides it's time to lift the curtain.

Fishers. They're called fishers.

We go fishing. Down over our bank. Where my cats go and then disappear.

Maybe if we go fishing, I could get a look at one. I picture something big and furry—I know that much—catching fish and washing it in its paws, like a raccoon.

I start in on my dad that night. Standing over him where he's stretched out on his back to get his spine back in line, I lean forward so I can see down into his face. "Can we go fishing?"

He ponders. "It's a little early, but I don't see why not, if it doesn't rain. I work Saturday morning, but maybe in the afternoon."

I nod, happy. "Do you need me to walk on you?" Sometimes I walk on his back.

"No, it's pretty good tonight, just a little tired."

"Should I dig the worms?"

"Don't have to until Saturday morning, but you can if you want. If you do it early, remember to put dirt in the can with them."

Right. Nothing more irritating than finding a bunch of great worms—not those little piddly things you can barely get on a hook—only to have them be dried-out dead on fishing day because you forgot the dirt. I mostly remember not to do that anymore, but sometimes I get overexcited.

"And poke holes in the plastic top."

Oh, right. I forgot about that bit.

I wait to dig worms until the next day, turning over the dirt in the garden patch. Daddy hasn't planted yet. It is early, but the ground is soft enough. The Maxwell House can at my feet starts to fill. I leave the ones that are too small, and I even leave the giant purpley night crawler I find under a rock. Partly because the last time I used one, the fish totally ignored it, but mostly because they're gross.

I do take his rock away, though, and roll it over the bank. Daddy needs the rocks out of the garden. He says most all of Vermont is like that, and our best crop is rocks. Fields and fields of rocks. When we learned about the Great Wall of China in school, I started thinking we should have a great wall of Vermont. We've got the rocks for it. Maybe I'll suggest it when I grow up and can vote.

I fill the can half-full of dirt clumps that hold about ten worms altogether, then take the little walk down to Bernie's piece of slate and sit on the ground. It's the spot we bury all the cats. I sit here to talk to them. I use this spot to talk to the ones that disappeared, too. Daddy planted a little pine tree next to it. "I'm going to go fishing this weekend and find a fisher," I tell my dead cats. I'm not sure what else to say. I don't know what I'm going to do once I find one. Still, I get a nice purring sensation, like they're rubbing up against me in approval.

They like the idea; I know they do. That's encouragement enough for me.

I leave the worm can in the shadow of the propane tank at the end of the house so it doesn't bake in the sun and go on inside.

"It's not raining hard. And isn't the fishing better in rain?" It waited until after my dad got home from work before it started. I could just scream.

"How about we play checkers, see if it lets up?"

I'm game, even though I can only beat him at checkers about a third of the time. It's so color-coordinated, like a flannel shirt. We play at the kitchen table, once, twice, three times. He looks outside. I can tell from the sound of rain on the windows that it's not letting up. I feel like crying. Besides the fisher hunt, I really like fishing.

He looks back to me and his mouth opens to speak. He pauses for a long moment, then says, "I think it's letting up. Let's go ahead, before it gets any darker out there."

I bounce up in glee and chase off after a raincoat. I could have sworn the rain hadn't let up at all! Seems almost harder to me. But he knows more about the weather than I do. Than anyone, really. He watches it every night, sometimes twice or three times.

We ignore the pelting rain and collect my worms and the old green fishing pole. It's pretty rusty, and the reel is rusty too, but it's still easier to fish with than the stick poles. The stick poles are thin branches from beech trees, with fishing line tied on the end. But our hooks are in good shape, and my worms survived.

It's dusky out, even at only 2:30 in the afternoon. Walking over the bank is treacherous with layers of wet leaves built up on the ground. We grab hold of trees as we descend the steep incline. It gets darker as the trees thicken around us. Since Daddy's right behind me, it's just cool and otherworldly, not scary. A leafy, mossy, green and brown escape. In seconds we can't even see the house above us, and all I'm thinking about is dodging spider webs.

We get to the first of our favorite places and settle. I bait my hook and drop it in the pool at my feet. After a few quiet moments of watching the water, I suddenly remember I'm looking for more than fish on this trip. Then I spend as much time scouting out the banks on both sides of the brook as I do watching for movement around the rocks in the water.

The rain hits the water and makes spreading, overlapping circles, drawing my eye. Black water bugs with long, bent legs skitter back and forth across the surface. This pool is big enough that the water actually sits here, instead of just rushing on like it does in some places. The mossy brown rocks shift under my feet, and I move very carefully when I want to change position.

Nothing nibbles. Nothing moves on either side of the brook.

After a bit, my dad suggests we try our second spot. I like it even better, because I sit on a big rock outcropping and it's flatter and more solid. The water is deeper, and there are usually more fish hanging around. I reel in and we move down the brook. I concentrate on walking as quietly as possible, though it's hard with the leaves. I don't want to scare the fish. I've always wondered how they hear you under the water. I picture them hearing our approach and swimming under the closest rocks, only to come out when we move on.

The other reason I like this second pool is because I'm that much further from the water, and I feel like I can talk to Daddy without the fish hearing. He must think the same thing because we're sitting watching two different fish dart back and forth in the pool when he suddenly says, "So. You know, kiddo, that Southern accent thing sort of worries your mother."

I nod, still watching the fish, guiding my worm through the water slowly. I do know. And I know he worries about her when she worries about us kids. But it's just the way things are. "I know, Daddy. I've tried to explain. People are going to expect it of me." I haven't talked to him about how I can heal with my hands. I haven't talked to anyone about it. They'd just worry, and they all worry about me too much already.

Or they'd think I was crazy. That's always a possibility.

"People who?"

"Just everyone." I know about faith healers, I researched. They're mostly all Southern men in suits on the television. I figured all this out a few years back when I first found out I could heal. I decided against getting a congregation of my own and hitting people on the forehead, because I'm not so sure about the religion thing. But people are going to expect me to talk like a faith healer, which means Southern.

Besides, once I got myself in the groove of the accent, I couldn't get out of it quite so easy.

That's all too complicated to explain, though, and I know from experience that when I try to explain things, people get confused. I change the subject to get his advice on how to spot a fisher.

"Do the fishers fish in the same good spots? If we're really quiet and still, will they come out to fish while we're here?"

Daddy looks surprised. "Oh . . . no, punkin'. Fishers don't fish. We won't see them. They live in these parts, but they probably hear us coming way off, and they run or climb a tree and hide."

"They don't FISH?" I'm scandalized. They're *fishers*. How can they not fish?

"No, they hunt. Squirrels, rabbits, mice, that sort of thing."

"And cats," I add darkly.

"Yeah, they'll take a cat as quick as anything. But they don't fish."

"Then why are they called fisher cats? That doesn't make any *sense*."

I think he's confused as to why I'm so intense about this, because he has that unsure look he gets when I start spouting something that sounds totally out to lunch. I'm used to that look on adults. But he presses gamely on. "I don't know why they're called fisher cats, come to think of it. Their name is just all over wrong, because they're not even related to cats."

"I thought that bit was because they *ate* cats."

"No, no. Maybe it's because they look a little like a cat, with the tail and general shape." His hands sketch a long, low body. "Kind of a stretch, but I guess they're sort of catlike. But if it was because of what they eat, they could better be called fisher chickens than fisher cats."

I'm incensed. What are people thinking? Naming something a fisher cat when it doesn't fish and isn't a cat, and *not* because they eat cats? That's just not okay. My face screws up into a scowl.

"I can take you to see a stuffed one up at Hogback. Your chance of seeing one live isn't so good."

That's better than nothing, but it doesn't serve my purposes. I'm not certain what my purposes are yet, but I don't think a long-dead fisher suits. Still, if I see the stuffed one, I'll know what I'm looking for and get a clearer mental image. Nodding, I bob my line up and down as the fish below me dart through the water, nowhere near my worm. "Okay. Tomorrow?"

"We'll have to check with your mother, but it's fine with me."

That taken care of, I order the fisher issue out of my head and just fish.

Hogback Mountain always makes me think we're going to drive right off into nothing. It's one of those roads that curves around so sharp that when you're coming to the bend in the road, there's nothing in front of you but huge sky and a major drop. Except right at the very point of the bend they built this gift shop and a platform with those little viewing glasses you can put money in and see things close up. We don't put money in because we're Vermonters, and we see trees close up all the time, but tourists fill them with quarters.

Mom was cool with taking a drive today, so after dropping Jen at work, we headed off. It's wicked cloudy but not raining anymore. The misty fog means fewer people hanging around the platform. Only one car sits in the parking spaces.

Mom and Laura wander the gift shop, but I head right for the stairs that lead down into the cool, darker rooms below. Glass cases stand between open shelves and freestanding pedestals. Vermont wildlife pose everywhere, frozen in time in the act of crouching, swooping, hunting, pouncing, standing clueless about to get eaten, or the ever-popular cowering in fear. Mostly it's birds under the glass cases.

I know it sounds ghoulish, but I never get tired of looking at stuffed creatures. I love the chance to study them so close, see all the details you never see in moving wild animals. They even have a catamount here.

"Evan. This one."

I tear myself away from the fox family and hurry to my dad. He gestures to an open exhibit where a large brown animal hunches, lips peeled back from the ivory of old teeth in a ferocious snarl. I back up, reaching for my father's hand. That fisher looks angry. It's fatter in the back end, the chest and shoulders narrow, almost as if its back is humped. The tail is bushy and long. I tilt my head to the side, transfixed. It looks nothing like a cat. If I was going to compare it to another animal, I'd actually say it looks like a miniature bear. There's one of those down here, too. A bear, I mean, not a miniature bear. I don't think there's any such thing as a miniature bear. But that's what the fisher reminds me of, except its muzzle is narrower.

No way would somebody mistake this thing for a cat.

"That doesn't look anything like a cat."

"No, not so much, does it? It's a weasel, actually."

"A weasel?" Wait a minute. I did weasels in school last year. I remember a lot about them, and the fisher is a lot bigger than what I remember. "A giant weasel?" I ask, skeptical.

Daddy laughs. "Sort of. They're part of the weasel family. Weasels, fishers, stoats, martins."

"Oh, okay. Because it's really big."

"Isn't it?"

"And what's up with the porcupine?" In front of the bristling fisher, a stuffed porcupine lifts its quills.

"They're good at getting porcupines. One of the few things that can get a porcupine without a nose full of quills. That's pretty much why they're back here in New England. After all the fishers got trapped for their pelts, and they were gone, the porcupines were hell on the timber and lumber companies. And houses and barns. The fishers ended up protected, so they could come back and get the porcupines under control. See those feet? It can climb like nothing you've seen. Its feet rotate so it can climb up or down, with a really good grip. It can climb down a tree face-first, not like most animals that have to back down. So it can get to porcupines easy, even after they climb a tree."

"But how does it avoid the stickers?"

Daddy hesitates. "They're mean. They just get right in there and attack and don't let go. When the porcupine turns around to show its back, the fisher jumps clear over it and is in front again. So the porcupine turns around and around and gets tired and confused."

The pause makes me think there's more to it that he thinks might upset me. I let it go, knowing that sometimes he's right. There's stuff I don't need to hear. Leaning my elbows on the shelf, I study the fisher from tip to toes. "Spends a lot of time in trees?"

"Yes."

A new idea forms in my mind even as Laura's voice calls from behind us.

"Daddy? Mom wants you."

He looks at me. "Okay?"

"Sure. I'm going to keep looking."

He ruffles my hair and heads for the stairs, ruffling Laura's hair on the way past. She laughs and follows him. I don't think she's fond of the dead animals.

I turn back to the fisher, leaning in as close as I can without touching. Then, glancing around, I reach out and touch the fur. As bristly as it looks, it's soft as I run my hand down the side. The body is rock hard, nothing like touching a living animal, no life glow. Soft as it is, the hair feels dry as well, and my fingers come away dusty. Wiping the dust on my jeans, I brush the fur of its face. There's no jolt of warmth like when I'm getting a healing pulse. Of course, this fisher is long past healing. Like I said, I can't raise the dead. If anything, though, my hand feels chilled by the touch. Suddenly it's a tiny bit shivery down here, surrounded by dead animals. I push past the sensation and move my fingers into the ruff of fur around the fisher's thick neck, staring into its glass eyes.

Then I get zapped. The electric charge shooting into my palm *hurts*. Nothing like the comfortable heat of healing; it feels more like the time I got shocked by the light socket when I touched the prong of a plug as it was connecting. I have the same reaction too, throwing myself backwards and clutching my hand to my chest. Staring at the inanimate object that should have absolutely no emanation whatsoever, I edge closer again, thumb rubbing at my sore palm. Peering into the glass eyes, I search for something, anything, even knowing the eyes are marbles.

Marbles that pick up an amber glimmer I'd swear wasn't there before, a glimmer way down deep that makes odd shadows flicker in the brown glass. A hum of static fills the air, and the fisher blurs at the edges, as if in a wave of heat. I hear footsteps on the stairs behind me. The very tips of the bristly fur glow red as my dad walks into the room.

"Finished?"

"Sure." But I don't move, waiting as he gets closer. The edging of red is still there, the marble eyes still shadowed. I want . . .

"Laura's going to get an ice cream, if you want one."

I don't want ice cream. I want . . .

"And we thought you might want to look upstairs, too."

Obviously, there's nothing out of the ordinary to him. He stands with his hand on my shoulder, eyes running over the glowing fisher and the same dead porcupine, without reacting.

It doesn't matter what I want.

I take his hand and let him lead me to the door, still watching as the red fades. By the time we start up the stairs, it's gone completely, and I figure I might as well have ice cream after all.

So, fishers do a lot of climbing trees. I can deal with that. I'm not the most athletic kid, but I can climb a tree. I think I can, anyway. My mother doesn't like us climbing trees because she doesn't think it's safe, but I know a tree that I climbed a little way, and I think I can get further up.

My need to see a fisher feels more urgent, not less, since the Hogback visit. I learned right off, when I found out about being able to heal, not to tell anyone about the weird things that happen to me. I sort of knew without knowing how that it just wasn't something people would react to well. I told my dead cats, though. About the glow and the eyes and everything. I still got the feeling they wanted me to find the fisher.

Well, *a* fisher. I realize my head has started thinking of it as *the* fisher. Probably means something. Likely my brain is telling me something again. I don't know what it is yet, though, so I don't worry about it. I recognize there's no way of me knowing if I find *the* fisher that specifically ate my cats. They're solitary, though, so chances are if I find a fisher in our woods, it *would* be the culprit.

That makes me wonder what exactly I might do when I find it, but I push that thought off, too.

"Mom, there's a car in the yard. Can I climb a tree?"

That's the rule. If we want to climb, we have to be in sight of the house, and there has to be a car in the yard. That way, in case we fall and break something, there's some way to get us to the hospital. We don't have a telephone, so we can't call an ambulance. Mom doesn't like telephones, and Daddy can't hear on them, even with his hearing aids.

She looks like she wants to say no. I don't usually bother her about climbing, and I know she'd rather I didn't. Probably because I'm more than a little clumsy, and again ... not so much with the athletic. Now that I have glasses, it's even worse. But Cat is home, and she has a car of her own now, and Daddy will be home from work in about fifteen minutes. She finally relents. "Okay, just be careful, and not too high."

I'm already running for the door, so I'm purposely not looking at her when I call back the lie. "Nope, not too high." I go up into the woods, straight to the really tall pine tree with all the close branches. If I can just pull myself up to get started, I can do this. I reach up to the lowest branch and tug, trying to lift my weight. I'm short, so it's a stretch, but with a swinging jump I get my leg up and over, and I'm on my way.

Only a quarter of the way up and I'm finding the flaw in this plan. Pine pitch. My hands are already sticky with it, and I *hate* sticky hands. Since it's too late now and I'm not about to climb back down to wash my hands off and get gloves, I just keep going. Halfway up, I can see my dad's truck backing into the driveway. I hold onto the trunk and settle my feet, watching him come down the path with his black lunch box in hand—or dinner pail, as he calls it. He disappears into the house, and I start climbing again.

Three quarters of the way up and the branches are

getting a lot smaller, but they're still close together, and I don't weigh that much. From here, I start looking around at all the other trees. I can see a lot farther from up here, just like I hoped. I keep going up and only stop when the top of the tree actually sways with my weight. Then I settle onto the biggest branch I can find, grip the trunk, and start scouting. I'm above most of the oak and beech trees and can get a look into their upper branches.

I look and look and pick pitch off my palms. It occurs to me that the trees I can't see well are the ones down over the bank, and since those are farther from the house, they would probably be the ones the fisher might like best. What are the chances I'd find it the first time out anyway? Frustrated and sticky, I'm about to give up when something moves just about on level with my eyes, somewhere further in the woods.

Searching out the movement, my eyes catch another flicker and focus on a splotch of brown amid the dark green of another large pine. I squint, and the splotch resolves into a long furry body, clinging to the tree like a giant squirrel. I can't believe it. I've actually found the damn thing.

Even as my common sense is whispering, "You're just not that lucky," my eyes adjust, take in more detail, and I understand why I'm seeing the fisher at all.

The thing parked itself in the biggest gap in the big pine's branches. The bushy tail is flicking back and forth, creating just enough movement to catch attention amid the greens of the woods. And it's looking right at me.

Across a distance far enough that I shouldn't be able to discern detail, our eyes meet and a brilliant flash of amber sparkles across my vision. I wonder if this is like the "eyes meeting across a crowded room" thing that happens so often in my sisters' romance novels. Sometimes they read easier than my school books, and I like the way they describe the guys, especially the ones with the red covers.

This definitely feels electric, like the books describe. And I guess you could say I'm intrigued, which the characters in the romance novels always are. Can't say I'm kindly disposed toward the critter though. If it wanted to be found, and it obviously did, couldn't it have made it easier than me climbing up this stupid tree? Now I'm going to have to get back down.

I'd have appeared to you on the ground if you'd just walked into the woods alone, idiot. It was your idea to climb the tree.

The voice registers in my skull like the muted crack and boom of fireworks going off, and I just about fall out of my tree. The sound almost hurts. Shaking my head to clear it, I glare across the distance. Great. Just great. It talks. Another surreal experience I can't tell anyone about. Not that there was any doubt, but here's one more thing to cement my freakiness. Fantastic.

No wonder my dead cats were all cool with me looking for the fisher. They knew it wasn't just any fisher. They probably even knew it wanted to find me. I'm sure knowing about things like that is easier for the dead.

Grumbling under my breath, I start back down the tree. Climbing down is a *lot* harder than climbing up, especially for a short klutz. I can hear a low buzzing hum of impatience from the fisher. Vaguely unpleasant. I block it out with limited success. Jumping from the last branch to the ground, I stumble and catch myself. Now my sticky hands are covered with dirt, too.

Relax. I don't stand on formality.

I walk in the direction of the magnanimous voice. He

sounded serious, which irritates me. Who does he think he is?

I know who I am, child. What I want to know is more about you. Continue approaching. You're almost here.

Ducking branches and stepping over roots, I push further into the woods. Off to my left is our well, and uphill to my right I hear a car drive by. I push aside a swath of branches too low to duck without crawling on my hands and knees. That's out, because there might be spiders in those dead leaves underfoot. Almost to the big pine he was in, I pause, wondering if I really want to meet up with a fisher who talks. I remember big, sharp teeth.

I won't hurt you. He sounds exasperated.

"Right. And I bet you'd tell me if you were going to."

You're too curious to turn back. Besides, I'll just keep waiting for you.

Shrugging, I push through the last few trees, and there he is, sitting on the ground on his hind legs, looking straight at me. He's even bigger than the dead fisher at Hogback. Sitting up like that, he looks huge. He extends a hand—paw—as if to invite me to sit down, but I stay standing. "What do you want?"

He blinks rapidly and his muzzle twitches. *Want? His mouth doesn't move with the sound. Honestly. You should be honored. I usually demand a sacrifice for an audience with me. Don't suppose you have anything to offer?*

I glare at him. "I'm fresh out of cats."

Small dog?

"If I did, I wouldn't hand it over to you!"

His lip lifts on one side of his muzzle in an obvious sneer. *Strange humans. So particular about which animals qualify as food. We're not nearly so picky.* Then, with a sudden lash of his tail, he changes the subject. *I want to talk. You've interested me for some time.*

That rings an odd bell. "Why me?"

His tail lashes again. *Surely you realize why anyone would want to talk to you. You're special, child.*

I can't contain the sigh. "Right. Special. Okay, so what does my specialness mean to YOU?"

Cynical little bastard, aren't you?

"Not really. Just tired of being special sometimes."

How odd. But then I've never presumed to understand humans. First you chase us down to wear us around your necks, then you ban that because porcupines chew through all your wood. So glad we can be of service.

"I don't trap and I don't wear fur, and you don't have to kill porcupines for us if you don't want. I don't care. I like porcupines."

Ah, but they're good eating. Difficult to resist. And plentiful, since no one else can get to them.

That twigs my memory, and curiosity gets the better of me. "Why are you all so good with porcupines, anyway?"

Because we're specialty killers. His pride shines in his voice. *We can tree them and then go up after them. On the ground, we can jump right over them when they try to turn quills on us, and we're fast enough to bite them in the face over and over and bleed them out. Then it's an easy case of flip and eat.*

My stomach turns. Daddy was right. I didn't need to hear about the face biting and bleeding. I'm not surprised he left that out. "Great. So if there are so many porcupines around, why do you have to eat cats?" My own reasons for finding him resurface in my mind, after the distraction of hearing he was looking for me.

Oh please. Cats go missing constantly, and we are not

the culprits you fools make us out. The coyotes kill more cats than we do, and I dare you to go try to have this conversation with their god. Coyote is much more reticent about direct audiences. And honestly now, if you're going to cultivate something that is the perfect size for a prey animal, and then slow it down by overfeeding it, and cripple it by softening it up and destroying its natural instincts . . . well, I'm sorry but you deserve whatever you get.

Opening my mouth to argue the point, my brain zeroes in on one statement. "Their God? Do you mean you're a—"

Of course. You couldn't tell? He looks affronted. *Who else but a god could manifest in a dead skin?*

"God. You're a God."

I'm a god, actually.

When I just look at him he sighs.

Small g.

"What's the difference?"

I find capital-G gods tend to be pretentious.

Alrighty then. "So, you're . . . god of the . . . fishers?"

The general weasel/stoat family. Minks, too. I tried for the otters as well, but they're not a very serious bunch. Nothing but antics. I let it go.

"Do all the animals have their own gods?"

Of course. I couldn't exactly presume to be god of deer, now could I? Although I'd be tempted to try. They have all the brains of domestic sheep. Which is to say none whatsoever.

Something about this puzzles me. "Gods, not goddesses? None of you have a goddess?"

The fisher god shakes his head so violently, for a moment I wonder if he's got something in his ear. *No no no. She wouldn't be pleased with lesser goddesses popping up everywhere. She would not be pleased at all.*

"She?"

Now see here! We came here to talk about me, not Her.
He stamps his foot.

"Actually I, came here to talk about my cats."

We've already gone over that.

"No, we haven't! You just blamed it on coyotes and
treated it like a done deal."

Coyotes . . . foxes . . . what have you.

"So you haven't killed any of my cats."

Of course not.

An anger I hadn't recognized cools behind my breastbone. I feel deflated. "Oh." If it wasn't him, how can I
ask him to stop?

I have minions for that sort of thing.

That takes a moment to sink in. "Minions?"

He lifts a paw and gives a rumbling growl. A soft red
glow suffuses his fur. The woods around us vibrate as
patches of brown separate from nearby trees and con-
solidate into animals. Three fishers and a variety of small
weasels edge forward and stop in a circle around us. I
stop breathing for a minute, all those beady little eyes
trained on me. It creeps me out that they were there, just
so still as to be invisible. It continues to creep me out
that they sit so quiet, *looking* at me.

"One of these killed my cats?"

*Not all of your cats. There were a couple of cars in-
volved, you'll recall.*

The anger is back, and this time I know it for what it
is. "But, oh, no, you guys aren't responsible for all the
cat disappearances. It's the coyotes." Sarcasm isn't my
best look, but I can manage it. "Why are they targeting
my cats?"

His head swivels to the side, and one paw lifts to fluff
his fur idly. *Ah . . . that would be my fault.*

Why am I not surprised?

Not intentionally, you understand. I was drawn to you, to what you are, without knowing why. So I took up residence in this general area, trying to find the source of the pull. My presence attracts more of my followers than might otherwise be in a particular area. And they do feel obliged to bring me gifts at times.

"Why didn't you show yourself? Why'd you let them keep killing my cats?"

I didn't know the pull was you. I just knew something was here. Something special. Like myself.

Being lumped in the same category as a giant glowing weasel isn't the most complimentary comparison I've experienced. I decide that making that observation out loud could be considered insulting, so I don't.

Then when you started thinking about me so much, I became more aware of the locus of the pull. You started actively calling to me. That made it easier.

"I brought you to me?"

Yes. Like a Disney movie come to life.

Now that's scary. I stare at him, trying to determine if he's kidding, but it's a difficult face for reading expression. "You lot know Disney movies?"

He snorts, and suddenly his expression is easy to decipher. *Please. I'm a god. Mr. Disney is roasting in a special hell reserved for those who take liberties with the animal kingdom.*

I feel my eyes go wide. "Really? You can do that?"

We all have our own influence.

Shaking that disturbing image off, I grasp backward for the thread I know I don't want to lose. "If I called you, then am I—"

Oh, yes. You've very likely called Others as well. Get a lot of deer in these parts?

"So I could be surrounded by gods and not know it."

Most definitely. Coyote himself could be out there snickering away with your name in mind. And may I assure you that is a scary thought indeed.

"So it's my fault my cats got eaten."

They don't hold it against you.

I sink down, sitting hard on the ground. A small weasel the color of chocolate with a beige face slinks closer and lifts onto his back legs, placing his front paws on my leg. Without thinking, I reach out and stroke a hand down his back. He nuzzles me. "And it's my fault other people's cats have gotten eaten."

They don't hold it against you either. At least, the cats don't. I can't speak for the people. If I were you, I wouldn't tell them about it being your fault.

The little weasel on my leg twists his head around toward his god and makes an odd noise, between a squeak and a yip. Then he bounces up into my lap and curls up on me, staring at his god with his teeth showing. One of the fishers swings his head toward the god and makes a low hiss, like an angry cat.

Oh, fine. I have the feeling the fisher god wants to roll his eyes. *It's not your fault. My followers insist I not leave you with all this metaphorical cat blood on your hands. Each animal acts on his or her own recognizance. Simply because I came here due to the pull of you does not mean you need to take responsibility for all the various results of my residency. Understand?*

"Yes." I don't elaborate that while I understand, I don't agree. I appreciate what his followers are saying. Instead, I change the subject. "So why do I call you? Before I started concentrating on fishers, back when you first just felt a draw."

The fisher god opens his mouth, and as one, the surrounding animals react. The squeaks, growls, and hissing noises startle me, and I remember to be a little scared. The god hisses back at them, his mouth opening wide, showing an alarming number of teeth. The collected followers subside, but an uneasy tension hangs in the air. The god turns his attention to me. Dark eyes stare into mine until I feel like I'm seeing straight through the pupils into that amber gleam deep inside. Finally, he says, *Haven't you heard the saying? Like calls to like.*

I puzzle over that, but it doesn't get any clearer. I'm not a fisher and I'm not a god. It's a nonanswer. I wish I could make sense of it, and I wish I knew why the animals reacted. The weasel in my lap is calm again, his head resting on my thigh.

"Now what, now that you know it's me and we've met?" I stroke the weasel on my leg with one finger.

The god stretches his body forward, and his front feet hit the ground. He walks toward me, his back end hunched so that his gait is odd. The surrounding animals retreat, but the weasel on my leg only lifts his head. The god skulks right up to me, until his muzzle almost brushes my arm. He circles me, and a crackle of static electricity raises the hair on my arms, on the back of my neck. I feel that same electric charge I felt in the basement on Hogback Mountain. If I touched him, I don't doubt I'd get zapped. My hands curl into fists.

The fisher god circles back into my line of sight, his fur glowing that subdued red again. His nose twitches as he leans in, directly in front of me. *I'd like an alliance. A partnership.*

"With me?"

No, with your Aunt Mary Lou. Yes, with you. Honestly, boy. One would think you really don't understand what your unusual draw is.

"I'm special," I sigh. "Right?"

You are. You heal. So, our partnership. You listen for me, you watch for me, and when I need you, you come here.

"And do what?"

What you do. Heal. It's a dangerous world, or didn't you know?

I think of some of the kids at school. Yes, I know dangerous. "So I heal hurt animals?" I can do that.

Exactly.

"I can do that. What do I get?"

He rises up onto his hind legs, looking affronted again. His lip pulls back. *Excuse me?*

"What do I get from our partnership?"

Have I mentioned I usually require a sacrifice to even have an audience with me? You're being offered an opportunity to use your gift in a very noble and rewarding way, for a god.

"You ate my cats."

The pause hangs heavy. *What would you desire, for offering healing when needed?*

"Stop eating my cats."

That's all?

The way he says that makes me wonder what I'm missing, what else he's getting out of this deal, and what else I should ask for. But that's all I had in mind. "Yes. Just leave my cats alone." Another thought occurs. "And protect them from other things."

Now see here. I'm not about to become a bodyguard for a feline.

"Then get some of your followers to do it. Just see nothing happens to any of my future cats. In the way of being eaten. I know you can't keep them from getting run over."

He inclines his head. *I can do that.*

Wow. That worked out well. For once there's a benefit to being strange. "Okay. If that's it, I ought to be going. My mother is probably freaking out."

It won't be the first time.

I have no idea what that's supposed to mean, but I've had enough of his cryptic pronouncements. Lifting the weasel from my lap, I scratch his head in parting and get to my feet. "I'll watch for you." I start back, lifting a branch and ducking under it. Sudden rustling tells me the followers leave too, and I glance over my shoulder. They're already gone, to a one. Only the god sits, perfectly still and watching me. I walk through the woods to our yard with the feel of his eyes on my back the entire way.

I scrub my hands until they're bright red but all the pitch still won't come off. I sit digging at it while Daddy watches the weather. When it's over, he turns off the TV, then sits back down on the couch. "What's up? You look sad."

"I just . . ." I stop. There's no good way to talk about any of this. I knew that years ago, and nothing has changed. Finally I say the only thing I can. "I think it's my fault all our cats disappear." I know it is. But I can't say that.

He's quiet for a few minutes, settling his arm over my shoulders. "Sometimes there's nothing you can do, Evan, no matter how much you want to. It's not your fault, it's just the way the world is. It's probably one of the hardest things to accept, but it's always there, especially when you feel responsible for something. You can love it so much you never want to see it get hurt, but you can't protect it from everything."

I think about how I feel when I'm around him—that

he can protect me from anything—and start to say so. But even as I'm thinking it, I remember him holding me the night Bernie died. I remember him telling me what happened, and I remember his tears. He couldn't protect me from that—not the death and not his hurting. I look up at him and see a similar pain now, in the lines around his eyes. It's not one I can heal away, any more than I can explain the strangeness that is me.

I know *I* can't climb in a box and never get hurt. I can't expect anything else to do the same for me.

"It's okay," I finally tell him. "You do a really good job anyway."

The lines around his eyes ease, then crinkle again as he smiles. The ache in my own chest relaxes a little when I realize that, in a way, I can heal some of that pain. I think if I could figure out how to explain everything that's so strange about me, he'd be pleased with me helping the fisher god. It's something he'd do.

The idea that he'd be proud of me if he did know cheers me up. One of these days I'll be able to explain to him about me. He'll understand.

As soon as I find the words.

BONE WHISPERS

By Tim Waggoner

Tim Waggoner's novels include *Pandora Drive*, *Thieves of Blood*, the Godfire duology, and *Like Death*. He's published close to eighty short stories, some of them collected in *All Too Surreal*. His articles on writing have appeared in *Writer's Digest*, *Writers' Journal*, and other publications. He teaches creative writing at Sinclair Community College in Dayton, Ohio. Visit him on the web at *www.timwaggoner.com*.

Kevin Blancmore slowed as he approached the old graveyard. It had been almost forty years since he'd been here last, and the place looked as if it hadn't changed in the slightest during that time. It was not a thought that provided comfort.

Kevin braked and pulled his Nissan Altima—on which he was two payments behind, not that it mattered anymore—onto the side of the road in front of the graveyard's black wrought-iron gate. There was no parking lot—the graveyard predated the road by nearly a century, he guessed—and Kevin scarcely had enough room to get his car off the road. There wasn't a lot of traffic out here in the country, and he doubted he'd have to worry about someone coming along too fast, not seeing his car, and broadsiding the damned thing. But even if they did, what did he care?

Kevin turned off the engine and pulled the keys out of the ignition, but instead of getting out of his vehicle right away, he sat for a moment, staring through the windshield and listening to the car's engine tick as it began to cool. He wasn't sitting there because he was afraid, though he supposed he had good reason to be. And he wasn't nervous, not even a little. He felt nothing, and that was the reason he sat behind the wheel of his car, hesitating. Considering what he had come here to do or, more to the point, to *find,* he should feel something. A moment like this ... well, it was why the word *momentous* had been created, wasn't it? It was potentially life-altering in the profoundest of ways and should be marked as such, if only inside his own heart. But just because he was aware that he should feel something didn't mean he would. It seemed he was as dead inside as any of the graveyard's residents, and all that remained was for the rest of him to catch up.

He unlocked the driver's side door and climbed out of the car.

The weather in southwest Ohio in early June could range from cool and mild to hot and sweltering. But that was Ohio, where the weather changed as often as people's minds. Unfortunately for Kevin, it felt more like mid-August, the air steamy, thick, and damp. Even worse, he still had on the suit he'd worn for Nancy's graduation, and the instant he emerged from the Altima's air-conditioned environment, sweat began beading on his forehead and pooling beneath his armpits.

He considered leaving his jacket and tie in the car and rolling up his shirt sleeves, but even though he would be more physically comfortable, he decided against it. A momentous moment like this called for a certain level of formality, so the suit would stay on and he'd just have to endure the discomfort. He could do that; after all, he'd had a lot of practice. An entire lifetime's worth it seemed sometimes.

Let's have a pity party for Kevvy-wevvy, he thought. *One, two, three—awwwww!*

Half amused and half disgusted at himself, Kevin walked across the uneven grass that covered the small strip of land in front of the graveyard—*Looks like the county's behind in their mowing*—and stepped up to the gate. The graveyard was enclosed by a salmon-colored brick wall that measured five feet high, nine feet on either side of the gate and at the wall's four corners where conical black-brick turrets pointed skyward. Kevin thought the graveyard's designer must've been going for a somber yet dignified effect, and he couldn't say the man had missed. The gate was in fact a pair, held shut by an ancient rusted padlock. Not locked, though. The padlock hung open on the gate, just as it had done during Kevin's childhood. He wouldn't have been surprised to learn that the padlock rested in the same exact position that it had then, untouched by hands all these long decades. Human hands, anyway.

A metal plaque was bolted on the turret to the right of the entrance, its surface dingy, the letters worn some but still legible.

QUAKER BRANCH MEMORIAL BURIAL GROUND. EST. 1957.

Kevin knew the date referred to the construction of the wall. The graveyard itself was much older.

He took hold of one of the gate's bars, careful to grip
a section where the black paint hadn't flaked off too
much—*Didn't come all the way here to get tetanus,* he
thought, almost smiling—and pushed. The gate resisted
at first, the bottom edge digging into the ground, and he
gave it a bit more muscle. Finally, the gate budged a few
feet, giving him enough space to slide through, even with
his less-than-modest gut. The gate hadn't made a sound
when it moved, no slow creaking or harsh grinding, and
Kevin recalled that it had been similarly silent the last
time he was here. Now, just as then, he was vaguely dis-
appointed. A proper cemetery gate should open with
some manner of sinister sound to establish the appropriate atmosphere.

Once inside, he paused to look around. Large oak and
elm trees bordered the outside of the graveyard, making
it impossible to see what, if anything, lay beyond. There
were no trees inside, no bushes, no greenery of any kind
save grass. Just as outside, the grass was uneven, almost
a foot high in some places, in others trimmed so close
to the ground that bare patches of dry earth peeked
through. There were a good number of gravestones, over
a hundred, he estimated, and they were divided into two
roughly even sections. On his left were the newer stones,
dating from around the time the outer wall had been
constructed. They were larger, more varied in type, and
the legends engraved upon them were still readable. To
Kevin's right was what he thought of as the old section.
Here the headstones were much smaller, set closer together, and more uniform in shape. They were colored
either stony gray or chalk-white, their edges softened
by the passage of one season after another and the
elements' less than tender ministrations. Kevin knew
from previous experience that the inscriptions—those

that remained legible, that is—were both simpler and somehow more elegant than those in the newer section. WILHEMINA MOTE, B. 1834, D. 1867. JACOB HOBBLIT, B. 1856, B. 1859. The birth and death dates were almost always closer together in that section, as well. Sometimes too close.

Past the newer section, nestled against the grave-yard's east wall, sat a simple wooden building, its sides gray, boards fraying in places as if the structure had been fashioned from cloth instead of wood. Two windows were visible from this angle, a door set between them, a small plaque affixed to the right of the door. Kevin couldn't make out the words from where he stood, but he didn't need to. He knew what the plaque said, could recite it from memory. THIS BUILDING IS A REPLICA OF A QUAKER MEETING HOUSE THAT STOOD ACROSS THE STREET FROM 1803 TO 1849. ERECTED BY THE BOY SCOUTS OF AMER-ICA, ASH CREEK TROOP, 1962.

The plaque didn't mention the fate of the original meeting house, and Kevin had always wondered what had happened to it. Had it burned down? Or simply grown old and fallen apart? *Happens to the best of us,* he thought. *The worst of us, too.* He also wondered why the scouts had chosen to reconstruct it. It seemed like a rather morbid project to Kevin, but then he'd never been a Boy Scout. Maybe it had been a jolly good time for those young upstanding citizens-to-be. Or maybe it had just been one more damn thing to do to earn an-other meaningless badge.

Looking at the meeting house—the *replica,* he re-minded himself—Kevin experienced a flash of memory so intense and visceral, for an instant it was as if he'd traveled back in time forty years. He was inside the meeting house, sitting with his back against the door, tears streaming down his cheeks. On the other side of the door was an excited snuffling accompanied by the sound of claws scratching against wood. From time to time there came a *thump,* both felt and heard, as something heavy shoved its body against the door in an attempt to force it open. And of course there were the sounds of his sobs and his plaintive whispered pleas. *Go away, please go away . . .*

Kevin gave his head a single sharp shake to dispel the memory, but while it retreated, it didn't go far. He felt moisture on his face, and he reached up and wiped it away, telling himself that it was only sweat and almost believing it.

The memory reminded him, as if he needed to be reminded, that there was one part of the graveyard he had up to this point assiduously avoided looking at: straight down the middle, back against the south wall. It wouldn't here now, not after all this time. So there was no reason not to look, right?

But the hole was still there, looking just as large as he remembered it. A three-foot circumference around which were scattered a number of old broken headstones, looking as if at some point they'd been flung forth from the hole and allowed to lay where they landed. And next to the hole, sitting back on its hind legs and gnawing a length of bone held clutched in its front paws, was a groundhog the size of a sheep. The creature looked at Kevin with its glossy black eyes, completely unfazed by the human's presence, regarding him impassively as it chewed on the bone, its teeth making soft *shhh-shhh-shhh* sounds.

Up to this moment the air had been still, but now a breeze moved through the graveyard, causing the branches in the trees that surrounded the outer walls to sway. The soft rustling of their leaves sounded to Kevin's ears like a chorus of whispering voices all saying the same thing.

Welcome back.

Kevin pedaled his bike faster, not caring that he couldn't see the road clearly through the tears in his eyes. Maybe if he went fast enough, the wind he kicked up would dry them. Or maybe he'd end up getting creamed by a car because his vision was blurred. Either way would be fine with him right now.

Houses flashed past: trees in the yards, cars in the driveways. Ranches, two stories . . . the same sort of homes that you'd find in town, except there was more space between them out here—sometimes as much as an acre or two. Though Kevin technically lived in the country, it was still close enough to town that there weren't many farms around, certainly none within a mile or so. It was late August, and he'd be starting fourth grade next week, not that he cared. He used to look forward to the beginning of the school year, but not anymore. Now he didn't look forward to anything.

The wind blowing against his face was hot and dry, and while it blew the tears from his eyes, its heat stung his face. He wondered if he was sunburned. Probably, he figured. He'd been out long enough. He couldn't decide whether he liked the pain, couldn't decide whether to keep feeling it or ignore it. He decided to worry about it later.

He'd been out riding since breakfast, and his Yellow Submarine T-shirt was soaked with sweat and clung to his scrawny body as though it were glued to him. His shorts were damp too, and he could imagine another kid seeing him, calling out, "Hey, did you pee your pants?"

and then bursting out with mocking laughter. Kevin would have to toss his clothes into the washer whenever he finally got home. He had to wash all his clothes, his sheets and pillow cases, too. And he had to do the dishes, both his and his mother's. If he didn't, the sink would become so full that cups and plates would slide off the mound and crash to the kitchen floor.

He wondered if his mother had any idea he'd been out this long, and if she did, was she worried? Not that she'd get out of her chair, let alone leave the house, if she was. Sometimes Kevin wondered what would happen if the house caught on fire. Would his mom just keep sitting in that old chair of hers, staring at the TV even after the air had become so filled with smoke that the screen was no longer visible? Would she sit there while the flames drew ever closer and began licking at her flesh? Maybe.

She hadn't liked leaving the house when Dad was alive, but he usually had been able to coax her outside. But now ...

Kevin didn't want to think about *now*, so he pedaled faster and concentrated on the stinging wind biting into his face.

Eventually he realized he was hungry, and he figured he might as well go home and make himself some lunch. He didn't care about food anymore; it was all so much tasteless mush to chew and swallow. But if he didn't eat, he'd become so hungry that he wouldn't be able to ignore his growling stomach, shaking hands, and throbbing head. It was easier to just eat and get it done with so he could avoid the annoyance. He'd ridden that day without any particular destination, just traveling up and down country roads, riding just to ride, pedaling so he wouldn't have to think or feel. But he was on Jay

Road now, only about a mile from his house. He could be home in only a few minutes—if he took the shortest route. Unfortunately, that would be riding past the old Quaker graveyard, and Kevin wasn't sure he wanted to do that.

He'd been to the graveyard a few times before but always with his father, never alone. It had seemed scary back then, but because he was with his dad, it was fun-scary, not scary-scary. But since his father died—almost a year ago, now, though it sometimes seemed to Kevin to be much longer—he hadn't wanted anything to do with graveyards and cemeteries, or anything else that related to death in any way. But if he wanted to get home fast, he'd have to go past Quaker Branch.

He almost took the long way. But it *had* been almost a year since his dad had succumbed to lung cancer, and Kevin *was* going to be in fourth grade, was practically a fourth-grader already. He figured it was time he started acting his age. He bet when Dad was a kid, he wouldn't have been afraid to ride past the graveyard.

That settled the matter. Kevin turned off Jay Road onto Hoke. His road—Culver—branched off from Hoke ... right after the graveyard. He thought about pedaling his ass off and flying by the graveyard at superspeed, but if he did that, he'd zoom right past Culver. There was no way he'd make the turn going fast; he'd end up in a ditch or sprawled on the street, scraped up and bleeding. He didn't care if he got hurt, but if he was injured, he'd have to clean and dress his own wounds, and he didn't feel like doing all that work. So he slowed as he drew near Quaker Branch, telling himself to keep his gaze fixed straight ahead and not look as he went past. But the graveyard was on his right, and it was set so close to the road that it was hard not to look. And there were memories within those walls . . . memories of him and his dad. In the end, he couldn't *not* look.

When he did, he braked to a stop in front of the black gate without being aware he was doing so. Through the gate's bars, on the far side of the graveyard, a large animal sat back on its haunches, its round head turned toward Kevin, wet black eyes staring at him. Its fur was brownish-gray shot through with coarse silver-white hairs, and it held something in its forelegs . . . something curved, white, and smooth. At first Kevin thought it was a giant rat—the creature looked to be three feet tall, if not larger—and it was plump, almost as round as a beach ball.

Kevin's imagination whispered through his mind. *You know how it got so fat, don't you? It's got tunnels all through the graveyard. It's broken into the graves, gnawed through the coffins, and—*

Kevin clamped down on those thoughts, clamped down hard. It wasn't a rat, it couldn't be. Rats didn't get that big . . . did they?

The creature, whatever it was, continued sitting there and staring at him, completely motionless. Kevin might have thought the animal was some kind of statue, or maybe stuffed and mounted by a taxidermist, so still was it. But despite the absence of movement, he knew it was alive. He could feel intelligence looking out at him from those wet black eyes, gauging, judging . . .

Then Kevin realized what it was that he was looking at. Not a rat, but a groundhog. Still a damned big one, though.

So it's a groundhog, his imagination said. *It still could've dug tunnels in the graveyard, still could be feeding here. Look at what it's holding . . . does that look like a rib to you?*

The idea was ridiculous. Groundhogs didn't eat meat . . . did they? Kevin wished his dad were here. He'd know. What's more, he'd tell Kevin that the groundhog had probably just burrowed its way underneath the wall around the graveyard, or maybe squeezed its furry bulk between the bars of the gate. It was just curious, just exploring. It didn't live here, didn't have tunnels here, and it certainly wasn't eating the remains of people, some of whom had been dead for more than a century. But Dad wasn't here to tell Kevin these things, and for some reason, they didn't sound as convincing when Kevin told them to himself.

The groundhog continued sitting and staring, but now it began to move. It brought the smooth white curved thing it held toward its mouth and—eyes still fixed on Kevin—began to chew on one splintered end. Even though the groundhog was at least two hundred feet away, Kevin could hear the sounds it made as it chewed as clearly as if it were sitting right next to him. Soft *shh-shh-shh* sounds, almost like someone brushing their teeth.

It wasn't a bone, couldn't be!

Before he realized he was doing so, Kevin started yelling at the groundhog.

"Get out of here! Go!"

He expected the animal to startle, drop the bone, and go running off in the galumphing-undulating way groundhogs had when they really wanted to move. But this groundhog just continued to sit, stare, and chew.

Shh-shh-shh, shh-shh-shh, shh-shh-shh . . .

Kevin opened his mouth to yell again, but before he could, the groundhog stopped chewing. It looked at Kevin for a long moment, and Kevin looked back, unable to tear his gaze away from the strange animal. And then the groundhog dropped the bone—if that's what it was—then fell forward onto all fours and began slowly coming toward Kevin.

Kevin's trance broke then, and he lifted his feet off the ground, jammed them onto the pedals, and got the hell out of there as fast as he could. He pedaled madly, and by the time he reached his house, sweat dripped off of him like rainwater, and while he had no memory of doing so, he realized he must've taken the corner turn onto his road at full speed and not wrecked somehow. He remembered something his father had once told him.

It's amazing what people can do when they're motivated, Kevin.

"No shit," Kevin whispered.

Kevin went out riding again after the first day of fourth grade. He didn't even bother going into the house after he got off the school bus. He just dropped his book bag onto the front porch, hopped on his bike, and took off down the driveway. He doubted his mother would know that he'd gotten home, let alone that he'd immediately left, and even if she did, he didn't care.

Kevin didn't have many friends, and none of them were in his class this year. He'd seen Mike Todd and Steve Tomlinson out on the playground at recess, and while he'd been tempted to tell them about the groundhog in the graveyard, for some reason he hadn't. It wasn't that he feared they wouldn't believe him—although Steve could be skeptical at times. It just felt as though he should keep the experience to himself, as if what had happened was private, just between him and the groundhog.

He hadn't been able to stop thinking about the giant groundhog, kept hearing the sound of the creature gnawing on its bone, kept seeing it coming toward him across the graveyard grounds ... The whole thing had been scary, sure, and he was scared now as he pedaled down Culver Road toward Hoke and the Quaker Branch Memorial Burial Ground. But he felt something else, too, something he hadn't felt in a long time: hope.

He remembered staying up one Saturday with his dad about six months ago to watch the late-night horror show, *Shock Theatre,* hosted by Dr. Creep. They watched the TV down in the basement because Mom was watching another movie upstairs, and she didn't want to change the channel. But that was okay. Kevin liked being down in the basement, alone with his dad, just the two of them. The film that evening had been *Thirteen Ghosts* with Vincent Price, and while Kevin didn't remember much of the story, he'd never forgotten one scene where a skeleton came out of a pool to stalk a pretty blonde woman in a nightgown.

During a commercial, Kevin had turned to his dad. "I don't like ghosts. They're creepy."

His dad put his arm around Kevin's shoulders and gave his son a gentle squeeze. "Yeah, that skeleton was scary, huh? But you know, I think there's something nice about ghosts, too. At least, about the idea of them. If you ever saw one, then you'd know that spirits were real, and that there's something more to life than just physical existence."

Kevin hadn't had any idea what his father was talking about, so he didn't say anything. But he understood now that his dad had already been sick and knew that he was going to die. He also understood what his father had been talking about. He didn't know if there was anything like a heaven for him to go to once he was gone. He'd been scared.

That was why Kevin hadn't been able to stop thinking about the groundhog. The damned thing was weird, no doubt about that, but if it was supernatural somehow, that meant that there was more to life than most people thought, that magical things could happen. The groundhog wasn't a good thing, Kevin was sure of that, but if bad magical things were real, good ones had to be too, right? He remembered something else his father had once said.

Where's there's shadow, there has to be light.

Kevin was headed back to the graveyard to see if he could find that light, even just a hint of it. Because if he could ... it meant that his father was maybe still alive somewhere, and not just a body sealed inside a coffin covered with dirt.

This time when Kevin reached the graveyard gate, he put down his bike's kickstand and climbed off. He walked up to the gate, shivering despite the temperature. He expected to see the groundhog come running toward him across the uneven grass, launch itself at the gate, claws scrabbling in the air as it tried to grab hold of him, curved flat teeth gnashing, eager to take a chunk out of his skin, tear away flesh to reveal the gleaming white bone beneath. Hard, fresh, young bone, so good for gnawing ...

But there was nothing. The graveyard was empty.

For a moment Kevin considered getting back on his bike and leaving. Instead, he pushed open the gate, which made no sound as it moved, and walked inside. He expected to experience some sort of eerie feeling—a chill rippling down his spine, maybe a sense that he was being watched. But he felt nothing beyond the heat of the day and a slight breeze that moved the air around without cooling things off. Well, he was here. Might as well take a look.

He started walking toward the spot where he'd seen the groundhog sitting.

He saw the hole long before he reached it. It was so big, he was surprised he hadn't seen it from the road. It was located only a few feet from the graveyard's southern wall, and the ground here was mostly bare, with only patches of dry, dead grass. The edges of the hole were rounded and worn smooth from years of use. How old could the groundhog be? Kevin had looked up groundhogs in an encyclopedia at the school library, and according to what he'd read, the animals usually lived two to three years in the wild, but they could live as much as six years. But somehow the hole looked older, much older, as if it had predated the burial ground, a natural formation that had been here since long before any humans had ever set foot upon the continent. It was a crazy thought, of course, but he couldn't shake it.

Kevin walked up to the edge of the hole and peered down. It measured nearly three feet across, he estimated, and there was no telling how far down it went. He couldn't see further than a few inches down. After that, the dry earth of its walls gave way to inky shadow that seemed so thick Kevin wondered if a beam of direct light would penetrate it. He wished he'd thought to bring a flashlight. Then he could've checked for himself. He was thinking about riding home to get one when he felt cool air emanate from the hole. It wasn't a breeze, exactly; more like air leisurely wafting forth from somewhere far away. It was cool and musty-smelling, kind of like a basement but more so. A basement built deep within the earth. Miles deep. Miles upon miles. A soft sound accompanied the air, kind of like the hush of ocean waves breaking on a distant shore. No, more like the whispering of voices. Hundreds, maybe thousands. So soft that Kevin could almost but not quite make out the words.

He lost track of time as he stood there, looking down into the darkness, listening to the voices as they continued whispering, more urgent now, as if they were desperate to impart a message to him, but whatever it was, he wasn't getting it. Maybe if he stepped closer to the hole, leaned down, cocked his head to the side so that his ear was nearer the source of the whispering ...

He got as far as sliding one foot forward when he heard a rustling in the grass off to this right. He snapped out of his trance and turned in time to see the giant groundhog running toward him. He had no idea where the creature had been hiding, but that wasn't important now. All that mattered was the damned thing was attacking. The voices grew louder then, and Kevin thought he might have been able to make out what they were saying, but he was too terrified by the creature coming toward him. He screamed, his voice drowning out the whispers, and he whirled around and ran toward the Quaker meeting house. He didn't look back to see if the groundhog pursued. He didn't have to.

He reached the house, grabbed the metal handle bolted to the front door, and prayed it was unlocked. It was. He ran inside, slammed the door shut behind him, and dropped to the floor. He pressed his back against the door just as the groundhog slammed into the other side with a heavy thump. Kevin sat there, listening as the groundhog began scratching at the wood, tears streaming down his face, and he begged the creature to go away and leave him alone. But the scratching didn't stop. It continued on and on ...

* * *

Adult Kevin walked up to the groundhog. The damned thing was even larger than he remembered. He didn't question whether it was the same creature. Of course it was. The beast sat only a couple feet from its lair. The hole looked the same as it had the last time he'd seen it, with the exception of the headstones scattered about. After he'd escaped the groundhog by breaking one of the meeting house's windows, climbing through, and running like hell for his bike, Kevin had returned to the graveyard one last time. He'd knocked down some of the older, smaller headstones—ones he felt confident he could carry—and brought them over to the hole. He tossed them inside, wedging them into the hole, stomping on them to pack them down tight. He'd known it wouldn't stop the creature, which he'd decided might *look* like a groundhog but was undoubtedly something else, but he had to do it, if for no other reason than he could pretend that he'd stopped the thing. He'd expected the beast to come after him at any moment, but the groundhog didn't show, and he'd left the graveyard safely, telling himself that he'd sealed the creature off from the world and no one need ever fear it again. He'd known even then that it was bullshit, but it was bullshit he needed to believe.

Now, four decades later, he walked up to the groundhog and crouched in a squatting position in front of it. The creature made no move against him, nor did it seemed fearful. It continued gnawing on its bone as it regarded him with its wet black stare. Kevin stared back, gazing deep into the darkness within those eyes, and for a few moments he did nothing more. But eventually he began speaking in a soft, tired voice.

"My daughter Nancy graduated high school today. I

didn't stay for her party, though. I . . . Her mother and I divorced when she was little, and Nancy's been uncomfortable around me ever since. Can't say as I blame her. I inherited my mother's less-than-sunny disposition, and I've battled depression all my life. And I don't think I ever recovered from the trauma of losing my father so young. At least, that's what all the therapists I've seen over the years tell me. It's been so hard for me. I can barely bring myself to talk with other people, and I can barely get out of bed in the morning. Medicine doesn't help. Just makes me groggier. But that's not the worst of it. A few months ago, I found out that I inherited something from my father, too. His cancer."

The groundhog remained motionless, but it stopped chewing the bone, and Kevin had the impression that it was paying attention to him. What's more, he had the feeling that it understood his words.

"No one knows. I didn't tell anyone at work. Didn't tell my ex-wife or Nancy. I wasn't planning on doing anything about it. Doctor says there's nothing *to* do. But as I was driving home from the graduation ceremony, I passed the highway exit for my hometown and remembered this place. Remembered you. So I turned around, got off the highway, and came here."

The groundhog cocked its head slightly to one side.

"To tell you the truth, I'm not really sure why I came here. Maybe I'm hoping that this time I'll finally find out whether there's anything beyond this life or not. Or maybe I'm just hoping that you'll make a fast end of me and spare me weeks of painfully withering away to nothing in a hospice." He paused. "I guess the real reason I'm here comes down to one thing: I've got nowhere else to go."

The groundhog stared at him for a long time, and

Kevin stared back, sweat rolling down the sides of his face and the back of his neck. He wondered if he'd try to run this time if the groundhog attacked, or if he'd just stand here and let the creature do what it would to him.

Finally, the groundhog dropped the bone to the grass and fell forward onto all fours. Kevin's stomach clenched in anticipation of the beast running toward him, but he held his ground. Whatever was to come within the next few seconds, Kevin had at least answered one question for himself: he wasn't going to run.

The groundhog looked at him a moment longer, as if it were trying to come to decision of its own. Then it slowly turned away and began walking toward its hole. When it reached the edge, it stopped and turned back to look at Kevin, and then it crawled in, its large, furry body sliding into the opening with ease. And then it was gone.

Kevin stood there for a moment, trying to understand what had just happened. When he'd been a child, the groundhog had attacked, clearly trying to kill him. But this time it hadn't displayed even a hint of aggression. He was sure it was the same creature, no matter how impossible that might be, so why hadn't it come after him this time? Was he too large to be considered prey now? Too old? And then it came to him. It was neither of those things. The creature hadn't attacked him because there was no reason to. He was for all intents and purposes already dead, both inside and out. He was no longer an intruder to be run off. He belonged here.

Kevin walked over to the edge of the hole, which was larger now, to accommodate the groundhog's increased bulk, and peered into the darkness within. He felt the same cool air on his face as he had when he was ten, smelled the same basementy odor, heard the same soft whispers. Only this time, he understood their message clearly. It was an invitation.

Kevin thought it over for a moment. Then he removed his suit jacket, folded it neatly, and lay it on the ground next to the hole. Then he got down on his hands and knees and followed the groundhog into darkness. As he made his descent—fingers clawing moist soil, hard-shelled insects scuttling through his sweaty hair and beginning to crawl beneath his damp clothing—Kevin realized that his father had been wrong about one thing. Where there was shadow, there wasn't always light.

Sometimes there was just deeper shadow.

WATCHING

By Carrie Vaughn

Carrie Vaughn is the author of a series of novels about a werewolf named Kitty who hosts a talk radio show, which now spans six volumes, including *Kitty Takes a Holiday* and *Kitty and the Silver Bullet*. She's also published over thirty short stories in magazines such as *Weird Tales* and *Realms of Fantasy*. She has a masters in English literature and lives in Boulder, Colorado, where she seems to be collecting hobbies. For more information see *www.carrievaughn. com*.

Paul stood in the middle of St. Mark's Square in Venice, arms limp at his sides, holding a small velvet jewelry box containing a diamond solitaire ring. His engagement ring. *Her* engagement ring, but she was walking away from him. No, running, pigeons scattering, flapping in her wake. Her last words to him: *I'm sorry*.

Right before that she'd explained that she'd been seeing someone else but hadn't had the heart to tell him because the trip had already been planned, and she should have told him, but she wasn't expecting this. And this moment he'd been dreaming about for months crashed to pieces. She was going to change her plane ticket and try to get a flight back home this evening. He could do what he wanted. And one of the most beautiful cities in the world turned to a hazy muddle in his eyes.

Mostly, he wondered why he hadn't seen it coming.

A pigeon landed on him, digging its claws into the shoulder of his polo shirt. Because if you stand still in St. Mark's Square long enough, the pigeons will mistake you for a statue and consider you theirs. Absently, he shook it away, but another came right behind it, and another, until he was slapping at them with both hands, rushing to get away from them. They cooed and flapped and shivered around him, but finally they left him alone. The whole square smelled of feathers and gasoline.

For all the tourists crowding Venice this time of year, he felt invisible. No one seemed to see him. No one noticed the little tragedy that had played out here. Street vendors shouted, gondoliers sang, bells tolled, as they had for centuries.

The only ones watching him were pigeons. Dozens of them, hundreds, looking at him, heads cocked, eyes— black, red, or orange—shining like beads. As if they were actually interested. As if they knew, and gathered around him to see what he would do next.

He resisted an urge to kick one, which would have been childish. But he was curious about whether it would get out of his way.

He sold the ring, called his office to say he wasn't coming back, and set out to backpack across Europe, as he should have done in college but hadn't because he'd been responsible. He'd done the right thing, finished his degree, gotten the good job, worked hard, climbed the ladder, met the girl of his dreams. The white picket fence and two point five kids would follow, and wasn't there a certain kind of happiness in that life?

So much for all that.

Eight months later, he hit bottom.

Bottom was a pair of holey jeans that needed washing, combat boots that didn't fit, five layers of shirts and sweaters, and a canvas jacket that made him too warm during the day, but the nights got cold so he didn't dare lose anything. He'd bartered bits and pieces of his corporate uniform and yuppie tourist gear along the way for his new disguise, the homeless rags that made people look away, that made him invisible.

But God, he'd seen Europe. Walked the streets in all the capitals, seen the monuments, the museums. He'd also spent whole afternoons sitting in parks watching children play, listening to parents call out to them in foreign languages. He'd shopped in local grocery stores, strolled through quiet neighborhoods. Seen things the guidebooks never talked about. He went everywhere, rode trains, ate great food, and stayed in hotels until his credit card maxed out. He kept going because he wasn't finished yet, wasn't ready to go home. The longer he stayed away, the less likely he would go home, simply because picking up the pieces would be too hard. The last of his cash brought him to Great Britain, where he discovered a network of footpaths that let him walk through much of that country as well. He'd probably never been in such good shape. Except he hadn't eaten well in weeks, and he was always hungry.

He sat on the steps of St. Martin-in-the-Fields, overlooking Trafalgar Square, and fed pigeons bits of scavenged bread. He kept thinking he ought to go home. He could call his broker, cash out what was left of his 401k—

But why? So much simpler to sit here all day, watching pigeons.

They'd followed him across Europe. Well, they hadn't followed him. It might have seemed like it, because they were everywhere, in every city, leaving their marks on every statue and monument, building nests in every available nook, no matter how many spikes or plastic owls people put up to dissuade them. He'd spent hours watching pigeons and had become an expert on them. Their coloration—grays, white bars on wings and tails, pale underbellies; heads shimmering with iridescent bands of green, purple, blue, or white, or brown, or some hybrid mix of all of them. The way they moved, strutting, preening, cocking their heads, staring warily as if unsure he would really drop a piece of bread. In flight, they were graceful, powerful. Almost beautiful. Many were injured, and he wondered what they did that so many of them lost toes. They didn't seem to mind; they just kept hopping, flapping, pecking, living.

Like him.

It's a sad life, isn't it? they seemed to say. So much work for so little reward. He tossed another crumb, and the reddish-grayish-green bird with the white ring in its eye looked at him, blinking, before pecking at the bread and trotting away.

"It really is," he said. Because even pigeons were suspicious of handouts.

Did you ever think you'd end up here?

"Nope." He sighed. But it was startling, how much he wasn't bothered by where he'd ended up. It was almost nice to be surprised.

He did wonder if he was going insane, because he'd been talking to pigeons across Europe. He'd had no one else to talk to. That wouldn't have been so worrying except

for how often the pigeons seemed to talk back. From
Barcelona to Bern to Lyon to Amsterdam to Copenha-
gen, they'd watched him. He'd sit on park benches, wondering what to do next, and they'd gather. He'd started
feeding them, even when he hadn't had enough to
eat, because he felt obligated. A pigeon missing a foot
would hop in front him, cock its head, and seem to say,
At least you have both feet. And he'd answer, "Well, yes,
you're right," and dig in a trash bin for cracker crumbs
to give it.

Trafalgar Square was full of pigeons. Not as many as
St. Mark's Square—apparently London had instituted
a feeding ban to cut down on the pests. But the pigeons
still came.

They gathered around him, lined up like an audience,
as if they wanted to listen.

"If I could fly like you guys, I think I'd go back home. I
think I'm ready." He knew he'd hit bottom then, because
he was ready to start crawling back up. Find another job,
pay off the credit card, tell stories for the rest of his life
about the months he'd spent slumming around Europe.
It almost sounded romantic.

A white pigeon with flecks of gray, as if it had been
spattered with paint, cocked its head.

But why? So you start all over again. For what?

He shrugged. "Because it's the right thing to do?"

How do you know this won't happen again?

He gave a bark of a laugh. "Because I'll ask her if she
wants to get married before I take her to Venice to give
her the ring."

Women. They're all the same.

He winced. Had he thought that, or the pigeons?

He was comfortable, sitting here on the steps, watching the cars curve around the loop, watching tourists

crowd around the lions at the base of Nelson's Column.
He could sit here all day watching, chatting with the
pigeons, who'd stay near him as long as he had something to give them. More reliable than women, for sure.
Maybe he hadn't hit bottom yet, if he wasn't ready to
move from this spot.

It's a sad world.

"Yes, it is," he said.

"Sir, you can't stay here. You need to be moving on."

He started; he'd dozed off. Someone was standing
over him. A man with a funny hat, smart blue uniform,
yellow safety vest. Police officer. Paul straightened and
blinked up at the officer, who was stern and insistent.

It made him sad. He'd begun to think of this spot of
stone as his very own.

A few pigeons still lingered, though he'd run out of
crumbs a while ago. As usual, they seemed oddly interested, turning their heads to look at him, then look at
the officer. He could almost hear them offering advice.
*Wouldn't it be interesting to hit him? Get yourself ar-
rested? That would be different.*

Then he definitely knew he hadn't hit bottom yet, because he stared at the cop and thought, yeah, he *could*
hit him. He could end up inside a British prison. Then at
least he'd have hot meals again.

"Sir, did you hear me? You can't stay here."

Go on. Shove him.

"Sir—"

Paul said, "Do you ever feel like they're watching
you? The pigeons, I mean. I know they're everywhere,
they're part of the scenery. But sometimes do you feel
like they're watching?"

Another pigeon cocked its head. The cop just looked
at him.

Paul shook his head. "You probably think that's crazy. That sounds crazy."

After a moment, the officer said, "You're American?"

"Yeah."

"How'd you end up here? Like this?" Here, in London, homeless, at the bottom.

He felt his mouth turn in a wry smile, his first smile in ages. "There was this girl, see."

The officer laughed, and Paul was glad he hadn't hit him. "Very sorry about that, sir. But I do need you to move on, right?"

Paul moved on, walking toward the river. A pigeon soared overhead.

At Ramstein Air Base in Germany, in an experimental command center situated far underground, a dozen technicians monitored computers, video displays, millions of bytes of data flowing constantly, and the satellite communications that fed the operation.

One of the techs looked up from her monitor, and the officer on duty, a male colonel in a crisp green Army uniform, walked over.

"Sergeant? What is it?"

"Sir, I have something strange going on with one of the tests," she said. She pointed to her screen, where a dozen windows each showed a different video feed, views of streets, buildings, skies, concrete, and crowds. Clicking a couple of buttons, she brought one window to prominence, along with a list of data points.

"Subject 53872. Acquired in Venice. Initial contact showed a weakened state of mind, highly suggestible. But something's changed. It's like he suspects. This is the footage we're getting."

The colonel watched for a few minutes. The video

showed a man, a ragged homeless bum, rough brown
beard on a gaunt face, tangled hair pressed down by a
torn knit cap, soiled canvas jacket with a collar sticking
up. The man stared directly into the camera, and his expression was pensive. His brow furrowed, his gaze was
searching. The sound was off, but he seemed to be talking as if the camera would answer him.

It happened sometimes. Paranoia could push test
subjects over the edge.

"How much data do we have on this one?"

"Eight months' worth, sir. It follows the usual pattern."

Satisfied, the colonel nodded. "Then it looks like it's
time to close this one out."

"Yes, sir."

The sergeant moved aside so the colonel could type
in his authorization code to conclude the test. The tech-
nician took care of the rest, entering a code to transmit a
preprogrammed message that shut down Subject 53872
and logging the results in the appropriate Psychological
Warfare Test Group file: Experiment 87, Subsonic Hypnotic Suggestion Transmitted via Remote Integrated
Cybernetics.

The colonel moved on, walking past a dozen screens
that showed hundreds of images, some of them static,
some of them turning, whirling, as if the camera were
falling off a building. In many of the images crowds of
birds gathered around, a tapestry of grays and purples.

Paul climbed over the guardrail halfway to the first
tower on Tower Bridge and sat on a precarious ledge, his
feet dangling. He watched the Thames flow under him.
It was a long way down.

You might as well end it now.

The despairing thought had followed him all the way

from Trafalgar Square. It might have started when he
didn't have the guts to hit the cop. That would have been
more interesting than this. But this time, the voice was
probably right. He didn't want to go on.

It's too hard. It'll be too hard to keep going.

"That's right," Paul murmured. It was all just too
hard.

Even here, pigeons followed him, strutting along the
ledge, cooing. One—was it the same mottled one who'd
looked at him so pointedly back at Trafalgar Square?
Hard to tell. Probably not, with billions of the aerial rats
flapping around.

You should just end it now.

The thing was looking at him. They'd always been
looking at him. They'd been following him, begging
from him, bothering him. Ever since Venice, where this
whole escapade started. What had gotten into him? He
really was crazy—not because he thought pigeons were
spying on him, but because no one acted this badly when
a woman dumped him. That was the crazy part, letting
the whole thing get to him like that.

But what if . . . What the hell, he thought. He was sitting on the edge of Tower Bridge getting ready to jump.
It wasn't like he had anything to lose.

He waited, very calmly, very quietly, barely breathing. The mottled pigeon didn't move. It just watched
him, head cocked, peering out of one eye, which shone
like glass. Paul counted slowly to three—then grabbed
it. Whipped out his hand and clamped it hard over its
neck.

"Gotcha!" He clutched the thing in both hands and
slammed it against the steel ledge. He pounded it over
and over again, until its skull burst, its skin split, until
blood and bits of flesh splattered out, until he was sob-

bing with despair and exhaustion. Because it really was just a pigeon, and he really was crazy.

But no—he spread the bird's remains in front of him, picking away bone and feather, peeling back skin, pulling apart its head. He found wires inside, a few coils of copper. A couple of microchips. Thin tubes where its eyes should have been—tubes with rounded glass ends. Camera lenses.

He wasn't crazy.

He looked around. A dozen more pigeons walked, strutted, flapped their wings. And how many of them had cameras for eyes? How many of them were spying on him? On everyone? It was brilliant—pigeons were ubiquitous, found in every city in the world. They could go anywhere, completely inconspicuous. No one would ever suspect.

"I should tell someone," he said. Oh, God—this was some kind of conspiracy. Who was behind this? Some government? Or worse—terrorists? Was that how they did it? They could go anywhere—"I have to tell someone!"

Rushing, he wiped his bloody hands on his coat, scrambled to his feet, reaching for handholds to pull himself back to the road. That cop, the one that had actually stopped to talk to him, where was he? Paul could tell him, he'd tell everyone, sell his story and make millions, he could start over again—

A pigeon landed on his shoulder, just like at St. Mark's in Venice. It picked at the fabric of his coat with its claws. Like it was trying to keep Paul from leaving. Like it didn't want him to go. He hesitated; it was just a bird. But what was it saying? He could almost hear it pleading.

But that was crazy, so he kept climbing. Then, the pigeon nipped his ear. Crying out, Paul batted it away, and it flew. But then another came, pecking at his hand. It hurt, but Paul couldn't let go.

The pigeons were everywhere.

A dozen of them flew at him, dove at him, wings flapping, beating at him. Individually, they were rats with wings, easily defeated, but together, like this, a swarm of them, all thrashing at him—it was too much. Paul screamed, crouched to try to escape, put up his arms to protect his face—and lost his grip.

He fell. *Then,* he hit bottom.

THE THINGS THAT CRAWL

By Richard Lee Byers

Richard Lee Byers is the author of over thirty fantasy and horror novels, including *Unclean, Undead, Unholy, The Rage, The Rite, The Ruin,* and *Dissolution.* His short stories have appeared in numerous magazines and anthologies. A resident of the Tampa Bay area, the setting for a good deal of his horror fiction, he spends much of leisure time fencing and playing poker. Visit his website at *richardleebyers.com.*

"Mrs. Porter is hysterical," the dispatcher said, "and not making a lot of sense. But apparently somebody named Molly collapsed."

"Shouldn't you send EMTs?" I asked. Like most cops, I'd once learned CPR. But I hadn't practiced in a long time, and anyway, what if CPR wouldn't do the job?

"I tried, but there's a tree down between them and Chiles Road. They'll have to go the long way around. You're close. I'm hoping you can get there faster."

"I'm on my way," I said.

I pulled my patrol car out of the Circle K parking lot

and headed down a flooded two-lane road only barely distinguishable from the overflowing drainage ditches on either side. The tires threw up dirty water. Broken branches littered the roadway or dangled above me. A telephone pole leaned to the side.

That was because it was September, 2004, and just hours ago, Hurricane Frances had hammered the little central Florida town where I was trying to make a new start. If you compared the damage to what Katrina did later to New Orleans and Mississippi, you might say we got off easy. But I'd never gone through any sort of hurricane before, and I was pretty damn impressed.

Despite the miserable driving conditions, it only took a couple minutes to reach Chiles Road, and Mrs. Porter had white numbers painted on her green plastic mailbox to point me to the proper dirt-and-gravel driveway. It dipped down, so the standing water was even deeper there than it was on the highway. Worried that the car was going to stall or get stuck, I made the turn anyway, managed to keep rolling past the live oaks growing on either side, and ended up in the yard—except that currently, it was more like a pond—in front of a doublewide trailer.

A woman knelt over a motionless body lying on its side and held the head up out of the water. I assumed I was looking at Mrs. Porter and Molly. Mrs. Porter was obese, fifty-something, and wearing a pink housecoat. Molly was a Labrador retriever.

For a second, I was annoyed. You don't call 911 because a pet is sick, especially in the aftermath of a natural disaster. But when Mrs. Porter looked up at me, I could read the fear and pain in her round, red, blotchy face even from yards away, and then I just felt bad for her. I climbed out of the cruiser and sloshed toward her through brown water and the sucking mud beneath.

"I don't drive!" Mrs. Porter wheezed. "You've got to take her to the vet!"

I suspected it might be too late for that. Molly didn't look like she was breathing. Still, I asked, "What vet does she go to?"

"Dr. LaSalle," she answered, and then I glimpsed a rippling curl of motion in the water on the far side of her.

I grew up in the city, so I don't know why I was instantly sure I'd spotted something dangerous. Maybe because of the Lab. Anyway, I pointed and yelled, "Watch out!"

Mrs. Porter looked around, and her reaction proved my instincts were on target. She yelped and tried to flounder in my direction. But one swollen, slipper-clad foot slipped out from under her, and she splashed back down into the water.

I lunged forward—as much as you can lunge, when you're wading—grabbed her by one doughy forearm, and heaved. Somehow, heavy though she was, I managed to spin her around behind me. Which gave me my first good look at the animal that was swimming after her.

It was a dark, mottled snake about two feet long, with indentations between the nostrils and the places where the eyes must be, though I couldn't actually see them while looking down from above. It darted at me, I kicked it, and it bit my foot.

Fortunately, the fangs didn't pierce my shoe leather. I kicked a second time, shook the snake loose, and flung it several feet away. It immediately swam at me again, and two others followed right after it.

I really wanted to run. But even if I could have made

it back to the cruiser ahead of the snakes, I couldn't have managed it while dragging Mrs. Porter along. So there was nothing to do but draw my Browning and shoot.

Even at short range, it's not easy to hit a target with a handgun, not when it's small and moving and you don't have time to aim. I emptied the whole magazine, and by the time I killed the last snake, it was right at my feet. Scared as I was, I was lucky I didn't blow my toes off.

Standing in a haze of smoke and the smell of cordite, I looked around for more snakes and didn't see any. Hands trembling, I reloaded anyway, then turned to Mrs. Porter, who was still on her hands and knees where I'd tossed her. "Are you all right?" I asked.

"I think so," she said, her breathy voice shaky like my hands. "Did the cottonmouths bite Molly?"

"I don't know," I said. But I figured they probably had, and hours later, when the vet examined the Lab's body, it turned out I was right.

But at first, I didn't think much more about it, and neither did anybody else. One poor snake-bitten dog didn't count for much when we had a whole town to put back together. City and county government focused on getting the power back on, the roads open, and the debris cleared. I worked a lot of overtime, craved a drink, and settled for attending early morning and late night meetings instead.

Meanwhile, water moccasins killed one person and diamondback rattlesnakes, another. I didn't see either of those deaths. But when a guy named Kropp called from Michigan to report that his mother had stopped answering the phone, I was the patrolman who went out to check on her.

Like many in the area, the house was a sort of ramshackle bungalow with a tin roof. Overall, it looked as if had been built decades ago, although the roll-up plastic storm shutters—which currently were up—had to be a recent improvement.

A dozen bright green lizards clung to the brick façade. Their black eyes stared as I picked my way over ground that was no longer underwater but still soft and sticky nonetheless.

The mere presence of the lizards wasn't odd. They lived all over the area, anyplace there were plants and bugs. I saw one or two whenever I went out of my duplex apartment during the day. But they generally skittered for cover whenever a human being approached, so it did seem strange that this bunch was staying put. Strange and, after my previous confrontation with local wildlife, maybe even a little bit creepy. But unlike the cotton-mouths, the lizards were tiny and completely harmless, so I managed to find the raw courage to step up on the concrete stoop and ring the doorbell anyway.

Nobody answered. I knocked and shouted, and no one responded to that, either. The lizards kept on staring.

I decided to walk around the house and see what I could see. I headed right, took a few steps, then glimpsed motion from the corner of my eye. I pivoted.

The lizards I'd been walking toward had held their positions. But the ones I'd started walking away from had darted along the wall and followed me. They stopped moving when I did, but it took them a second. Just time enough for me to see what they were doing.

But had I *really* seen it? It seemed more likely that my eyes were playing tricks on me. I headed left.

Now the lizards on the right scurried after me. The ones on the left stayed put until I passed them, then joined the parade. And whenever I stopped, the reptiles did, too.

Okay, this really did seem weird, but I reminded my-self I knew nothing about lizards. If I did, maybe I'd understand that what they were doing was normal.

In any case, it couldn't have anything to do with Mrs. Kropp, and she was the reason I was here. I took a breath and went back to checking the house. The lizards continued to supervise.

The air conditioner was a stumpy metal box with rounded corners sitting on the ground next to the east side of the building. It wasn't running, which came as no surprise, considering that Mrs. Kropp had left a number of windows open. The one above the AC unit had a hole poked through the bottom of the screen. A small hole. I couldn't have stuck my hand through without tearing it bigger.

But a snake could slide through.

Not that there was a bit of evidence that a snake actually had. But once the thought occurred to me, it stuck in my head.

So you can imagine how eager I was to go inside the house. But the son had given permission, and it seemed that someone should.

Mrs. Kropp had left the back door unlocked, so I didn't have to break in. I resisted the urge to enter with gun in hand. I didn't want to scare her to death if it turned out she was simply hard of hearing.

First, I smelled the rotten stink. Then I heard the buzzing flies.

Mrs. Kropp had been slimmer and nicer-looking than Mrs. Porter, but I judged she was about the same age. She lay on her bedroom floor with multiple wounds—paired punctures—on her face, neck, hands, and arms, and legs. Maybe on the rest of her body, too, but her yellow pull-over and baggy tan walking shorts made it hard to tell.

It was scary to realize that the snake or snakes that had bitten her might still be in the house. But the lizards crawling on the walls spooked me just about as badly.

I told myself they couldn't be the same animals that had followed me around outside. They hadn't really come through the hole in the screen, then raced through the house to watch my reaction when I discovered the corpse. No, obviously these were different lizards, camped out here to eat the insects that came to eat the body.

I exited the house even more cautiously than I'd entered, then called in the death. Along with the usual ambulance and investigators, Animal Control showed up to look for the snakes. They didn't find them. The reptiles had killed their victim and escaped back into the great outdoors.

I caught the Animal Control officers when they were tossing their snake-catching equipment—poles with hooks on the ends and sturdy canvas bags that looked like mail sacks—into the back of their van. "I think I know how the snakes got in and out," I said. "Want to see?"

The shorter of the pair, a redheaded, freckled guy who smelled of cigarette smoke, shrugged and said, "Okay."

I led them around to the side of the house. No lizards followed us. Maybe the activity centered on the corpse was more interesting.

"The way I see it," I said, "a snake could probably climb up on top of the air-conditioning unit, then move from there onto the windowsill. It could press its nose against the screen until it broke, then crawl on in. There's a chair on the other side of the window, so when it was ready, it could climb back up and out."

The freckled guy frowned. "I guess a snake could do all that. But I don't think it would."

"Me neither," said his partner. He was missing the last joint of his ring finger, and I wondered if an animal had bitten it off. "A snake will come into a house if it happens to find a way. But climbing, then *forcing* a way in? I just don't see it. I don't know, maybe if the hole was already there. The hurricane could have ripped the screen."

"Probably not," I said. "It didn't tear any of the others, and she would have had her new storm shutters down. But if my idea's wrong, how do you think the snakes got in and out?"

"There's a hole at ground level," said the freckled man, pulling a pack of Marlboros and a disposable lighter from his pocket. "We didn't find it, but it's there somewhere."

And that was that. Since they didn't even like my snake theory, I didn't see much point in telling them my crazy lizard story.

Snakes killed someone else the very next day, and that was when the local TV stations and newspapers decided to make a big deal out of the story. They had a point. Florida averaged five deaths by snakebite per year. Our little piece of the state had racked up almost that many in a week.

Herpetologists explained that it was simply a fluke. Snakes didn't ordinarily hunt in packs, nor did they hunt humans. If we left them alone, they'd leave us alone and help us out by killing rats and other pests.

I imagine some of the local residents found the experts' line reassuring. Others went hunting, to get the snakes before the snakes got them.

Whether or not that was an overreaction, it was largely an exercise in futility. The town was on the I-4 corridor and close enough to Tampa for commuters to drive back and forth, so the developers had us in their sights. But the area was still pretty rural—*very* rural, compared to what I was used to—with plenty of strawberry fields, pastures, barns, thick stands of palmetto, and creek beds. All perfect places for a copperhead or diamondback to live and, if need be, hide.

Since the damn snakes had nearly bitten me, and I'd been the first officer at the scene of Mrs. Kropp's death, I got interested enough to find out the details of each incident. And after the fifth death, I reluctantly decided I ought to talk to my boss.

Chief Davis was a stocky guy with a ready smile, a receding hairline, and faded blue tattoos on his forearms that dated back to his tours of duty in Vietnam. He'd decorated his office with plaques and framed newspapers commemorating the department's more notable achievements, which mostly involved either raising money for disadvantaged kids or busting meth labs.

He waved me to a chair. "What can I do for you?" he asked.

"I've been thinking about the snakebite cases," I said.

He snorted. "You and me and everybody else around here. It's a crazy situation."

"Yeah. But there's a pattern to it."

He cocked his head. "How so?"

"All the victims have been white women between the ages of forty and sixty, living alone. Mrs. Porter, the woman who almost got bitten, meets the same description."

"I noticed that, and it is a funny coincidence. But then, according to the professors, this whole thing amounts to one giant funny coincidence."

I hesitated, then took the plunge. "Here's the thing. When you have several people with the same characteristics turn up dead in quick succession, it can be because you've got a serial killer on your hands."

Now it was his turn to hesitate. "You're kidding, right?"

"I'm not saying that's what's happening, but maybe we should look at the possibility."

"I don't think there is one. You're talking about a killer who uses trained snakes as weapons, right? And you *can't* train a snake. They're too dumb."

"But what if someone figured out a way? It would explain the snakes hunting in groups and going after people so aggressively. Killing a dog to lure the owner out into the open—"

"That's just your interpretation of what happened."

"—then biding their time, waiting for a good moment to sneak up on her. Forcing their way into a house. The scientists say none of that is normal."

"Okay, but when you had your run-in with the water moccasins, did you notice anybody standing back and giving them commands?"

"No."

"Then that pretty much blows your theory, doesn't it?"

"Maybe. But I'd still like to know: Has anybody noticed anything else unusual? Something that didn't make it into the written reports?"

"Like what?"

"Anything. Maybe something involving some other kind of animal. Like, I don't know, lizards." As soon as the words were out of my mouth, I wished I could take them back.

Because, although he'd been patient up till now, he finally reacted the way I'd feared he would. "John, I have to ask this. Have you been drinking?"

"No. I swear. I'll take a breathalyzer if you don't believe me."

"That's okay. I do. I guess I'd smell it on you if you were. But maybe you could use a day or two off."

"Really, there's no need. I'm not crazy. It's just that weird things are happening, a couple of them right in front of me, and I'm trying to figure them out."

He eyeballed me for another moment, then said, "All right, if you say so." His voice got softer, the way you talk when you want to be gentle. "But you know, even if we did have a human killer running around, you wouldn't be the guy in charge of catching him. You're not a detective anymore. Maybe someday you will be again, but for now, you're just a uniformed officer."

"I know."

"So, until they ask us for backup, let the wildlife officers worry about the snakes."

I tried. I didn't want to lose my job, and, especially now that Davis had pointed out the weaknesses in my logic, my suspicions seemed crazy even to me.

But then snakes killed another woman. She was white, fifty-one, and had lived alone. And despite my better judgment, the continuation of the pattern pushed me into phoning an old friend in the FBI office in Philly.

After I asked him to do me a favor, it took Charlie a couple days to call me back. I was sitting on the couch watching a National Geographic Channel documentary about reptiles when he did. As I muted the sound, he said, "It took some work. You owe me."

"What did you find out?" I asked.

"Back in 1996, they had a serial killer murdering middle-aged Caucasian women in the Orlando area."

"How?"

"Jack the Ripper style, with a knife."

"Did they catch him?"

"No, and after eight victims, the killings just stopped."

"Were there any suspects?" On the TV, a python un-hinged its jaw and started swallowing an antelope.

"A guy named Derrick Horn. He definitely fit the profile. Abused kid, wet the bed, set fires, tortured ani-mals, bounced in and out of foster care, detention, and the mental health system. The psychologists who evalu-ated him said he pretty much hated everybody, but his late mother most of all. And the murders stopped after he got hurt in a car crash."

"Sounds like they had a winner."

"You'd think, but they could never pin anything on him. Anyway, after seven months in the hospital, he headed down I-4 and settled in *your* county. Maybe he didn't want to stay in a place where local law enforce-ment was convinced he was a bad guy."

"Jesus Christ," I said.

"What's going on down there, John? Why did you want to know this stuff? I checked, and nobody seems to think you've got a serial killer running loose in your little podunk town."

"It's complicated," I said. "I'll explain if I ever get it sorted out. For now, just tell me one more thing. Did Horn have anything to do with snakes or reptiles?"

"If he did, it's not in the file, and the guys I talked to didn't mention it."

After I got off the phone, I sat and tried to figure out what I had. The answer was basically nothing. Whether or not he matched the profile, it was entirely possible Derrick Horn had never murdered anyone. Even if he had, that didn't mean he was doing it now. He didn't ap-pear to have any connection to snakes, and in any case, as Chief Davis had pointed out, no one could train reptiles to wander around on their own and kill people of a particular race, sex, and age.

For maybe the hundredth time, I told myself to let it go. I'd already thrown away one life, drunk away one career and one marriage, in Pennsylvania. Wasn't that enough for me?

As it turned out, maybe not.

Not long after, another middle-aged white woman got herself killed, despite all the public-service ads that had begun to appear telling people how to stay safe from snakes. None of them had warned her that half a dozen diamondbacks might hide under her car, wait for her to approach, and then lunge out all at once, with nary a rattle to tip her off to the danger.

And I decided it couldn't hurt just to take a look at Derrick Horn. After all, I really was a cop. If I had a decent excuse and didn't harass the guy, it wasn't likely he'd call the station and complain.

As Mrs. Porter and Mrs. Kropp had, Horn lived on a sizable lot on the outskirts of town. His brown concrete-block house looked newer, though, and unlike its neighbors, it had a paved driveway and a ramp running up to the door. The dark green van parked in front of the garage had a handicapped sticker on the bumper.

Charlie had told me that Horn had gotten hurt. Apparently the crash had left him permanently disabled.

There were two ways of looking at that. The sane one was to realize that a crippled guy couldn't possibly go roaming over rough ground and through brush to catch or give commands to a bunch of snakes. The crazy one was to think that injury could explain why a psychopath who preferred killing with a knife would switch to using trained animals instead.

I climbed out of the cruiser, headed for the ramp, then

faltered. Because several lizards clung to the front of the house, and like their counterparts at Mrs. Kropp's, they stayed put and stared at me as I drew near. A couple even scuttled toward me, as if for a better look.

I took a deep breath, then hiked up the ramp and rang the bell.

To my surprise, the door cracked open after just a second, even though the man inside was in a wheelchair. I assumed he must have looked out the window and seen me coming. He would have needed a head start to get to the door so quickly.

I studied him as best I could through the narrow opening. His accident had left him skinny as a pencil and twisted and lopsided to boot. Your immediate response was to feel sorry for him, until you noticed the narrow, mud-colored eyes.

They were cold eyes, guarded but not scared. As if he had something to hide but was confident he could keep it concealed from the likes of me.

Or maybe, after a lifetime of brushes with the law, he just didn't like cops.

"Mr. Horn?" I said.

"Yes."

"I'm Officer Santelli. Could I talk to you for a minute?"

"About what?"

"The snake attacks."

"What about them?"

"Is there any chance we could talk inside?" I smiled. "It's hot out here, and you're letting the air conditioning out of the house."

He hesitated for half a second, then said, "Okay." The electric motor of the wheelchair whirred as he backed it down the entrance hall to make room for me. He maneuvered into the first doorway on the right and led me into his living room.

Which was a mess. Piles of books sat all over the furniture and the carpet, too. The musty smell of old paper tickled my nose.

Horn parked himself in front of the computer desk. "You can move something to make a place to sit. The maid service comes once a week, but I don't let them clean in here anymore. I could never find anything after they did."

I cleared a spot on the couch. "I imagine you know that a couple of the attacks occurred less than a mile from here."

"Uh huh."

"So we're going around the neighborhood for a couple reasons. One is to make certain everyone's being as safe as possible. Have you checked your house to make sure there's no way for a snake to get in?"

"Well . . . not really. But I only bought the property and had the house built a few years ago." With settlement money from the accident, I suspected. "I keep the AC on and the doors and windows shut. I'm sure it's fine."

"It's still a good idea to take a look. I can do it for you if you'd like."

He frowned. "I can do it myself if I decide it's worth the trouble."

"Whatever you say. The other reason I'm here is to ask if you've seen any snakes. If we could find them, we could kill them."

"Sorry, no."

"What about dead animals in your yard? Or, are there animals you're used to seeing that you haven't seen lately?"

He snorted. "Since you thought I needed you to inspect the house for me, you can probably understand that I don't spend a lot of time outside."

"Sure." Since I had a bad feeling about Horn, I wanted to prolong the conversation, but I was running out of questions. I glanced around. "Anyway, reading all these books must keep you busy."

"Yes, it does. So if there's nothing else—"

I picked up books, looked them over, and got a surprise. Under other circumstances, I might have dismissed the volumes as superstitious bullshit, meaningless as a supermarket horoscope or an issue of the *Weekly World News,* but they were a little more unsettling if you happened to come across them in the home of a suspected homicidal maniac with weird lizards crawling around outside. Still, I tried to look as if I were simply curious. *"Dead Gods. Inhabitants of the Crooked Hours.* Something in French, I think, with what looks like a half man, half jellyfish stamped on the cover. What is all this stuff, anyway?"

He shrugged. That was vaguely unnerving, too, because one shoulder hitched higher than the other. "Mythology. History. Philosophy."

Against my better judgment, I gave in to the urge to push him at least a little. Grinning like I was kidding, I asked, "Not devil worship?"

He sneered. "Are you religious?"

"Not me." Which was true, give or take that higher power the program tells us to trust. "But I imagine you've got some Baptist and Pentecostal neighbors who'd be upset if they saw these. They'd figure you practice black magic and perform human sacrifices."

He eyed me for a moment, maybe trying to decide just what, if anything, my reference to murder actually meant. I kept on doing my best to seem like I was just making conversation.

Eventually he said, "I know. That's why I keep my interests to myself."

"So, *are* these books about black magic?"

"If you're talking about something connected to Satanism and Christianity, no. But since ancient times, a few people have held a view of the universe completely unrelated to any of the major world religions."

"You mean, they believed in different gods."

"Partly. Some that lived in outer space or inside our own brains. One hibernating at the bottom of the ocean." He smiled. "A dragon king to rule over cold-blooded creatures and all the things that crawl."

That last example startled me. I hoped he hadn't noticed. "And I guess people prayed to those gods just like the Baptists and Pentecostals pray to theirs."

"And got the same answer: none."

"Not that I believe in this stuff or anything, but do you know that for sure?"

"Well, let me put it this way. If you were to study enough of this material, if it really got inside your head, you might find yourself tempted to experiment, at least in a harmless, half-assed kind of way."

"And then, when nothing happened, you'd know the 'dead gods' aren't real."

"Right. Although the true believers always had excuses for when the magic didn't work. The worshiper didn't have enough willpower or didn't perform the ritual with the necessary precision to break through the wall between realities."

"I suppose that would have to be a pretty thick wall."

"So they say." His smile widened. "That's why a Dutch

cultist named Gansevoort recommended working magic during huge storms. Supposedly, the violent weather helped break open the barriers."

That little factoid jolted me even more than his reference to the reptile god. And after I got out of there, I drove around and tried to figure out what it all meant.

If I let my imagination run amok, I could construct a scenario based on what Horn had told me. After his injury, it had been impossible for him to continue killing in the same way as before. So he'd turned to occultism to learn how to murder women with magic.

It didn't get him anywhere until Frances blew through and cracked the wall between the worlds. Then, at last, he made contact with the dragon god.

The god gave him the power to reach out with his mind to find reptiles, see through their eyes, and control them. Venomous snakes became the weapons he used to kill. Lizards were the scouts who located his victims, stood watch outside his house, and allowed him to monitor a location after the murder, to gloat over the excitement when the body was discovered.

Yeah, right.

I didn't need Chief Davis to point out the weaknesses in this particular theory. For starters, if it was true, why the hell—aside from the fact that he was a head case—would Horn even hint about it?

Well, maybe I'd succeeded in convincing him I knew nothing about his past and didn't suspect him of anything. If so, it might have given him a thrill to indicate his guilt to a dumb cop who didn't have a clue what he was talking about.

In any case, the real objection to my idea was that it seemed impossible even to me. I didn't believe in witchcraft or unknown gods any more than the next guy.

Or at least I never had. Maybe I wasn't quite as sure anymore.

The hell of it was, I couldn't even see anywhere to go, any way to prove or disprove my suspicions. If Horn was finding and guiding snakes by mental telepathy, even putting him under direct surveillance wouldn't help. I wouldn't see him do anything incriminating.

So I did nothing but fret and get spooked whenever I saw a lizard. It felt as though they were watching me, although I never caught one doing anything peculiar enough to make me certain. Meanwhile, copperheads killed another woman, and Hurricane Jeanne wandered around in the Atlantic.

The town didn't worry much about the latter. By that time, people were too busy being scared of snakes. Besides, the forecasters said Jeanne probably wouldn't make landfall in Florida at all, and even if it did, it would likely only affect the Atlantic coast.

They were still saying it on the afternoon when I walked out of my duplex, came down the steps, and felt a tiny sting on the back of my leg, just above the ankle. It didn't smart any worse than if a no-see-um had bitten me through my pants and sock, but I glanced around to see what the problem was.

Banded with black, red, and yellow, coral snakes were crawling out from under the porch. The one in the lead had already bitten me. It was hanging on and, if I could believe the National Geographic Channel, chewing.

Maybe I should have seen the attack coming. But I didn't think Horn believed I was a threat to him. Why should he, when I scarcely believed it, either? I can only assume that over time, he decided it had been reckless to share his story even in the form of hints and insinuations and wanted to make sure I didn't repeat it.

I tried to spring away from the coral snakes. Somehow, I tripped and slammed down hard on the ground. Before I could scramble up again, the reptiles were all over my legs. I felt more little stings as their fangs jabbed and gnawed their way into my flesh.

I grabbed them and pulled them loose. Ripping their teeth out of me hurt worse than the bites did. I threw them and they immediately started slithering back at me. Some of them bit my hands as I reached and snatched, and ended up dangling from my fingers and palms.

I realized I couldn't stay where I was until I removed them all. They kept coming back faster than I could get rid of them. I ripped several off, then jumped up and ran with two more still hanging on to me.

The other coral snakes chased me, but I reached my cruiser ahead of them. I scrambled inside, slammed the door, rolled down a window, and tried to deal with the reptiles that were still biting me.

I didn't have too much trouble yanking the first one off and tossing it outside. The second let me go of its own accord and started to crawl under the seat. I grabbed its tail just before it disappeared and chucked it out, also.

Then I fumbled my keys out of my pocket, started the car, and hitched it back and forth, crushing snakes beneath the wheels. I could just feel the bump whenever I caught one.

The survivors scattered and fled, while I did my best to kill them all, including the ones that crawled from the dirt driveway back onto the grass. My tires cut scars in the lawn.

Finally, no matter how hard I looked, I couldn't see any snakes that were still alive. Rage and disgust lost their hold on me, fear welled up to take their place, and I realized I had to get to a hospital.

Maybe I should have called an ambulance. But I was already sitting in an emergency vehicle, and according to the National Geographic Channel, it could take hours for the symptoms of coral-snake poison to appear. I turned on the siren and chase lights and pulled out onto the road.

I found out pretty fast that either I was more susceptible than the average victim or the documentary hadn't been talking about people bitten so many times by so many different snakes. First, my mouth filled up with spit, and no matter how often I swallowed, it came right back. Then my hands got numb.

My eyelids drooped, and I felt sleepy. Once, I actually must have drifted off, because the world seemed to skip, and suddenly the car was left of center.

Not long after that, my vision blurred. Fortunately, by then, the hospital was dead ahead. I stopped the car in front of the ER entrance and stumbled inside.

A nurse hurried over to me. "Coral snakes," I said, spilling drool down my chin. I hoped she understood. My voice was slurred.

She called for help. She and an orderly walked me into a curtained-off examination area and hoisted me onto a bed. And since I'm still alive, they and the rest of the staff must have gone on helping me, but I passed out and missed the rest of it.

I woke in a dark room. For a few seconds, I was disoriented, and not just because it was an unfamiliar space. Outside the window, the wind roared, and the rain pounded like a jackhammer. It made me feel as if it were three weeks ago, and Frances was doing its best to level the town.

Then I noticed the wires attached to my chest, the round little Band-Aids on my puffy wounds, and the IV in the back of my hand. I realized I was in the hospital, and that brought my memories of recent events rushing back.

I took stock of myself and decided I felt well enough to get up. I detached myself from the heart monitor and hanging bag of saline solution. Then, feeling awkward in my hospital gown, I headed out into the hall.

It was gloomy there, too. I realized the area had lost electricity, and the hospital was relying on its generator.

A short, plump woman with a pretty round face and shiny black hair hurried out of the nurse's station to intercept me. "Mr. Santelli," she said, her Hispanic accent barely noticeable, "you shouldn't be out of bed."

"I feel okay," I answered. "Are we really having another hurricane?"

She frowned. "Yes. Can you believe it? Jeanne came ashore exactly where Frances did and is following the same path. Is that bad luck or what?"

And I thought, you've got no idea.

Because, crazy as it was, I now truly, completely believed that Derrick Horn could control reptiles with his mind and was using them to commit murder. The coral snakes had chewed all the skepticism right out of me.

And, believing that, I also had to assume that a second hurricane gave Horn a second chance to commune with the dragon god. He was liable to come out of it with even more power to hurt other people.

Somebody needed to stop him, and since I was the only one who knew, it would have to be me.

I had to talk to a doctor before the nurses would give me back my stuff and let me sign out of the hospital AMA. I told him that as soon as Jeanne blew through, the town would need every available cop, and my dedication to duty won him over.

By that time, it was three A.M. When I stepped out onto the covered porch, the night was as dark as any I'd ever seen, with no moon- or starlight leaking through the cloud cover, and scarcely an electric light burning anywhere. It was only a few yards from the door to the space where someone had parked my cruiser, but my clothes were plastered to my skin by the time I made the sprint. I twisted the key in the ignition, turned the windshield wipers on high, and found they barely helped at all. The rain was pounding down too hard for the blades to clear it.

Poor visibility was only one of the reasons why no one with any sense was on the road. The wind shoved me around as I crept along. I drove through standing water so deep that I was sure it would splash up inside the engine.

Lightning flashed, thunder banged, and sparks fell. A pole toppled in front of me, dragging broken power lines along with it. I stamped on the brakes and realized from the mushy feel that water had definitely gotten inside them. I hydroplaned to a stop just short of a collision. Shivering in my wet clothes, I sat for a moment, waiting for my nerves to settle, then dropped the cruiser into reverse.

By the time I made it to Horn's place, the weather had gotten even worse. When I climbed out of the car, the rain stung like gravel falling from the sky and made it impossible to see for more than a few feet. The wind howled and almost knocked me over.

I waded around the car and took the Ithaca 37 out of the trunk. I figured that a shotgun blast could kill several snakes at once and also knew that as long as I picked up my ejected shells, forensics wouldn't even be able to identify the make of scattergun fired at the scene, let alone my individual weapon.

Which was a definite plus. Because if this ever came back on me, I wouldn't have much hope of convincing anyone that I'd had a legitimate reason to break in and kill a paraplegic sitting alone in his own home.

Deprived of electricity, that home was as black as all the surrounding houses. I slogged toward it, and the rain battered me. Damn, it smarted! I tried to take comfort in the thought that at least it would keep Horn's lizards from spotting my approach. They couldn't be standing watch now. The downpour would wash them from their perches.

Something moved at the edge of my vision. I turned and looked directly into the wind and the rain it blew in my face like a stream from a fire hose. Squinting, even blinder than I'd been before, I could just make out a long, low shape. I figured it was either a log or some man-made object floating in the floodwater. The important thing was, I could tell it wasn't a snake. It was far too big and bulky.

But then I realized it was coming straight at me, faster than even hundred-mile-an-hour winds could explain. I saw the lashing tail and the stumpy legs.

Shock froze me for a precious instant. I'd heard there were alligators in the area, but I'd never seen one, and, since Horn hadn't used them to kill any of the women, I hadn't expected to run into one now. The reptile was nearly on top of me before I shouldered the Ithaca and fired.

The blasts tore into its head, and it stopped moving. I just had time to feel relieved before the jaws of a second gator snapped shut on my calf. In the dark and the rain, I simply hadn't noticed it. It yanked my leg out from under me, and I splashed down in the water.

The National Geographic Channel had told me what

to expect next. The alligator would start shaking me or rolling over and over to tear me to pieces.

I jackknifed up into a sitting position, twisted, and managed to get the animal in front of my gun. Not caring whether some of the scatter hit my leg, I fired at the gator's snout and eyes.

It jerked at the impact, then flexed its tail to start the death roll. I fired again. That shot blasted chunks from the back of its head and seemed to finish it.

I looked around for other gators. When I didn't see any, I pried my throbbing leg out of the reptile's jaws.

It was gashed and bloody, but maybe not quite as bad as it looked—and felt. I stood up cautiously and found I could limp around on it.

Even after I turned on my flashlight for a moment, I could only find one of my spent shells in the floodwater. I'd just have to hope it would wash the others far enough that nobody else would ever find them, either.

As I sloshed on toward the house, I wondered if Horn knew I was coming. If his mind had been inside the gators when they attacked me, then yes. If he'd simply given the animals orders and left them to stand guard, then maybe not. The Ithaca really boomed when it went off, but the hiss of the wind and clatter of the rain might have been enough to mask the noise.

I told myself it didn't matter if he knew or not. I'd already proved I could handle snakes and now alligators, too. What else was there?

The front door was locked. I had a bump key, though, a souvenir from my years as a detective, and it only took me a few seconds to get it open.

It was even darker inside the house than outside, and as I crept down the entrance hall, I peered for any hint of motion to indicate the presence of a snake. The animal didn't have to be on the floor. It could be on a piece of furniture, or even coiled in a light fixture on the ceiling, waiting to drop on me as I hobbled underneath.

But I didn't spot any snakes or anything else alive. Not until I turned into the room that Horn had turned into his library. There, amid the heaps of books that looked like tombstones in the dark, I could just make out a vague shape inside the wheelchair.

As I shouldered the Ithaca, I caught a rank animal smell competing with the odor of old paper. I aimed, and my target shot out of the chair, thumped down on its belly, and slithered toward me. It gave the impression of a leech or a thick-bodied snake, and it charged with the sinuous speed of a predator built to crawl.

I'd arrived too late to keep Horn from praying or the dragon god from answering. But this time, the blessing had come at a price. The spirit had restored his ability to move around unaided, but it had stripped him of his humanity in the process.

Maybe Horn didn't think it was such a heavy price. He'd already been inhuman on the inside.

I fired. Horn kept coming. I backpedaled and emptied the 12-gauge. He still kept coming.

By then, I'd retreated all the way back to the front door. I groped behind me, found the knob, and fumbled it open. At the same time, I dropped the Ithaca and pulled my pistol from its holster.

Horn raised his head, then struck at me like a rattler. The impact slammed me backward, out the door and off the stoop. I lost my grip on the Browning. Horn and I splashed down in the floodwater tangled together.

The bite he'd delivered to my stomach hurt. It didn't kill or paralyze me, though, and when lightning flashed, giving me a better look at him, it revealed the reason why.

He hadn't finished changing. His head was still a little bit human, and evidently his teeth were, too. They weren't capable of injecting poison quite yet.

Unfortunately, he had another way of attacking. His body twisted around mine like a boa constrictor. I didn't know if he could crush me, but he didn't have to. He only had to hold my head underwater.

I jerked my right arm free before he could immobilize it and punched him repeatedly in the face. He faltered. I heaved and loosened his grip on the rest of my body. Grabbed him by the neck, rolled him underneath me, and held him below the surface.

He thrashed, and his tail pounded me. I was terrified that I wouldn't be able to hold on. But maybe the fear gave me strength, because I did.

Until he finally stopped struggling. I clutched him and kept my weight on him for a while longer, making sure he wasn't playing possum. Then I floundered off him, flopped down on the stoop, and gasped for breath.

Tired and hurting as I was, the cleanup felt like almost as much of an ordeal as the events leading up to it. It had to be done, though. I found the Browning, picked up the Ithaca and the spent shells from inside the house, and wiped my footprints away. Then I dumped Horn in the trunk of the cruiser, drove to the center of a bridge, and dropped him into the rushing water below.

And basically, that was the end of it. Nobody questioned the story I made up to explain my injuries. It took more than a month for a neighbor to report that Horn had gone missing, and then no one connected it to me. So far as I know, no one ever pulled his body out of the river, although it's certainly possible someone did. The finder wouldn't call the cops if he couldn't tell the remains were human.

It was time to put the whole thing behind me, but for some reason, I couldn't. Instead, I did research, trying to find out just how often problems like Horn came along. Not situations involving reptiles, necessarily, but events that were horrible and unexplainable.

It turned out, more often than you'd think. And I supposed that if a person was smart and valued his life, he'd do his best to steer clear of them.

But what did my life amount to, anyway? Entry-level police work and choosing not to drink one day at a time. It wasn't awful, but compared to what I'd lost, it was nothing to get excited about, either.

And that's about as close as I can come to explaining why I did what I did next.

First, I educated myself. I got hold of some of Horn's books, and reading them was a good start. And when I felt ready, I turned in my badge and went hunting.

One way or another, the new job pays the bills. It gives me nightmares, too, but there's always a meeting somewhere when I find that I can't sleep.

THE WHITE BULL OF TARA

By Fiona Patton

Fiona Patton was born in Calgary, Alberta, Canada, and, grew up in the United States. In 1975 she returned to Canada and now lives on 75 acres of scrubland in rural Ontario with her partner, Tanya Huff, six and a half cats, and a tiny little Chihuahua that thinks he's a Great Dane. She has written six fantasy novels for DAW Books, the latest being *The Golden Tower*. She has also written more than two dozen short stories, most of them for DAW anthologies edited by Tekno Books.

The soft spring rains had come early to County Meath, causing a blush of pale green to spread across the fields and hills surrounding the royal palace at Tara.

Stretched out beside the low stone wall that separated the dozen kitchen plots from the more formal herb gardens, Brae Diardin of the Ulaidh Fianna lifted her face to the breeze, breathing in the fresh scents of newly turned earth and blossoming fruit trees with a sleepy smile. The late afternoon sun filtering through her copper hair caused the outline of her otherworldly form, a white Sidhe hound with red ears, to shimmer about her shoulders. One ear twitched lazily at the high, musical call of a lark in a nearby copse of birch trees and the lowing of a cow in the distant, gray-washed pasture fields.

Brae yawned.

She and her company of twenty-eight warriors, including her three siblings, Isien, Tierney, and Cullen, had wintered at Ushnagh in County Westmeath, where the five great provinces of Ireland convened. With their legendary Captain, Fionn mac Cumhail, also in residence, it had been an eventful season, and the small community of Druids at Ushnagh had been relieved to see the back of them come spring.

The much larger community at High King Cormac mac Art's Court of Learning at Tara were not particularly happy to receive them, but after obtaining Sub Captain Goll mac Morna's promise that he would personally keep the rowdy band of hunters and warriors in check—especially the Sidhe hound children of Diardin—they had grudgingly made them welcome. Goll had made good on his promise, keeping Brae and her siblings busy in the surrounding forests patrolling and providing meat and game for the Court.

Brae gave an unimpressed sniff. They were only staying long enough to refit for their journey south to Drombeg in County Cork—a fortnight at most. How many druidic feathers could they possibly ruffle in that short a time?

A shriek of outrage shattering the afternoon tranquility answered her question.

"Brae, that blasted whelp of yours has been in my garden again!"

Brae opened one eye. Her new hound, Bala, a female brindle whelp just five months old, lay stretched out beside her, great, oversized paws covered in dirt and fine young shoots of . . . Brae squinted down at them . . . some plant or another. Tucking them surreptitiously out of sight, Brae raised herself up on one elbow, schooling her expression to one of purely innocent curiosity.

Moifinn, Senior Druid at Tara's Court of Learning, was stumping towards them, brandishing her gnarled hawthorn walking stick in the air like a club.

Deciding at once that flight was the better part of valor, Brae scooped Bala up under one arm and vaulted over the wall, sprinting for the surrounding woods with the old woman's shouted invectives snapping at her heels, dodging through the thick stands of oak, birch, and alder trees, barely encumbered by the ungainly dog in her arms. It was only when Moifinn's voice faded that she paused for breath. Setting Bala onto her own paws, she threw herself down on the ground and, as the dog began to investigate a nearby stump covered in club moss, she gazed at her fondly.

"And how does she know it was you digging in her patch, anyway," she said. "It could have been any hound, or hare, or deer . . ." She yawned again. "Or a really big Sidhe mouse for that matter. This close to the woods, she's only asking for trouble. Druids: all about sacred and never about practical."

Bala's tail thumped in response as the whelp began to scratch at the soft earth by the stump, clods of moss and dead, rotting leaves flying out from between her back legs.

"Just as I thought," Brae added with a nod. "It could have been anything. But just to be on the safe side, we better stay out of Moifinn's way for an hour or two."

Changing swiftly to hound form, she joined Bala at the tree stump, thrusting her nose into the pile of leaves with a joyful woof.

The two of them spent the rest of the afternoon wandering the woods, exploring and hunting, until the sun dropped below the spires and pennants of Tara. Then, they made their way home with a brace of coneys to mollify Moifinn.

An egregious frown met her the next morning.

"What?" she demanded. "Bala hasn't been anywhere near your patch."

"No, but something has." Thrusting one finger out, Moifinn pointed at a trail of deep indentations, trampled plants, and large brown piles of manure on the carefully tended pebbled pathways that ringed her herb beds.

"That's not hound, that's . . ." Brae took a deep sniff. "Cow."

"Not my cows."

Keeping well out of reach of Moifinn's walking stick, Duir mac Linne, the local farmer who tended to Tara's herds as well as his own, shrugged deeply.

"No?" The sweet tone in the Druid's voice was more of a warning than a question. "Then how do you account for that?" The finger thrust out again, this time towards a telltale break in the fence that separated the gardens from the nearby fields and the accusatory trail of hoof marks and broken bracken that wound over and through it.

The farmer rubbed his chin thoughtfully. "Don't," he said after a moment.

"Try."

"Well, it's likely cows. But not my cows," he added as

a vein in Moifinn's left temple began to throb dangerously. "I moved all my cows to their spring pasture in the
south fields three days ago."

"Then whose cows are they?"

The farmer shook his head. "Don't know."

"Find out."

Brae's jaw dropped. "Why me?"

"Because your whelp trampled through my garden
yesterday; because you trampled through my garden last
year; because I need someone who can track them with
nose to ground, because you and your worthless siblings
were supposed to be guarding the northern perimeter and
should have seen them coming. And because I said so!"

The last words were snarled so vehemently that Brae
found herself backing up a step. Even Bala, who'd begun
to growl at the Druid's threatening tone, now slunk behind Brae, tail between her legs. Feeling much the same,
Brae turned her attention to the trail of broken foliage.

"I'll sniff around," she promised.

"You do that."

"Maybe it wasn't cows." Shifting fluidly from his
hound form, Brae's younger brother, Cullen, glanced
up from the deep indentation in the center of a badly
mangled juniper bush. "It's got a strange scent."

Brae shook her head. She'd enlisted the aid of her
three siblings, and together they'd gone over every square
inch of Moifinn's herb garden, trying with little success
not to cause more damage. "It was cows," she stated,
pausing a moment to sneeze as the heavy odor of crushed
peppermint and catnip assaulted her nostrils. "The tracks
are cow tracks, the dung is cow dung, and the smell is cow
smell. The scent you're getting is mashed juniper buds

along with it." She growled in frustration. "The problem is," she admitted reluctantly, "that I can't figure out how they got here. I followed the trail, and it led to this little portal grave in the north field, and that was it."

Her older brother, Tierney, snickered. "Faery cows?"

"Looks that way."

His twin sister, Isien, frowned. "You'd better show us."

As Brae had told them, the trail lead through the broken place in the fence and across the north field until it disappeared before an ancient, overgrown portal grave. The meadow grasses at the entrance had been badly trampled, clearly showing the effects of cows' hooves; but, long since fallen in, the entrance was unnavigatable. The siblings, along with their four hounds, spent nearly an hour snuffling and digging around its entire perimeter until they threw themselves down on the ground in frustration.

"Now what?" Cullen demanded peevishly, pulling a burr from his hound, Chekres', back leg.

"We wait, I suppose," Brae answered, "to see if they come through again."

"Then what?"

"Give them to Duir?"

"How? Have you ever herded cattle before?"

"No, but how hard can it be?"

"As hard as getting a horn up the arse," Tierney supplied.

All four snickered.

"What if they don't come through again?" he continued.

"Then it's going to be a long wait without a horn up the arse."

Cullen grimaced as his belly rumbled. "Wish we'd brought some lunch," he complained.

"We still can," Isien answered. "There's no reason we all have to stay here all day. "You and Tierney head back to Tara and fetch some food. We'll make a picnic of it. If no cows show up by nightfall, we'll take it in turns to guard the entrance until dawn."

"And if no cows show up by then?" Tierney demanded. "We can't spend an entire fortnight here."

"You tell Moifinn that."

"Oh, no," Tierney shook his head vehemently. "Brae tells Moifinn that. Because it was your hound that got us into this in the first place," he added as Brae opened her mouth to protest.

"Oh." Brae hunkered down with her back against the portal grave. "I still think it could have been anything in her patch," she grumbled, fondling Bala's ears absently. "She didn't actually see you there, exactly."

Beside her, Bala began to dig in the hard earth before the entrance, dislodging stones and plants in her fervor. As the strong scent of ravaged catnip wafted over them, Brae gave a resigned sneeze.

"That's not a cow."

"No."

"That's a bull. A young bull . . ." Brae twisted her head to get a better view between the distant animal's back legs. "But still a bull."

"Yes."

The moon had risen high in the sky, casting a bright, clean light across the darkened field. Brae and Tierney had taken over the watch from Isien and Cullen nearly an hour before and had settled in with Bala and Tier-

ney's hound, Tukre, a hundred yards from the entrance,
listening as Tara's main bell tolled three. One by one,
lulled by the cool, spring breeze and the mating sounds
of crickets and frogs, they'd fallen asleep.

Only to be jerked awake by the otherworldly crack of
the portal grave's entrance stones being thrust aside as a
large brown and white cow emerged. Dropping her head,
she'd cropped at the plants by the entrance, and once
again the pungent smell of catnip had wafted past them.

Tierney'd covered Brae's nose at once, muffling her
sneeze, but the matriarchal cow had paid them no heed
as another, smaller cow became visible behind her.
Another followed, then another and another until finally a herd of nearly a dozen perfectly normal looking cattle had stood grazing placidly in the shadow-cast
field. The matriarchal cow had waited a moment, then
given an impatient low as if to a reluctant calf, and, finally, the last of the herd had emerged into the bright
moonlight.

Now Tierney peered at the animal as well. "It's a
white bull," he pointed out, catching hold of Tukre's collar as the dog began to growl. "With red ears."

"Faery bull or Sidhe bull?"

"Can't tell from here."

"If it's a Sidhe bull, we could talk to it, explain how
it should keep out of Moifinn's patch before she sacrifices it for Tarbh-feis or something. Bala, be quiet." Brae
caught her whelp by the muzzle as, following Tukre's
lead, she began to growl as well.

"We could," Tierney agreed reluctantly, "but if it's a
faery bull, it might skewer us before we had a chance to
open our mouths. It's got really big horns."

The renewed lowing of the matriarchal cow cut off
Brae's answer. As the young bull joined her, she turned

and, with a purposeful air, made for the distant palace with him by her side and the herd cows trailing after.

Brae swallowed. "Um, I don't suppose Duir got a chance to mend that break in the fence?" she asked in a worried tone.

The sound of fence rails cracking like twigs made Tierney wince. "I don't suppose it really matters," he answered.

"Great. Moifinn's going to skin me."

"What should we do?"

"Get help keeping them out of her patch."

"From Duir?"

Brae shook her head. "It'll take too long. No, one of us has to go get Isien and Cullen, and the other has to start heading the cows off before they wreck the place." She paused as Tierney hesitated. "What?"

"Nothing, it's just . . ." He flushed in embarrassment. "They have, you know, really big horns."

"So? They're cows. We fought a giant weasel last year; it had really big claws. How much worse could it be?"

"There're more of them, and one of them's a Sidhe bull."

"Might be a Sidhe bull."

"Either way, it's a bull, which means it belongs to someone else, which means we can't just kill it even if it tries to skewer us. That cuts down our chances."

As Brae opened her mouth to argue, the crack of another fence rail sounded in the distance. "All right," she agreed reluctantly. "We'll both go for Isien and Cullen, then the four of us'll tackle the cows. We're Sidhe hounds, we should be able to herd a . . . herd without getting skewered. And in the morning we find out just exactly what kind of bull it is. Agreed?"

"Agreed."

* * *

"It sounds familiar. Wait here." Cnu Deireoil, Chief Bard of the Ulaidh Fianna, turned, his bright yellow hair gleaming in the sunlight that streamed through Tara's main library windows. "Don't touch anything."

The four siblings obeyed, grumbling.

Brae and Tierney had roused their siblings at once, and the four of them and their hounds had spent the rest of the night trying in vain to contain the herd as they wandered throughout Tara's herb gardens, placidly ignoring the dog pack snapping impotently at their heels. The white bull had seemed to pay particular attention to the plants at the southern end of Moifinn's garden while the matriarchal cow looked on approvingly and the others trampled about doing random damage to shrubs and herbs alike. When the dawn sun had finally broken over the distant forest, they'd all headed back across the north field and disappeared inside the portal grave once more. After noting that the entrance was again as impassable as before, the siblings had gone in search of Cnu Deireoil.

Now, the Bard returned cradling a huge, leather-bound book in his arms long before boredom caused them to disobey his directive.

"Here we are," he said, setting the book down on the small, carved dais in the center of the main reading room. "In Cattle Raids, as I expected."

"That doesn't look like the book Moifinn made me memorize Cattle Raids from before I joined the Fianna," Brae noted.

"That's because it isn't," Cnu answered, turning the creamy smooth vellum pages with a loving expression. "This is a very special, very rare edition that grubby little Sidhe hounds aren't allowed to touch. Or anyone else for that matter," he added to take the sting from his words. "Even Moifinn hasn't read from this book."

"Because she's a grubby little Druid?" Cullen asked with a gleam in his eye.

"No, because it's mine. I wrote it. Now be quiet a moment. Yes, here it is. Tain Bo Cuailgne: the story of Donn, the brown bull of Cooley."

"This is a white bull," Tierney pointed out.

Cnu raised one golden eyebrow at him, and he subsided with a barely audible mutter.

"Donn," the Bard continued once silence reigned again, "was the sworn enemy of Finnbhennach, the white-horned, or white bull of Connacht."

He glanced up to see if this would elicit another comment, but when all four Fianna kept quiet, he returned his attention to the book. "Finnbhennach was owned by Ailill, consort to Queen Medhbhan of Connacht, and raised with her own herd of royal cows."

Brae coughed apologetically, and Cnu glanced up with a flat expression. "What?"

"Um, the Queen of Connacht isn't called Medhbhan," she offered tentatively.

"No Queen of Connacht has ever been called Medhbhan," Isien added. "And none of them have ever had a consort named Ailill."

"No, not yet," Cnu replied with a crafty gleam in his blue eyes. "But I'm not talking about the past or the present. I'm talking about the future. The tale speaks of Donn and Finnbhennach fighting a great battle across time itself, and it's from these earlier travels that I gleaned this story. They fought backward and forward, each taking new forms as it suited their struggle: animals, dragons, demons, and birds."

"But not people?" Tierney asked.

Cnu sighed. "No. The story only makes mention of those four."

"So its a shape-shifting future faery bull traveling with a herd of cows owned by royalty," Isien noted.

"Which means we can't kill them," Tierney said to Brae with a pointed expression.

"And that means we can't eat them either," she noted with regret. "Too bad. They looked really tasty."

"And not an actual Sidhe bull we could reason with," Isien finished firmly, glaring them both into silence.

Cnu closed the book in a snap. "Essentially."

"So now we know what it is, but we still don't know why it's here, how it got here, or what to do about it," Isien growled a few moments later as they threw themselves down beside Moifinn's damaged garden once more. "It's clearly not fighting this other bull yet. It's practically still a calf."

Brae snorted. "Not from where I was looking," she scoffed.

"Then look again, little sister; a mature bull's bollocks are much, much bigger."

Tierney and Cullen snickered loudly at the word, then subsided as Isien cast them a scathing glance. "It's likely just mucking about looking for nice, tender herbs to eat," she finished.

Plucking a leaf from one of the few undamaged peppermint plants, Cullen gave it an experimental lick. "You'd think it would have plenty of nice, tender herbs to eat where it comes from," he noted with a grimace, wiping his fingers on Chekres' pelt.

"It probably does," Isien answered. "But you know how cattle are, they're always after fodder in somebody else's field. And there's lots of very lovingly druid-tended fodder here." Her outstretched arm took in all of Tara's herb gardens.

Brae glanced around with a thoughtful expression. "Funny how it only mucked about in Moifinn's patch then, isn't it?" she asked, with a sneeze as Cullen waved the crushed peppermint leaf under her nose.

The others frowned at her. "How'd you mean?" Tierney demanded. "There's dung everywhere."

"Sure, but that was just from the herd wandering around. We saw them, remember? Mostly the cows just munched away on the grass around the fence line, but the bull went straight for Moifinn's patch."

"So what's so special about it?" Isien asked.

Brae shrugged. "It's all vetch to me," she said with another sneeze. "Nasty to smell and just as nasty to eat."

"You know who we have to ask then, don't you?" Isien said.

As one, her three siblings nodded glumly.

"But we don't *all* have to be here when she answers, do we?" Cullen asked with a hopeful expression.

Brae rounded on him with a snarl, and Tierney stepped quickly between them. "Yes, pup," he said to his little brother in a firm tone. "We *all* have to be here."

"Catnip, peppermint, dragons blood, cinquefoil, and thyme. That was the worst of what got *eaten*."

Moifinn glared down at Bala as if the whelp had been responsible for the damage, and Isien moved forward before Brae could take offense at the unfair accusation and say something that they would all regret.

"So, what would all that do for a bull?" she asked brightly.

"Give it a bad case of the runs," Moifinn replied in a sour tone.

"Looks like it succeeded then," Cullen noted, wrinkling his nose.

Tierney shook his head. "That's what it's always like," he whispered.

"Ew."

"Enough," Isien snarled at them both. "I meant, what are they usually used for?"

"Many times many things; the same with all herbs," Moifinn snapped. "Cleansing potions, love potions, creating a psychic bond with your cat. Do you think it has a cat?" she asked, the dangerously sweet tone in her voice once more. "Protection, prosperity, to cure nightmares or cure impotency. Don't you dare laugh," she warned, glaring at Tierney and Cullen.

"We weren't," Tierney protested.

"Bollocks, you weren't."

All four siblings stared at her, trying hard not to break up laughing, and after a moment the Druid allowed herself small chuckle. "Yes, well, I suppose that was a bit funny," she allowed, then frowned. "You say it was a faery bull?"

"A legendary faery bull," Brae explained, quickly recounting Cnu Deireoil's tale of Finnbhennach.

Moifinn glanced down at her garden thoughtfully. "Cinquefoil, thyme, and dragons blood are all important elements in strength potions, useful if one was to fight another creature of equal or greater ability. Peppermint and dragons blood again are used for change. And catnip is most particularly the key ingredient in magical shape shifting." She nodded to herself. "It's preparing for battle.

"But that's notwithstanding," she added with a scowl, "you keep that great roast of beef out of my sacred

herbs or he'll become just that: a great roast of legendary faery beef."

"So, now we know what it is, and why it's here," Isien
said, ticking the points off on the tips of her fingers. "But
we still don't know how it got here or how to get rid
of it." Throwing herself down by the break in the north
field fence, she wrapped one arm about her hound
Keenoo's neck, laughing as he turned around to swipe at
her face with his tongue.

"How do cows usually get where they aren't wanted?"
Cullen asked, joining them on the trampled grass. Chekres immediately dropped his head in his lap, scratching
at him with one huge paw until he dug his fingers into
his ruff.

"They just break through the fence and go, like
here."

"So, what fence did they break through to get here,
in the bull's past that is?" Tierney asked as Tukre head
butted him until he sat as well.

Isien shrugged. "Probably the portal grave entrance.
Everyone says they're magical, and we used one like it
ourselves last year to get to Ynys-Witrin outside normal
time, remember?"

"But this one's been plugged up and undisturbed for
years."

"Err . . ."

As one they all turned to Brae.

"Actually, it hasn't," she admitted ruefully as Bala
began to dig in a pile of cow manure at her feet. "I was
up there, um . . . the day before yesterday, and Bala was
rooting around the entrance. I thought she'd found a
rabbit hole or something, so we both had a go at it until

we starting scratching about in that stand of catnip. Then I pulled her off."

"So, *you* broke through the fence?"

"I guess. We threw up a lot of stones. But I didn't think we'd thrown up enough to let an entire herd of cows get through."

"Think again."

"So, should we try to seal up the entrance again?" Brae asked, peering anxiously over Cnu Deireoil's shoulder.

The four siblings had returned to nag him with questions about portal graves until he'd finally set the sheet of music he was reading aside and returned with them to study it for himself.

"I don't think you can," he replied, bending down to peer into the collapsed entrance tunnel. "Such places were sealed magically as well as physically, and the spells have long since been lost. Whelp . . . what's your name?"

"Bala," Brae supplied.

"Bala, remove your nose, thank you." Cnu pushed the whelp to one side as she tried to shove her head between him and the entrance.

"Even the most accomplished of Druids would have difficulty resealing the entrance to any degree today," he continued. Crouching, he ran his hand along a clump of young catnip sprouts cropped almost to the ground, and behind him, Brae sneezed. "Likely they were drawn to the catnip at the entrance, and, once that was consumed, they followed the scent to more in Moifinn's garden." He glanced up. "You could try planting a faery ring at the entrance. It's believed that cattle will not step over one, but I don't suppose that any of you know how to do that."

All four siblings shook their heads.

"And Moifinn . . . ?"

"We'd really rather not ask her," Brae said hastily. "If we could help it. She's in a bad enough mood already what with having to replant all her herbs and shrubs."

"Not to mention bullying someone else into shoveling up all that cow dung on her paths," Cullen added.

"And with all your knowledge and all your books . . ." Isien began.

"We thought maybe you might do it," Tierney finished. "Please."

Four Fianna and four brindle hounds all looked at him hopefully, and Cnu sighed. "I'll see what I can dig up on the subject," he promised. "But it may take some time to set it in place," he added, raising his hand to forestall a premature celebration. "A day or two even. You'll have to do what you can to guard Moifinn's garden in the meantime. And if you can't keep them out of it, I can't help you with her reaction."

Four Fianna and four brindle hounds all slumped unhappily.

"Think it's holding?"

"I don't know. Maybe. It should be. Cnu's very smart."

"But he's not a Druid."

"No."

Five nights later, the four siblings and their hounds crouched behind a low rise where they could keep an eye on the portal grave. They'd been there every night since the Bard had set his faery ring in place, and so far there'd been no sign of cows, faery or otherwise.

Now Brae gave a wide yawn. "Finnbhennach might

have eaten all he needs to," she noted, pulling absently at Bala's ears. The whelp echoed her yawn, showing a mouthful of pointy, white teeth, before settling back with her head in the crook of Brae's arm.

"Either way, the company's leaving for Drombeg first thing in the morning, so after tonight it won't be our problem," Tierney answered from where he was lying stretched out with his head on Tukre's flank.

Cullen snorted. "I hate waiting like this," he complained. "Couldn't we start out early? We could be advance scouts."

"We might have been able to if we'd thought about it sooner," Isien replied. "But Goll won't appreciate being woken up on the eve of a long day's travel. We'll have to wait."

Cullen slumped against Chekres. "I wish we could time travel," he muttered.

"No you don't."

The sudden overloud sound of cracking from the portal grave's entrance cut off their argument at once. Jerking upright, Brae gaped at the huge creature who suddenly appeared standing with one large, front hoof squarely planted in the center of Cnu Deireoil's faery ring.

"Guess it didn't hold," she breathed.

Isien craned her neck so that she could peer over her sister's shoulder. "That's not Finnbhennach," she noted in an awed whisper.

"No."

"That's a brown bull."

"Yes. And he's a lot ..." Brae peered out at the animal. "Older," she finished.

Tierney and Cullen joined them at once. "Think that's Donn?" their younger brother asked.

"If he is, it's a good thing for Finnbhennach that he ate all the catnip and such from Moifinn's patch already," Tierney answered.

"But Moifinn's spent the last four days replanting it."

"Yes, but it won't be ready yet."

"Then why's he here?"

Tierney shrugged. "There are other herbal patches at Tara besides Moifinn's."

"Think he's headed . . ."

Isien snapped at them irritably. "Be quiet," she hissed. "We'll know soon enough."

The distant lowing of Duir's cows in the field sounded faintly over the trees, and as they watched, the brown bull lifted his head and sniffed the night wind with two great breaths from his huge nostrils.

Tierney chuckled. "Watch and learn, little brother. Food isn't the only thing a bull might break through a fence to find."

The bull's body began to ripple like quicksilver in the moonlight; then, from one breath to the next, a vast, brown dragon suddenly towered above the field, its long, red tongue darting out from between its flashing teeth to taste the wind. As all four hounds began to bay hysterically, it launched itself into the air. It circled over the portal grave with a great pumping of leathery wings, and the four Fianna got a excellent look between its legs before its black silhouette disappeared over the trees.

Tierney coughed. "Well," he began, shouting to be heard above Tukre's deep bass barking. "It certainly won't need to worry about . . ." He paused.

"Shape shifting?" Brae offered as she tried unsuccessfully to calm Bala down.

"Right, shape shifting, that was what I was going to say."

"Wish I had shape shifts like that," Cullen noted, then yelped as Isien smacked him on the back of the head. "I'm just saying he was very . . . older," he added.

Isien turned to Brae. "Shouldn't we do something about this?" she shouted, then turned with an exasperated expression. "Keenoo, shut up! It's gone!"

Her hound subsided with a resentful look, then turned on Chekres, nipping him in the ear. Cullen's hound yelped, then slunk quietly behind the youth's legs.

"Like what?" Brae asked, finally just clamping her hand around Bala's mouth to silence her.

"I don't know," Isien continued, glaring at Tukre, who quieted at once. "Warn Duir maybe?"

"About what?" Tierney laughed. "I don't think it plans to eat them."

"Dragons do eat cows," his twin pointed out.

"Yes, but bulls don't."

"Do bulls mate in the springtime?" Brae asked with a frown.

"I think they mate whenever they want to, but it's an otherworldly bull; it probably doesn't matter."

The timbre of the distant lowing changed to something that was definitely not fear, and all four Fianna grinned widely.

"Well, I guess that answers that question," Tierney chuckled. "So," he asked, stretching his back out. "What do we do now, go watch?"

Brea yawned. "Oh, yes, that's so tempting. No. If we're not going to go tell Duir that his cows are cavorting with a strange bull, we might as well get some sleep." Stripping off her tunic, she tucked it under her head. "Tomorrow we leave for Drombeg, and when we next come to

Tara, I'll bet Cnu has a whole new chapter in his story about Donn and Finnbhennach." She yawned again. "I wonder if we'll be in it," she added sleepily. Then, changing as fluidly to her Sidhe hound form as the brown bull had changed to its dragon form, she nudged Bala up against her stomach and closed her eyes.

One by one, her siblings followed her lead until four white hounds and four brindle hounds fell asleep to the distant lowing of satisfied cattle.

DEAD POETS

By John A. Pitts

John A. Pitts is a transplanted Kentucky boy living in the Pacific Northwest. He's a long time writer of speculative fiction whose work has appeared in such magazines as *Talebones,* as well as the DAW anthologies *Swordplay* and the forthcoming *The Trouble with Heroes.* John recently signed a three-book deal with a major genre publisher. Visit his website at www.japitts.net

Offal, carrion, rot, and decay. Panic rises in Katie as she staggers across the living room to shut the French doors. The stench of death rides the autumn wind.

For a moment, she stands frozen, staring out at the rose garden, searching in vain for the source of the stench. With eyes watering and throat clenching she shuts the doors and reels to catch herself on the back of the couch.

Dear God in heaven.

She crosses to the kitchen, one hand over her mouth. The urge to gag flits through her as she runs a cloth under the tap. Once she covers her mouth and nose with the damp cloth, she rifles the cabinet for anything to overcome the smell.

Half a can of air freshener later—Piney Woods—she collapses on the veranda and flips open her cell phone.

No signal, of course. She lays the phone against her forehead and watches the dust motes dance in the last rays of sunlight. The breeze has blown across the garden for days now, and the intoxicating aroma of heat and roses has teased her mind with memories of her childhood and days with no end.

Now, something, or someone, has been eviscerated in the garden and fermented in the heat of the day. With the evening's shifting of the breeze, she now suffers the full brunt of the carnage.

Her stomach churns, adding the tang of bile to her already overloaded senses. This is not what she wanted. Nothing in her cute little house seems appealing any longer.

The odor slithers into her psyche, addling her thoughts. What in the verdant grove could be . . . She sits bolt upright. Oh, it couldn't be!

She slips on her sneakers and holds the cloth to her face with one hand, grabbing the fireplace poker with the other. "Please don't be Grandma," she whispers as she flings the doors open again. The odor has subsided a bit, or perhaps she's just getting used to it. In either case, she steps gingerly from her house and stalks around the path through the three trellises flowing with wisteria. The raucous call of a crow causes her to jump, smacking the fireplace iron against a trellis with a bang.

"A raven caws in the gloaming night," she whispers, clutching the poker to her chest.

"our darling girl stands a'fright
abattoir's wind has come of late
blows the ire of Sweeney's gate"

Three years of English literature and her fear thrills with hackneyed poetry. The sigh that escapes her lips buzzes behind the drying terry cloth. Death lingers nigh, she thinks, walking beneath the wisteria.

She clears the end of the hedgerow and crosses the lawn. No bodies strew the lengthening shadows. The windows of her grandmother's house are open, and she hears singing from the kitchen.

Okay, Grandma Eloise has not been butchered. That's good.

Her heart lightens somewhat as she walks the path beneath the growing dusk, careful to step on only the white stones. Safe, she thinks, when her feet touch the porch. Safe at last.

The door squeaks a bit as she opens it. Grandma straightens from the oven and places a beautiful bundt cake on the counter. The overwhelming smell of sugar and eggs, vanilla and ... lemon of all things ... washes away the blight of death.

"Playing robber?" Grandma asks.

Katie smiles behind the terry cloth and shrugs, placing the fireplace poker on the table beside the cake. "Sorry, Grams. Something horrid has happened in the garden, and I thought perhaps you'd been murdered."

"Oh, my," Eloise says with a shake of her head. She places the oven mitts on the countertop near the sink and rinses her hands. "Murdered, you say?"

"Yes," Katie says with a vigorous nod. "The smell is overwhelming."

Grandma laughs then, a light, airy trickle that causes

her eyes to scrunch up and a rosy glow to brush her cheeks. "Oh, my child. It's that fool butcher bird."

Over jasmine tea and steaming lemon poppyseed cake, Katie learns of the shrike that nests among the thornier hedgerows and its proclivity for impaling its victims on the long thorns of the hawthorn hedge. How scrumptiously morbid.

"It's nesting now," Grandma assures her. "But after a few weeks the little ones will be gone, and the aroma will die back."

"Lovely metaphor," Katie says, toying with a bit of glaze on her third slice of cake. She slumps over her plate, her left hand cupping her right ear. "I'd hoped to enjoy the last days of Indian summer before the rains return and the world runs gray with pain."

Grandma sniffs and sips her tea. "Your grandfather hated that bird, you know?"

Katie straightens. "Hate is such a strong word."

"Loathed, perhaps, would be better," she offers. "If that bird hadn't kept the voles on the run, he'd have burned the hawthorns down to spite that creature."

"The stench is quite something," Katie agrees. "I can just see the epic battle, man versus nature." *How lovely,* she thinks. "And only his love for your roses stayed his hand in the end?"

"I don't know about all that," Grandma says. "I know he'd have egg on his face come the spring if the garden club got wind of him chopping or burning anything."

"Oh." Of course it was nothing so grand.

The briefest of smiles creases Grandma's cheeks. "But he did plot that bird's death on more than one evening over a stiff whiskey and a full pipe."

Katie stands, catches up both their plates, and sets them in the sink. Out there in the dying light, she thinks, the bird snatches its victims unawares and hangs them to die, slowly, on the vine. She thinks of Poe and Keats, staring into the yard.

"Are you all right, dear?"

Resolve floods through Katie, who turns and nods once. "I shall take up the noble cause." She smacks one fist into her opposite palm. "I will strike the blow my ancient fathers failed to strike."

"Watch the ancient talk." Grandma also stands and brushes her hand across Katie's shoulder. "Let the bird raise her little ones."

The tone of her voice is obvious, but Katie pretends not to hear. Outside, the shadows push the final pools of light into oblivion.

"Tomorrow I will scout the terrain."

Grandma pauses her hand on Katie's shoulder, squeezing it once before letting her hands fall to her side. "Tomorrow you could call your mother and see about returning to school."

Oh, that was the ploy, was it? Katie narrows her eyes. "I see. Perhaps it is you I should be wary of." She hugs her grandmother with a grin. "In league with the foul bird, methinks. Trying to drive me from my humble home?"

Grandma steps back, holding Katie at arm's length. "It was the gardener's home before he moved to Florida," she says raising her eyebrows. "And you are welcome to stay there as long as you need."

Katie gives a little curtsy. "Thank you."

"Let us hope your needs change."

For three weeks, Katie scours the vast yard dressed in a beekeeper's hood and an old army gas mask she acquired at that fashionable surplus store in town. With a long pair of barbecuing tongs and a box of biodegradable bags, she haunts the hawthorn, recovering the shredded and decaying bodies of field mice, crickets, small birds, and an occasional snake.

Each night as the stars appear between the scuttling clouds, she burns a block of cedar or mesquite. The fire dances in the brazier, gold and red, a pagan's delight, while she buries the day's body count in the vegetable garden.

Even when hunting, she rarely thinks of anything but poetry—T. S. Eliot, of course, is first on her mind, but there is also Byron, or Tennyson in a pinch. *The Deader the Better,* her favorite shirt proclaims on the front. *Read Dead Poets,* reads the back.

The shrike is not idle all this time, by any means. For every partial mouse or decapitated mole she discovers and inters, the butcher bird finds others. The nest remains hidden from Katie, but in the morning as the smell of coffee and bacon fills her home, she hears the song of the little ones, crying for their food.

The irony of her stuffing bacon into her yap as she listens to the hungry cries of the baby birds is not lost on her. The tragedy haunts her in the quiet moments, but after a hearty breakfast and a brief nap, she dons her warrior attire and hunts the elusive carrion fruit.

The weather has begun to turn wet again, as it is wont to do in the fall. Katie keeps the wood stove going much of the evenings to beat back the chill.

The plaintive cries of the young fell silent days before, and the reek of decay fades. Still she prowls the shadowy corners of the garden, searching for her nemesis. It is in this fervor, her holiest of crusades, that the abomination appears to her through the morning mist.

It is the twenty-third of October when it changes. She will recall it for the rest of her days. The morning mist has burned off, and the weak sun toys with the shadows as she sojourns this day. New territory, she deems. Look where she's failed to look. That is the way of it. But the prize is not always what one expects.

Tucked in a corner of the garden, behind Grandpa's prize-winning *R. roxburghii plena,* her vision shatters, her heart is sundered. Amid the longest of the hawthorn's wicked plumage the shimmer of the gossamer wings catches her eye. She pulls aside the helm and mask and leans forward—

> face of bone china
> tiny skirt of marigolds
> bosom impaled in cold cruel death
> —thus ends the lightness of heart.

Her legs give way and she falls to the ground. The rain soaks her as she sits in the mud, studying the lifeless fey. It isn't until Grandma kneels beside her, draping her in a blanket and pulling her to her feet, that Katie realizes the day has gone and the shadows rule the garden.

"Did you see," she asks as Grandma pulls her into the little house. "Did you see what our Sweeney Todd has done this day?"

Grandma does not say a word. She strips Katie of her wet and muddy clothes. As each garment is shed, beekeeper helmet, gas mask, sweatshirt and jeans, a bit of the anger and horror slips past the gate. By the time the shower is running and the windows are fogged with steam, Katie stands in the heat of the water, weeping.

She weeps until the water runs cold. The icy fingers drive her to a dry towel and her favorite clothes. When she emerges in her college fleece and an old pair of sweats, Grandma has the stove pinging and the cocoa steaming in oversized mugs.

Katie curls into a blanket on the divan, her feet tucked beneath her and the steaming mug held tight in her hand.

Grandma sits in the rocker across from her, near the stove. "Do you recall your summer here?" she asked. "When you were seven?"

Memories of long drowsy days in the sun puts a smile back on her face—playing with her dolls as the walls of thorns protected her from the rush of the world. "Yes. Those were wonderful days."

"Do you remember how your doll disappeared one afternoon? How you cried in Grandpa's lap because your best friend in the whole wide world had been stolen by some villain?"

This puzzles Katie. She does not recall any trauma here in the garden. Nothing horrible has ever happened in her memory. "Are you sure it was I?" she asks finally.

Are you sure it was I.

Are you sure it was me.

Grandma sighs. "Yes, dear heart. It was you. The pixies were thick that summer, having been driven from the forests near Redmond in all the construction. Raphael, the gardener, found your doll in the hawthorn among the shrike's recent meals. The cloth was torn and much of the yarn hair was missing, but the way it had been impaled on the thorns scared Raphael. He left soon after, swearing that the fey had cursed you.

"This house has sat empty all this time."

"Sixteen years," Katie breathes. "And all this time, have you seen the pixies?"

"Not a one," Eloise says. "Your grandfather found several impaled on the thorns, like your doll, like the voles and the sparrows. The butcher bird, your Sweeney Todd, will take what it needs. That year, your grandfather had wanted to protect you from the horror and did as you have done, clearing the dead, hiding the food. The shrike resorted to what it could. Once the first pixie had been taken, things began to go wrong."

Katie sits up, "Wrong?"

"Tiny things at first. The milk went bad within a day, cakes fell, the odd missing sock." She touches the side of her face, her eyes lost in history. "Your mother knew immediately what had happened. The mark on your face," she trails off.

Katie touched her own face, finger tracing the mark she carries. Wine stain, she had always been told. But what if?

"Fairy marked," Grandma says. "You were too old to steal, as pixies are fond of doing, and trading one of their own for you was not feasible. Instead they took a bit of you, a small touch on the cheek to remind us of the part we played in the butcher bird's depredations."

"And why did you allow me to repeat his mistake?" Katie asks. "Why did you not warn me of the appetite and the need to feed? Why did you allow me the crazed notion that I could fight this bird and risk the wrath of the fae?"

"This is not poetry, girl. This is real life. Your Byrons and Keatses will never be enough for you. You are cursed and blessed in ways we cannot imagine."

Katie sips her chocolate and falls deep in thought. In her mind's eye, she sees the fairy kiss that graces her cheek, a burned red cluster of wing beats and angry, wailing fists.

"I found the pixie that day," she says, finally. "I pulled it from the thorns and hugged it to my face, thinking it a toy. I remember the soft mewling as it died against my cheek, its blood stinging my flesh."

Grandma stops rocking and stares at her. She holds her hand over her mouth and moans. "It is the bird's nature to find its food, no matter the source," she whispered. "She must feed her young."

"But we interfered," Katie says, feeling overly hot. She flings the blanket aside and stands in her fluffy pink bunny slippers. "I'm not crazy. I remember the pixies and the way the trees glowed with their magic on Samhain. I remember you leaving gingersnaps and root beer on the wrought-iron table in the back, so the pixies would leave you alone."

"And then the shrike began nesting nearby. At first we loved the pageantry, the way it courted with such amazing dances and songs. Then when the voles were under control, we celebrated. It wasn't until that October, with the pixies in the trees and the autumn sun blazing overhead, that we realized the price one must pay for certain favors. The roses have never bloomed more full. The shrike was a harbinger of prosperity and balance."

"But the fae pay the price with their blood."

"It is but an animal," Grandma says. "A simple bird like many others."

"No," Katie says, setting her mug on the table and moving to stare out into the rain. "It has become tainted, as have I."

She catches her reflection in the mirror, the scar on her face that drove her inward, to poetry and her inner world. "It has eaten of the flesh, fed its young on the magic. It has become voracious. Seeking that which it has only tasted for one season."

"But surely it is not the same bird."

Katie turns to her grandmother. "I believe it is. I believe it hunts the hawthorn and roses in search of more than mere sustenance."

She sits back down on the couch, pulling the blanket over her legs. "We must find its nest. We must make certain that it cannot thrive."

"And the pixies?"

"This land has been in our family for generations," Katie says. "It is blessed and cursed, as I am. I believe we owe it to the fae to remove this scourge."

"But, it is just doing what comes natural."

"Natural?" she asks. "I don't think natural is in the equation any longer."

The lights dim, and the fire's glow is the only light in the room. Katie sits alone in the garden house, whimpering as the rain pelts the windows.

The rocking chair sits empty, a vague whiff of vanilla and lemon reach her, driving the memory of softer times.

She stands at last, walks to the window, and stares up at the empty house. The butcher bird haunts her dreams, haunts her garden.

But tomorrow, she will find its nest. She will end the madness that has afflicted her all these years. Her cell phone lies on the table, its battery long dead. It never got a signal here at the estate, as it is.

Her college days are long past her, her family gone to the great beyond, and yet the memories haunt her. Fae touched, her grandmother had told her. And still she finds the eviscerated remains of pixies and fairies. The butcher bird eludes her hunt, but its children starve.

SUPER SQUIRREL TO THE RESCUE

By P.R. Frost

P.R. Frost resides on beautiful Mt. Hood in Oregon. She hikes the Columbia River Gorge for inspiration. She is an omnivorous reader, having taught herself to read before entering kindergarten. Her sister claims this was so she wouldn't have to wait to learn how to write so she could begin penning her stories. At science fiction/fantasy conventions she can be found hanging out with filkers and costumers. P.R.'s musical tastes are as omnivorous as her reading, ranging from classical to Celtic to New Age to jazz and, of course, filk.

A crack of thunder and a flurry of wind broke my concentration. I looked out at the bright blue sky. A cold east wind blew down the mountain pass clearing away any trace of a storm.

Another burst of noise.

"What the ...?" I extricated myself from my lap desk filled with my computer, a stack of note cards, and a sleeping cat.

The psycho Siamese hissed at me as she jumped to the floor, a ball of indignant cream and pewter fur. Wait a minute, psycho and Siamese is redundant.

How do you spell "catittude"? S-I-A-M-E-S-E.

A closer look out the window showed the source of the out-of-season thunder. "The murder of crows is back, Dyflyn," I sighed to the cat.

She hopped up onto the windowsill. Instantly the fur along her spine stiffened, her ears came up to a point, and she crouched down, shoulders twitching. Or was that itching? A strange clicking sound came from her throat.

"No, you can't go hunting those crows, Dyflyn," I admonished my companion. Her name meant "imp" in Welsh, and it suited her.

She clawed the glass and hissed again.

"Two hundred fifty crows fighting over one ear of corn at Elliot's feeder next door are too many." The sea of writhing black feathers covered my yard, the next-door neighbor's yard, the street, and the sidewalk across the street. It looked like something out of a Hitchcock movie.

At that point, Elliot, mid-seventies, fit, trim, and bald as an egg, emerged from his kitchen door into his drive-way carrying a baseball bat. "Shoo!" he shouted, waving his weapon. "That's not your corn."

The crows looked at him for about two seconds with amused expressions, then returned to squabbling over the ear of corn stuck on a spike in the middle of Elliot's impressive array of feeding stations.

Their beady black gaze lighted on me through the window. Intelligence. Cunning. Evil.

I shivered and stepped back.

Elliot retreated and reemerged with a pair of frying pans. He banged them together and shouted some more.

The crows just laughed at him and moved on to the gazebo the size of my bathroom filled with sunflower seeds.

I gave up. Deftly I moved my workstation to the den at the back of the house. Dyflyn would follow me when she got tired of posturing at the crows. The crows didn't care. They just wanted more food.

Or to take over the world.

Before I settled in the recliner, I checked my own modest bird feeders on the back deck. The hanging one still held about half a load of sunflower seeds. Two chick-adees and a yellow finch perched on it as it spun. Below it, up against the railing, the screened tray of seeds had been licked clean. "Greedy jays," I half laughed.

This time of year, as the solstice approached and an arctic high pressure sat east of the mountain, spilling frigid air through the passes and the Columbia River Gorge, I didn't begrudge any of the critters a good meal. So I dumped another two cups of oily seeds on the tray and went back to work.

Dyflyn wandered in a few moments later. I quickly saved the marketing plan for the local hair salon. The cat sat and washed her paws. I saw the cunning look in her eyes and braced myself. She jumped onto the lap desk, spilling papers, note cards, Post-its, and pens in eighteen directions. She wormed her way around, drap-ing herself across my arms between the laptop and my elbows.

"Fine, I'll watch the birds for a few moments and pet you. But then I've got to disturb your imperial highness to retrieve all that stuff on the floor."

She huffed and settled deeper. A deep purr erupted

from her throat. My pulse calmed and matched her rhythm.

"You know that if you want fresh litter and gourmet tinned food, you are going to have to let me work."

No comment.

"Look, you territorial tyrant, I know this is your lap and I have no right to make you share it with something so ordinary as marketing plans, bookkeeping, payroll, and taxes for fifteen small businesses, but you are going to have to move."

Dyflyn's attention swiveled to the sliding glass doors. A squirrel sat in the middle of the seed tray stuffing hundreds of seeds into its bulging cheeks.

All the birds had fled.

Not just any ordinary squirrel. The local pests are Douglas Squirrels (named for the legendary naturalist David Douglas). They measure about four inches in body length, not much bigger than a standard chipmunk, have a rusty belly, and brownish brindled fur.

This guy looked easily three times that size, maybe more. Much bigger than even the gray squirrels that infested the valley. But he had the coloring of our little Dougies. I'd seen ostrich feather boas less full than that plume of a tail.

"Where did you come from?" I gasped in awe. He looked up a moment, as if he'd heard my words, then returned to stuffing his mouth.

Dyflyn chirped at him, preparing to leap at the glass. She did that quite regularly, scaring the small black bears that visited the deck after dark. They'd all gone night-night for the winter and spoiled her fun.

The squirrel barked. He sounded like a Chihuahua. He was bigger than most of them.

Dyflyn backpeddled across the den in surprise.

Since I had to get up anyway, I grabbed the phone and carried the handset back to the den. Number six on my speed dial connected me with Elliot's house.

"Ginny!" I said when Elliot's wife picked up on the first ring. "Have you seen the super squirrel?"

"Oh, my, yes, Penny. He ate an entire ear of corn yesterday, just after dawn, before the crows landed."

"What kind of squirrel is he?"

"I looked him up in the books, and he must be a cross between our Dougies and a California gray. Gray biggers we called them as kids," Ginny said.

I pictured her settling into her love seat with footrests. She didn't have much else to do other than watch the wildlife surrounding us. MS left her weak and depressed most of the time. We chatted at least once a day.

"I thought I heard rumors of a gray bigger finding its way up here last year. I'm surprised it could cross breed with the Dougies," I mused.

"Oh, you know rodents. They'll breed any way they can."

The squirrel sat up on its haunches and scanned the deck. A crow had dared hop onto the railing.

I said a nasty word as I examined the engorged nipples on her swollen belly.

"What's the matter, dear?" Ginny asked, quite concerned.

"The squirrel is female and preggers."

"Oh, dear. I fear that one gray has started a bigger problem." She laughed at her pun. "Should we call Fish and Wildlife?"

"I'm not sure," I hedged. "This gal is bigger than any squirrel I've ever seen, even a gray bigger."

Ginny dismissed my misgivings. "You've seen some of those wolf/dog hybrids. The pups can grow larger than either parent. That's all it is."

I only half believed her.

Visions of teenage mutant ninja something-or-others danced through my head.

"Do you remember the rumors of a toxic waste dump in the wetlands off Salmon River Road? Some kids found abandoned barrels that were leaking."

"Oh, that was three years ago. And the barrels contained nothing more toxic than the dregs of diesel fuel. Elliot checked it out."

But he didn't report them to the authorities and have the dregs tested.

"Just because the barrels were *labeled* diesel doesn't mean they *contained* diesel. The barrels are still there. Still leaking, and this squirrel is as big as a toxic waste dump mutant."

The squirrel charged the deck railing. The crow fled in an awkward clash of wings and loud squawks. His cronies lined up on Elliot's fence and protested mightily. Deafeningly.

If Big Mama out there could discourage the crows . . .

Big Mama went back to stuffing herself with sunflower seeds. I named her Cass.

The crows attacked the kitchen skylight. It sounded like machine guns or a jackhammer. A herd of elephants would be quieter tromping across my roof as they changed places in a unique dance.

End of work for the day. No way could I concentrate with that racket.

Time for a walk. Dyflyn had other ideas.

She watched me from the top of the recliner back with one eye open. The rest of her seemed ready to nap.

I donned the usual assortment of wool socks, boots, cap, scarf, and coat over my wool sweater and jeans.

The second I opened the front door two inches, Dyflyn scooted through.

I dove to grab her, slipped on the ice, missed the railing, and came up with a fist full of loose fur and a face full of slushy snow.

"I'm gonna get you for that, Dyflyn. You're supposed to be an indoor cat!" I yelled after her.

She twitched her tail at me saucily.

Okay, end the walk idea. I couldn't leave with the cat out. We have coyotes who eat cats. Though I pity the coyote who might tangle with Dyflyn. So, I dug out the last set of outdoor lights and strung them around a rhododendron conveniently near the house and the multioutlet strip.

I was standing in the middle of the street trying to decide if the extra layer of white was overkill to the display when what to my wondering eyes should appear, but a distressed cat with super squirrel on her tail.

Dyflyn dashed up the western red cedar at the center of the yard. Great. Now I'd have to get the extension ladder out and try to persuade her down.

The squirrel raced up the tree in pursuit.

I bit my lip in trepidation. The cat and the squirrel were almost the same size. Which one would I end up transporting to the vet?

Three seconds later, the squirrel headed back down the tree with Dyflyn hot on her tail. They ran around the base of the tree, up the rhodie, made a jump to the carport roof, reversed, leaped over to the cedar, clung for several precarious moments while I watched with my heart in my throat, then continued the game up and down and around, over, under, around again. They threaded through the deck railing posts like a dog agility course. They climbed and scooted, blurs of liquid fur.

An audience of neighbors gathered in the street. We cheered on the competitors in this strange contest and commented on the bizarre parentage of the squirrel.

Eventually they paused in heart-racing truce, each perched on a different granite boulder. They stared at each other for several long moments.

I crept over to Dyflyn, hoping to catch her while she rested. I'd get scratched. That was better than losing her to a rabid squirrel bite.

I was almost upon her when she sat up, ears cocked in alarm.

I stopped short, afraid she'd spotted me and prepared to run again. But all of her attention was on the squirrel. Cass ended the staring contest, turned, and hopped to the next boulder down in the terracing. This rock had a mesh of multicolored lights spread across it. Idly, she began chewing the twisted green wires.

Dyflyn chattered and yowled. Even she knew better than to chew light cords, especially when the lights were lit.

"No! Get away." I started toward the squirrel, waving my arms.

Cass began to twitch. Blue energy arced and crackled along her fur.

I dove for the power strip, slamming the off switch with my fist.

Too late. The super squirrel gave one final convulsion, legs stiff, brindled fur standing on end, smoke leaking out of the engorged teats, and keeled over. She landed in a soft nest of orange cedar tailings, only a shade darker than her tummy.

We stood there in stunned silence. My heart stuttered for a beat or six.

Linda, the neighbor across the street, ran for her house crying.

"It's a goner and good riddance," Elliot grumbled. "Worse than the crows, eating more'n its fair share of corn." He turned and stomped through his back door.

We didn't have a crow problem until he started putting out the corn.

The party broke up, and I was left alone with my cat to catch. And a dead squirrel.

I sighed to disguise the quivering of my chin.

Dyflyn ceased chattering and stared at the dead animal. She sat immobile. Unbelieving?

I grabbed the chance and scooped her up in my arms. She twisted wildly. I clung tighter, afraid she'd dash off again. We compromised with her head on my shoulder, staring back at the squirrel.

The soft flutter of her heart near my ear reassured me that she lived. Her silky fur comforted me.

Once inside, I threw Dyflyn onto my bed and closed the door. With her safe inside, I scrounged around the spare bedroom closet and found an empty shoe box I'd been meaning to recycle and hadn't gotten around to yet.

The ground was frozen. Not a good time to try digging a grave. I should have just carted the carcass off into the woods and left it for the crows. Strangely, they kept their distance as I used a shovel to deposit the dead squirrel into the box. Then I clapped the lid on it and stuffed it into the shed. Somehow in the last hour I'd developed an odd bond with Cass. She deserved better than to be left as carrion for those nasty crows.

"Who said life in the mountains would be quiet so I

could get more work done?" I shook my head as I settled with the laptop in front of the gas-log fire. Dyflyn liked stretching out in front of the heat. I think I turned it on to soothe her after her adventure more than to warm my icy feet.

I opened a spreadsheet and began plugging in numbers.

Dyflyn prowled around the love seat, under the foot-rest, across the hearth, under the Christmas tree. She banged her head against a bell on the lower branches and jumped backward four feet. She gave me the "I meant to do that," look and levitated to the windowsill. And there she sat for over an hour staring out at the strangely quiet winter afternoon.

If I didn't know better, I'd say Dyflyn was mourning a dear friend. She'd only known Cass for ten minutes.

I felt a bit mournful myself.

A snow flurry swirled, blocking our view of the street. Or were those tears in my eyes?

In my neck of the woods we say, "If you don't like the weather, wait a minute. If you don't like the forecast, change the channel."

A warm south wind blew up about midnight bringing bucket loads of rain. At some point I heard the shed door bang open. Not unusual with gusts this strong, so I went back to sleep with a promise to get the local handy-man to realign the door. Like I'd been promising myself for the past three years.

Dyflyn woke up at the noise and began prowling again, peering out the window and chittering softly to herself.

The freezing level shot up to pass level. By morning the last of the snow had melted. The ground thawed enough that I figured I could give Cass a decent burial after breakfast.

"I don't need your help, Dyflyn," I told her. She crouched by the door while I donned my usual layers of outdoor gear. So intent was she on getting out, she completely ignored the crows trying to drill holes in the skylight.

"Time for a preemptive strike," I said as I grabbed her and tossed her into the bedroom. Just barely, I managed to close that door before she scooted out again. She pawed at the frame and dug under the door, mewing pitifully.

"Sorry," I lied as I exited the house. When I peeked over my shoulder I saw her sitting in the bedroom window glaring daggers at me. I wondered if she'd accept the bribe of a can of gourmet cat food.

Probably not.

The shed door swung back and forth in the remains of the wind. I grabbed the shovel first, then looked down at the spot where I'd stashed the shoe box coffin.

The lid lay in tatters beside the box. The box was empty.

My heart sank. Some beast, probably a coyote, had taken advantage of the loose door and seized Cass's dead body.

I sighed as I replaced the shovel and dumped the box in the garbage can. Somewhere deep inside me, I said a small prayer for the squirrel. She deserved better. But this was nature's way. I should just let it go.

Sadness made my steps heavy and slow as I retreated indoors and went about my morning chores.

I hung the bird feeder and replenished the seeds in the screen tray before settling in for a morning of work in the office. The phone rang.

Great, another excuse to put off actually working.

"I thought the squirrel died," Ginny said without preamble.

"It did."

"Then what is gnawing the corn cob like an old-fashioned typewriter?"

Carrying the phone, I dashed to the window that overlooked Elliot's parade of feeding stations. At the end closest to my bedroom, he'd stuck a corn cob on a spike in the middle of a small ledge. Sure enough, a huge squirrel the size of a small dog, with the rusty coloring of a much smaller cousin, methodically worked her way up and down the cob, removing the kernels one by one, row by row.

"Huh?"

"It must be another one from the same litter," Ginny muttered.

"Would two sister squirrels both be pregnant out of season at the same time?" I asked. Cass had risen up to catch the tip of the cob, exposing her swollen belly. She looked even bigger, all over her body, not just in her belly, than she did yesterday.

"Penny, are you sure she was dead, not just knocked out?"

"I didn't feel for a pulse," I snapped.

I tried to picture the shoe box. The lid had been shredded in long gashes from very sharp parallel claws. The box with its bit of tissue paper had remained undisturbed. A coyote would have left tooth marks in the cardboard. Could Cass have torn through the lid to escape?

Dyflyn joined me at the window, pacing back and forth along the sill, meowing. At every third pass, she'd rise up on her hind legs and paw at the glass.

The ubiquitous crows shifted. First one, then five, then fifty, lining the gutters of my house and Elliot's. They rocked side to side from foot to foot. At first they moved randomly, then gradually fell into a unison dance. Back and forth in a hypnotic and silent ritual.

Dyflyn crouched down, ears flat, front paws edging forward silently.

I'd had enough. Time to take back my neighborhood from this avian invasion.

Grabbing a coat as I ran, I dashed out the front door, heedless if it closed tightly. For the first time in my life I wished I possessed a firearm. Preferably a shotgun loaded with bird shot, or rock salt, anything to get rid of the black menace lining the roof trees and gutters.

Cass nodded to me and resumed her work on the corn cob.

I looked up, assessing what I had to do to convince the crows to move away, about three hundred miles away.

Just then the crow on the near end of my gutter swooped and jabbed its beak at Cass's head. Then it landed in one smooth glide at the end of the line across the way. The lead crow on that side took its turn, repeating the motion. This time it came up with a tiny tuft of squirrel fur in its beak. It landed with a triumphant caw that echoed between the houses.

Elliot appeared on his steps inside the carport with two pot lids in his hands. He banged them together in a shrill clash.

The crows ignored him.

I headed for the garden hose neatly coiled inside the shed. By the time I'd attached it to the spigot, Dyflyn had escaped the house and climbed the four by four that held up the feeding station next to Cass and the corn.

The next crow in the queue lost a tail feather to Dyflyn's claws. She snarled in disgust that she hadn't drawn blood.

Cass finished with the corn and took notice of the

flurry around her. As the next crow dive-bombed toward her, she ducked and rolled into a tight ball.

The crow missed and noisily protested his disappointment at no fur trophy.

I aimed a spray of cold water toward the roof line. A crow rose straight up and down again. It croaked curses at me that made my hair stand on end. I kept up my watery barrage, forcing the line of crows away from the gutter's edge.

Dyflyn caught the edge of the cascade. She hissed and spat, rightly blaming the birds as the cause of her getting wet. But she didn't leave her post.

Amazing.

Then Cass uncoiled from her hedgehog roll. As she unfurled, she grew bigger and bigger yet.

My aim with the hose faltered, drenching the ground rather than the enemy.

Blue energy sparked from the end of each hair on Cass's pelt. More than just puffing up with air to intimidate a rival. More than flexing her muscles. Her eyes glowed with the same blue electricity. Her fur bristled and took on darker, more metallic hues. She bared her teeth, and they elongated. Her claws grew almost as long as her stretching arms.

Blue flame shot from each knife-sharp talon.

The four-by-four post vibrated with the strength of her transformation. I felt the tingles of those sharp flashes all the way through my feet to my knees. My hands shook. I dropped the hose and wrapped my arms around myself to ward off atavistic awe.

Cass's fur stiffened, flattened, forming overlapping panels of plate armor. She became the Incredible Hulk of all squirrels.

My heart skittered, and I knew fear.

Elliot stared at her gape-jawed, forgetting to bang his pot lids.

Down the post of the feeding station Cass flew, up the woodpile stacked neatly at the side of Elliot's house. Then she leaped to the roof with Dyflyn hard on her heels.

They slashed and tore, snarled and hissed. Crow after crow hit the ground, disemboweled, wings broken, heads smashed. If Cass left one living, Dyflyn finished it off. And they moved on, to the next and the next.

Five died before I remembered to breathe.

Ten met their grisly fate before the crows got the idea this was no longer a safe place for them. The flapping of wings sounded like a single clap of thunder as they rose. With telepathic precision they circled and wheeled. One foolhardy hero made one more attempt to land beside the empty corn cob.

In a magnificent leap, the armored squirrel soared from the roof to the ledge, gouging beady black crow eyes as it landed. This bird fell too, pierced to the brain.

As one, the flock turned in the air and streaked west toward the valley and more hospitable climes.

They'd have to begin their world domination elsewhere.

Cass descended from her perch with dignity and scampered off into the woods.

Dyflyn came down more awkwardly. Still, she was full of herself and stropped my ankles until I praised and petted her with due admiration.

"Gonna freeze tonight," Elliot said around a toothpick. "Might as well leave the buggers. Easier to handle when they're stiff. I'll bag 'em and put 'em in the garbage first thing in the morning before the truck comes." He retreated with his pot lids.

By the time I'd put the hose away and gone inside, Dyflyn had settled in front of the fireplace. The look she gave me clearly said that I needed to turn on the gas log so she could dry off and warm up properly. I obeyed.

I also put out extra seeds on the back deck tray.

I never saw Cass again, though the sunflower seeds disappeared at an alarming rate all winter long.

By spring the crows hadn't come back.

But if they do, there's an entire litter of oversized squirrels ready to take them on. Dyflyn trains them regularly with games of follow my leader and catch me if you can.

I don't think I'll put out holiday lights again though.

This story is dedicated to
Lilac
My own dyflyn of a Siamese
5/5/1998—1/4/2008

HER BLACK MOOD

By Brenda Cooper

Brenda Cooper has published fiction in *Nature*, *Analog*, *Oceans of the Mind*, *Strange Horizons*, the anthologies *Sun in Glory; Maiden, Matron, Crone; Time After Time,* and more. Brenda's collaborative fiction with Larry Niven has appeared in *Analog* and *Asimov's*. She and Larry have a collaborative novel, *Building Harlequin's Moon*, available now in bookstores. Her solo novel, *The Silver Ship and the Sea*, was released in 2007. Brenda lives in Bellevue, Washington, with her partner Toni, Toni's daughter Katie, a border collie, and a golden retriever. By day, she is the city of Kirkland's CIO, and at night and in the early morning hours, she's a futurist and writer. So she's trying to both save and entertain the world, with sometimes comical results as the two activities collide and, sometimes, blend. Neither, of course, is entirely possible.

The doorway to the High Hills exists within a water-fall that exists within an arts festival that exists in

*Laguna Beach, California, once every summer.
Many of my stories have passed through this doorway. I hope you enjoy this one.*

Summer sun beat down on Carly, washing out her
skin and the sawdust under her feet and dulling the
bright green and purple glazes on her mother's pottery.
The air had become a veil of heat-shimmer between
herself and the path she squinted down.

Nothing but tourists in bright shorts with sweaty faces.
Of course, the tourists were welcome for their wallets.
But she wanted her mom. Or Marla the women's shelter lady or Jack the handyman or anyone else she knew,
for that matter. It was a drag to be stuck in the booth;
she had to post a sign, carry the cashbox, and worry the
whole time if she even went to the bathroom. She dug
her toes into the hot sawdust and wiped sweat from her
face and sighed, still looking.

If only she could just leave. She'd met some girls
down on Main Beach, runaways living on the lawn by
the boardwalk all day, flirting and laughing. She'd even
made friends with one, a tall Latina girl named Toy who
came by the booth once in a while. Maybe Toy would
come today, and her mom wouldn't get drunk until after
the festival closed, and Carly could go to the beach with
Toy and ask her and her friends some of the thousand
questions she had. Where did they sleep? How did they
eat? Where did they go when they left Laguna Beach
after the festival?

It would be fun to go with them, wherever they went.
Not that she would. She picked up a rag and rubbed
the sawdust leavings from the platters and bowls on the
lower shelves, still watching.

There. Finally. Not Toy, but her mom. Hobbling up the

ever-so-slight hill between the entrance wall and their
booth, walking even slower than the tourists, as if she
were fifty instead of thirty-five. When her mom finally
stood inside the booth, she smelled of this morning's
whiskied coffee and the two or three bottles of cheap
wine from the night before. Now that she was here,
it was hard for Carly to remember why she'd wanted
her here, even though she had. Carly mumbled, "Good
morning."

Her mom's eyes fastened on Carly's, and a thin smile
touched her lips and cheeks, making her look almost
healthy for a moment. "How's it going?"

Her words slurred a little. Not enough for a customer
or a cop to recognize, but Carly heard it. Damn her mom,
anyway. "It's almost three o'clock, Mom. I'm hungry."

The older woman shoved her fist into her pocket as if
there might be money there.

There wasn't, of course. She glanced at the cashbox.
"How'd we do so far?"

Carly looked away, barely keeping her voice even. "*I*
did okay. *I* took in sixty-four dollars so far, even in the
heat. Mostly mugs, but also the purple dragon platter."
*And another twenty-five I hid against the winter because
you won't.* But she didn't say that since then the twenty-
five would disappear.

"So take four dollars and go get lunch."

Anger licked up Carly's spine and flushed her face.
"Four dollars? That's a stale hot dog from Mumbly
Pete's. I opened six hours ago. And I get seventy-five
cents an hour?"

"C'mon Carly. You know we have expenses."

She'd hoped so hard this winter. After Carly'd started
sleeping in the women's shelter on bad nights, her mom
had gotten worse. Then one morning Carly found her in

tears, slumped over the rickety fake-wood kitchen table in their studio. She'd raised her head and sworn she'd become a good mom. She'd pinky-sworn to stop drinking. She signed up for a regular twelve-step program and quit drinking for a full month. Even though the month had ended with a binge, it had been better for a while. It really had.

But not anymore.

A tear pulled itself into shape in the corner of Carly's eye, and she turned away so it wouldn't drive her mom to yet another drink. Carly reached into the cashbox and took out a twenty. *That* would buy lunch. There was a thin back entrance between their booth and the jewelry booth that faced toward the aisle behind them, and Carly was skinny enough to slide through a place her mom couldn't follow.

The tear slid down her cheek and another one gathered, and she licked it coming down, a trick she'd taught herself as a kid. If you catch a tear before it falls, you can stop crying. Only this time, once she licked off the tear, it became an anger-stone in her belly.

Damn.

How come her mom couldn't get her shit together? Marla and everybody else told Carly it wasn't about her, but even if it wasn't because of her, Carly should be able to help her mom. Except she never could.

The twenty-dollar bill in her pocket seemed as heavy as the tear-stone in her belly. She'd never stolen from their kitty before unless it was to save money to buy food in the winter, when there was no place to sell her mom's pottery. She could take it back—she would take it back—but that didn't take away the fact that she'd stolen it. One of the buskers or mummers would have shared food or a few dollars with her; they were always willing. Anyway, she should have done something other than stealing the twenty.

She built up enough mad at herself and her mom that the tears stayed away as she stalked though the crowd.

Little kids squealed and splashed in the pool in front of the waterfall door. A ragged red towel had been draped over the NO WADING sign. Even the moms, who pretended they were chasing children, cooled their feet in the shallow pond while looking guilty. Carly waded right through them, managing not to step on anyone, walking into the rock wall so fast she didn't have any time for doubt.

That was the only way she could go through this year. Running at the wall and trusting that the door didn't dare refuse her. Last year had been easy, and the first year had been cake, as if the stone melted for her. But then, she'd been scared instead of mad. Jack had told her the trouble was because now she was mad instead of hurt, and the magic of the door didn't like anger. But how was she supposed to stop being mad? Her mom was falling apart. Her grades sucked from worry, and she never knew where she was sleeping for sure till she saw how drunk her mom was any given night. Maybe by next year, she'd be so mad she wouldn't be able to come at all.

But it worked now. On the far side, she realized she'd been holding her breath. She stopped, feet planted on the hard dirt, back against the stone she'd just walked through, and inhaled the fresh air of the High Hills. The place on the far side of the waterfall door.

Maybe she should just stay here. The faintest whiff of an ocean breeze licked her face and sent her salt and seaweed and the thin distant cry of gulls. Her stomach rumbled. She'd forgotten to stop and buy lunch. Stupid. Well, it was still lunchtime over here. Time in the High Hills was behind time in the modern world, the real world. Sometimes Gisele knew she was coming and brought extra.

Overhead, the sky shone pale summer-blue, but to the west, white and gray clouds billowed over the ocean. The feel of rain prickled the skin on Carly's bare arms. Just downhill, the familiar meadow was summer-brown, thirsting for the storm, and sere brown hills dotted with scrub oak surrounded her on all sides. A clutch of houses nestled behind the westernmost oak grove, all of the houses and most of the trees invisible from here but just ten minutes away on foot. She stalked across a wooden bridge over a thin stream that meandered through the meadow and walked down the path on the far side. The High Hills didn't lighten her mood any, nor did the first fat drops of warm rain hitting her shoulders and nose.

As if the clouds had warned everyone inside, Carly didn't pass a soul before getting to Gisele's door. She didn't knock—why knock when Gisele always knew when she was coming? She found her mentor bent over, carving a fist-sized fish, her gnarled hands moving surely under the bright battery-operated desk lamp Carly'd brought over for her last summer. Gisele's thin gray hair tumbled over a faded green shawl draped over her shoulders. An old ginger tabby, Tab, curled on the wood-pile behind the old woman, and bestirred herself long enough to lift her heavy head and drop it back to her paws. Wood blocks of various shapes and colors piled on the desk to Gisele's right, and on her left a basket had been filled with finished carved animals, each delicate, detailed, and still dead.

Gisele's eyes widened in surprise before her gaze softened. "Carly. I hoped you'd be back."

Before Carly could say anything, Gisele's attention returned to the fish. Of course. It was always that way when Gisele was finishing a carving; the life in the wood demanded her focus.

Carly looked around the cluttered workshop. No visible food.

She shrugged, as if there were anyone watching her to see, and went to the basket of finished animals. She began picking through, looking at each one. Her hand wouldn't be steady enough for a horse. Not today. Gisele must have a special order for fish—there were a dozen. They didn't interest Carly. Nor did the border collie or the dachshund. A broad-shouldered lab waited to become a black lab or a chocolate lab or a golden lab. Carly fisted the dog, rubbing its wooden snout with her thumb.

Not right.

Maybe none of the animals wanted her to paint them alive. After all, she was a thief, and she'd abandoned her mother.

She closed her eyes and murmured to herself. *Choose.* She carefully reached deep into the basket, trying not to slice her thumb on a sharp fin or ear. Her hand emerged with a fat frog. Its wide belly was already blond wood, its humped and knobby back a darker color. Exaggerated eyes dominated the fat face and the front legs bowed inward. Its haunches looked well-muscled and powerful. A jumping bullfrog of some kind.

Very well.

She settled herself into her own spot, a low desk in the back of the room, surrounded by paints, brushes, and rags. One glance confirmed that Gisele remained lost in her fish. Carly closed her eyes and held the frog to her for the briefest moment, less time than she had ever spent looking for the heart of a being. Who cared, after all? It was just a frog. It felt heavy and solid, easily a pound or maybe one and a half, as heavy as a big apple or a medium-sized stone. Her hand ranged to a deep gray-green, settled for a moment, then passed it, stopping on the shade of black that existed in new winter boots until a moment after you put them on.

She dipped the ends of a medium-sized horse-hair brush into the paint, and drew it dripping dark along the back of the frog's head and in a wide stripe down to the nub where its polliwog tail had disappeared. Again, and again, each line touching the other, the paint sliding into the tiniest crevices as it softened the wood toward flesh. The great bumps along the frog's back got her darkest gray, and the soft parts of the belly a softer grey, but mottled and demanding a few drops of red that turned to buried veins as she painted them on.

Gisele and the whole room, remained largely silent, the only sounds the soft splash of Carly's brushes and the snick-snick pause, snick-snick pause of Gisele's carving knife. Most days this silence was more restful than oppressive. But most days she would have chosen a horse.

The last thing Carly reached for was the eye-black, which slid from her fingers. The bottle rang sharply against the small ceramic cup Carly had mixed the belly colors in.

The frog didn't want black eyes? What now? Green eyes for a black-bodied frog? Her mood wasn't getting any better.

The eyes had always been eye-black. Of everything. Horses and dogs and fishes and goats and birds. Always. The eyes were the last step, the final windows into the being.

She reached to dip her brush into the thickening gray paint in the ceramic dish.

It didn't feel right, the brush too light.

She stared at the frog, giving a near-silent whisper. "What do you want?"

It didn't answer. It was, after all, still dead, even though its skin felt cooler and more supple. It held the paint well, barely losing any to her fingers.

She pondered.

Her thoughts drifted to the stolen twenty in her pocket and she imagined her mom stumbling though helping some faceless stranger buy candlesticks or a set of mugs or a great round serving plate. No wonder she couldn't figure out what to do with the frog. She wasn't giving the damned thing any attention.

She brought it close to her face and stared at the eyes. Then she poured two great drips of eye-black into the gray belly paint, watching the black and grey mingle, a few traces of red staining it here and there. Her brush slid easily into this paint, and she gave the frog its eyes.

It blinked in her hand.

The frog had turned out to be a dark thing, all black, barely lightened by gray, mottled, the only other color the flecks of red on belly and eyes. It stared at her, rocking back so its weight concentrated in the long bony back feet. Its back elbows—or whatever they were on a frog—dug into her palm so sharply she cried out.

Gisele turned toward her, her eyes startled and her mouth falling open.

The frog smiled.

It had teeth.

It leaped at her. Fast and hard. She flinched back, throwing a hand up for protection and knocking the frog

away. It landed on the ground on its back, feet scrabbling against the air for nonexistent purchase.

The wooden fish Gisele had been working on clat-
tered to the floor.

The old woman leaped up faster than Carly had ever
seen her move, then squatted on the ground, staring at
the black frog. When she looked up at Carly, her old
yellow-blue eyes were full of something Carly couldn't
quite name: fear or anger or both. Her whisper sounded
like a hiss. "Did I not teach you to create the mood of
the animal as you paint?" She didn't wait for an answer.
But she picked the frog up, setting her palm on its belly
and curling her fingers around its back. As she lifted it in
the air, its back feet pressed against her splayed thumb
and it nearly leaped free, all the time smiling so the im-
probable teeth showed.

Gisele kept her arm extended, keeping the frog far
away from them both. She regarded it for a long time,
and when she turned to look at Carly, she seemed to be
looking at some pitiful being. Her voice held pity, too.
"You've created a monster."

Carly stiffened.

The frog thrashed.

Gisele said, "Take it. You must kill it."

Carly had thrown up all over the teacher when they'd
made her dissect a frog at school. "No," she said. "No. I
won't kill anything."

Gisele shifted the frog to her other hand, her arm
shaking a little. Carly couldn't make the old woman
keep the heavy thing. She held her hand out, expecting
Gisele to drop it into her open palm. But Gisele shook
her head. "Two hands. It's strong."

Carly drew in a sharp breath, and a shiver of fear ran
up her arms. She held the bullfrog at arm's length, as

Gisele had, and it twisted and flopped and then, with a great effort, braced both its legs and hopped onto her shoulder. Its sharp teeth dug into the fine flesh of her earlobe just as Gisele swatted it. It leaped from her shoulder to a nearby shelf. "Catch it!" Gisele demanded, "But don't let it bite you."

"What?" Carly blinked. "You carved a vampire frog?"

It was the wrong thing to say. All the softness left Gisele's face. "Catch it."

Carly swallowed, still mad, maybe even madder. The frog watched her, as if assessing her ability to capture it and deciding she didn't have a chance. She stood still in front of it, the frog a foot above her head on the shelf. It didn't move except for the rise and fall of its fat sides as it breathed. She forced every muscle of her face and back and legs to stay still, moving only her hands . . . slowly . . . slowly. Her arms rose to shoulder height. Hard rain spit against the dusty window, startling her, making her move a bit too fast.

The frog flinched but didn't move.

Carly's hands neared the bottom of the shelf.

The frog leaped past them both, seven, maybe eight feet away, landing among the scattered paints and brushes on her desk. It dipped its long tongue into the mix she'd painted its eyes with, just a touch, the tongue a blur of movement between teeth. It leaped again and again. Once it came near Tab, and the cat rose faster than Carly had ever seen the old thing move, the fur on its back straight up so the cat looked twice its size and, briefly, young again. The frog gave Tab a glance before it hopped away, finally stopping as far from the two women as it could get.

Carly wanted to scream. Everything, absolutely everything she had ever painted alive had been sweet. True, the small paint pony had been skittish, and one dog had run away for two days before coming back, hungry and thirsty, riding in on Gisele's boot. They'd all been soothable. They'd all gone on to be children's pets or parts of traveler's wagons.

The great black frog didn't look soothable. It looked like a kid's nightmare. Its very existence made her hot and angry. First she'd been trapped in the hot booth, then she'd stolen from her own mom, her belly was rumbling empty, and now this stupid frog.

She turned to look at Gisele. "How?"

Gisele sighed. "That frog is your black mood."

"Oh, no. I didn't make it black. It wanted to be black." She remembered how her hand had gone to black. The animals always picked; they guided her hand. "You taught me to stay open and be a conduit for the animal's soul, for what it wants. The frog wanted this."

"And the desires of a block of wood are all that gives them personality? With all of our animals? Your feelings don't matter?"

Our. Gisele had said *our animals*. So she had something to do with it, too. And why couldn't Gisele just spit out whatever she was trying to say, instead of making Carly answer questions? "Maybe you should help me catch the frog."

"Why do you almost always paint the horses? Isn't that your desire?"

"The horses are pretty."

Gisele started advancing on the frog. "You do a wonderful job with them. You like them, maybe love them, and you picture them as proud and tractable. No apprentice has ever done so well with horses."

Apprentice? She tucked the word away for later.

"You have to catch it," Gisele whispered hoarsely. "How do you feel about frogs, anyway?"

"Compared to horses? They're fine. I mean, who cares . . . whatever's wrong with that frog, it's not because of me. It can't be." Could it?

"Why not?"

They rounded the corner of Gisele's big work desk, now halfway to the frog. "I don't know. I just know it's not my fault."

"We all have a black side."

Carly frowned, but they were getting close to the frog, and she didn't want to say anything to startle it. If this was her black side, it was damned ugly.

The frog blinked it heavy-lidded eyes and let out a single loud sound that was more bark than croak and then leaped onto Gisele's shoulder. Carly reached out to grab it, but it leaped again, this time heading toward Tab. "Maybe I will kill it," Carly muttered.

"You have to. You have to fix this," Gisele said as she turned, too, both women drawn toward a high hiss from the cat. The bullfrog had managed to land on Tab's back, and the cat shook and screamed, but didn't move. Maybe it was too old to carry such a heavy frog. The frog's head was buried in the cat's neck. It looked as though the frog should slide off, but it didn't.

Carly started toward the two animals, but Gisele grabbed her arm and held her back. "Watch!"

Maybe the cat would kill the frog. The frog's muscular back legs scrabbled across Tab's back and the cat's howl turned to a scream of pain. Tab's tail twitched behind her.

Carly tried to wrench free from Gisele. The old carver's hands were strong, her grip impossible to eel out of, so tight Carly feared that if she did make forward progress she might pull the old woman over and hurt her. She couldn't take her eyes off the fight in front of her. Tab sank down under the weight of the bullfrog, crouching, then leaped up into the air. The frog finally slid off. Tab backed up against the wall, hissing angrily. For a long moment the two stared at each other. Then the frog jumped up onto a chair and then onto a table.

Maybe it was over.

The frog bounded from the table onto the ginger cat's back. Tab crumpled under the weight and velocity of frog's leap and let out a pained scream. The frog opened its mouth and bit the cat, tearing at its ears and savaging its face. Tab didn't fight any more, or scream, or make any more noise. She just shrank under the frog, which seemed to be growing on top of her.

"The damned thing is going to kill Tab!"

"Don't curse," Gisele said. "Tab knew it. She told me today."

"The cat told you a wooden frog was going to kill her?"

The frog leaped away, bigger, leaving Tab lying splayed face and, belly down on the woodpile. Carly froze at the dark slash of blood that soaked the back of Tab's neck. Gisele dropped her hand from Carly's arm. "No. She simply said it was her day to die."

"She is dead. She's dead!" Carly walked over to the still form. Blood had pooled under the cat's head and stained the wood blackish red. She touched the cat with a finger, and it moved like a lump of clay might move, or any other dead thing.

Carly felt dizzy. Did the cat die for her? Gisele talked to animals, and even Carly did, a little, to the horses and dogs and goats she usually painted. So the cat had known it was going to die and told Gisele. She believed it. Maybe. Bloodsucking frogs and dead cats who lay down on woodpiles to die. She'd been coming here and painting animals alive for three summers now, and even so she barely believed in the High Hills when she wasn't here. The anger had all left her with Tab's death. Even though all the cat had done in the last year she'd been living here was sleep, and even though Carly had only seen her maybe ten times, the old cat had become part of her haven here. She'd liked it. Carly half-expected Tab to turn into wood, except all the magic she and Gisele made was small and Tab was, had been, full sized.

A soft indrawn breath drew Carly far enough outside of herself to look over at Gisele. A single tear ran down the old woman's cheek and splashed onto her cloak. Gisele was hard on her sometimes, like today, and she was sad. Incomparably sad. But Gisele wasn't her mom, and didn't drink, and didn't run away, and didn't lie to her. Carly pulled Gisele into her, ignoring the dead cat and the murderous frog. "Is it Tab? Why are you crying?"

Gisele shook her head, and another tear slid down her cheek.

"I'll help you bury Tab," Carly whispered to the old woman. She'd hardly been nice to anyone today, not herself, not her mom, not Gisele, and maybe—maybe she'd killed the cat. Remotely. If she hadn't painted the frog when she was so mad ... Oh damn. Her own eyes started leaking warm, salty tears down her cheeks. "I'll go find a shovel."

Gisele pulled a little away from Carly. "Don't open the door."

Carly blinked at her.

"The frog will get out."

Oh.

Gisele started crying harder, papery sobs like her papery skin.

What was Carly supposed to do? "If it's not Tab, then why are you crying?"

Gisele turned away and looked around her workshop. "Surely I have a box around here somewhere. I'll put Tab in that until you catch the frog."

Now the old woman sounded like Carly herself, avoiding a question. Carly tried to use her command voice, the one she used with her mom when her mom was drunk. "Tell me why you're crying."

Gisele sank down to sit on a large block of wood that waited to be broken up to become carving blocks. In spite of the rain, dusty light from the high window gave a brighter cast to her old gray skin, made her look almost transparent. "My boy."

Carly knew the story but only because Jack had told her. Gisele had never said anything.

"You're like my own boy, who went through the magic gate and went away. He used to have your strength, and there was one day he did what you did. A friend of his— Steven—beat him up over something the way boys do when they're twelve—I never found out what for, but Jory came home one day with a black eye and a bruise on his cheekbone and so much anger I didn't recognize him. He came out here without me—which he wasn't supposed to do—and he painted a poison snake." She paused. "He put it in Steven's house."

"Did the snake kill his friend?"

The old woman's shoulders started shaking, and Carly knelt down in front of her, so she looked up at Gisele, and took her hands. Gisele gave a little bit of a half smile. Her tone softened. "I've not been a good teacher. I should have taught you about your dark side and what you could do. At least told you. But you were always so happy to be here."

"I thought it was a dream to be here. A good dream. It makes me happy."

Gisele wiped at her cheeks and looked quietly at Carly.

"What happened? What did the snake do?"

"It killed Steven's baby sister."

"How awful." Carly checked to make sure the frog was where she'd last seen it. It was. "So you knew it could kill Tab," she whispered.

"You needed to know it, too." Gisele answered. "Maybe now you'll have the strength to kill it."

Carly shivered. She didn't want to kill anything. She didn't even kill spiders at home; she put them outside. "No."

Gisele looked away from her as if Carly'd slapped her.

Carly clutched the old woman's hands harder. "I won't kill it. Not here. But I'll catch it and take it back. It will just be wood there, and it will have teeth, and it will stay black, and it'll remind me not to get so mad." And she'd take back the twenty and buy her mom a lemonade for the heat, which would just be slipping into a warm night.

Gisele turned her gaze back to her, blinking at her, as if trying to decide what she thought of what Carly'd just said. She glanced at the frog and back at Carly, and at Tab's still form and back at Carly. One more tear, just one, rolled down her cheek and she sniffed. "Okay."

"You miss your son, don't you?"

Gisele didn't hesitate. "More than I can express. But there's no point in hanging onto things you can't change. You have to get on with life."

"Yeah." Maybe looking at the frog would give her

enough strength to tell her mom that if she didn't stop, Carly was going to find another job and start saving money. And maybe this time Carly would do it even though her mom wouldn't stop. Or maybe she'd leave school and her mom, and come back here and ask Gisele to take her for the winter as a full time apprentice. Whatever, she'd better make some decisions before the gate wouldn't open for her at all any more.

She sighed.

It was going to take strength to catch the frog. "Do you have anything to eat?"

Gisele smiled. "I have some cheese and an apple in my drawer." She hobbled round to the front of her desk and used her carving knife to cut the apple in two. She handed half to Carly, along with half the cheese. Carly chewed on the cheese and watched her black mood, contemplating how to catch it.

Three hours later, the summer storm had finished blowing through, and the long-beamed afternoon sun poked in the window, burnishing a few pennies and a pile of wood nearly gold and throwing long shadows across the workshop and burnishing some items gold. Gisele had carved two matching fish and was starting to expose the tall fin of a third, so focused she hardly seemed to be in the room at all. At this stage, even her knife was fairly quick, just a low snick, snick, break, snick.

Tab waited patiently in a box.

Carly sat back in her chair, the desk in front of her neat and tidy, her paints put away for the day. She glowered at the frog.

The frog sat on a windowsill, more catlike than amphibian, and watched her back.

Carly's stomach was empty again, and she'd banged her elbow—twice—trying to catch the frog. She'd found an old towel that used to be white, and now it trailed out of her hand and across the floor beside her.

The frog was faster than her. Nastier. It was teasing her, Whenever she got near, it got away; then it sat and waited for her to get near again. It was ugly. Why the heck had she painted the thing ugly? And how ridiculous was it to be sitting in a world that might be imaginary chasing a big black frog she'd painted to life around a little crowded room? She was even effectively trapped in here by the frog.

She giggled.

And her giggle turned up into a full laugh.

Gisele glanced up and raised an eyebrow at her.

If only her friends, or even her mom, could see her now. Even putting her hand over her mouth so the towel draped down like a bib didn't stop her laughing. It made her laugh harder.

The frog jumped down on the desk in front of Carly.

She threw the towel over it.

Frog and towel jumped up off the table at her.

She gave a little scream and caught the bundle up. She made sure she had all of the edges of the towel.

The frog struggled.

Carly grinned.

Gisele looked over at her and winked. "I thought you were going to take all day to figure out how to catch that frog," she said dryly.

It took Carly a second to get it. "Laughter! It breaks a bad mood any time."

"Best go home now," Gisele said.

Carly glanced at Tab's box. "I need to—"

"Go home," Gisele interrupted her. "I'll deal with Tab after I finish this fish. I told Tom Jenson he'd maybe have to help me with that this morning anyway."

Carly tied up the edges of the occasionally squirming bundle of towel and frog with twine, making sure some air could get in, and that the knots wouldn't come undone. She kissed Gisele's rough, wrinkly cheek and whispered, "Thanks. I'll be back."

"I know."

Carly carried the frog carefully, both so she wouldn't hurt it and so it wouldn't bite her. As soon as they passed through into the noisy, bright early evening, the frog stopped kicking. She peeled off the towel and grinned. The long-toothed frog had been caught with a truly evil look in its eyes, the kind that would remind her how being angry was filled with unintended consequences. But it was also a little funny-looking with its long teeth, to remind her to laugh at the look in its eyes. At herself.

Their booth was nearly empty. Just her mom, sitting in the chair by the cashbox, frowning. A quick look convinced Carly she'd only sold a few things; a good day left the shelves half bare until they brought in stock. Her mom looked up as Carly came in. "What's that?"

"A frog. I made it." Carly opened her hands so her mom could get a good look.

"That's . . . a. . . ."

"Ugly," Carly finished for her.

"A little. Except it looks so real."

Carly nodded. "I had help." Maybe her mom would ask where she learned how to carve frogs, or anything else for that matter.

Her mom didn't. She just shrugged. "Some days, my pottery doesn't come out right either."

"Sorry I was gone so long."

Her mom stood up and started prowling around the booth quietly. She was smiling at Carly, but her tone of voice had that little edge that meant she was missing alcohol. "I was getting worried about you."

"I know, I didn't mean to be gone so long."

"Look, I'm hungry. I'll go get us food, okay?"

And herself a drink. She'd just gotten back. They hadn't spent five minutes together, and if she left she wouldn't be back for half an hour. Or more. And she'd be half drunk when she got back. A sharp edge on the wooden frog dug into Carly's palm as her fist tightened, and she let it go and let out a long breath. "I'll go with you."

"I can do it."

Carly grabbed the cashbox. "It's not that busy tonight. We can be back in a few minutes."

"But—"

Carly shook her head. "No drinks. Not yet. I want your advice."

Her mom's eyes widened. "About?"

"I'll tell you on the way." Maybe about where she should look for a job this summer. Or about whether or not Carly should go live in the women's shelter sometime. Or just about anything. She couldn't keep her mom from drinking, except maybe for the next hour. But she could stop being mad at her and start planning on a future. Surely her mom knew she was going to grow up sometime. Or maybe not. But she could show her. She set the "Pay at the next booth" sign in the window and took her mom's arm. As she led them toward the food booths, Carly smiled.

NINJA RATS ON HARLEYS

By Elizabeth A. Vaughan

Elizabeth A. Vaughan is the author of *The Chronicles of the Warlands* and *Dagger-Star*. She still believes that the only good movies are the ones with gratuitous swords or lasers. Not to mention dragons. At the present, she is owned by two incredibly spoiled cats and lives in the Northwest Territory, on the outskirts of the Black Swamp, along Mad Anthony's Trail on the banks of the Maumee River.

It was a dark and stormy night.

Well it was, damn it. The cold air slapped me in the face as the glass doors of the ER waiting area slid open. Any warmth my tattered bathrobe held was gone in an instant as the wind wrapped around me. The rain had stopped for now, but the entire parking lot gleamed under the lights, as did the ambulances, their flashing lights reflecting off the puddles and my van.

My bloodstained slippers were soaked as I slapped across the parking lot. I cradled my purse and those damned discharge instructions as I fumbled for my keys.

I opened the passenger side door, set the purse carefully on the seat, and then slammed that sucker shut with all my strength.

I was pissed, and who could blame me?

Nothing like being attacked in your own home by a hideous, stinky white possum and his ninja hench-rats at an ungodly hour of the morning. We'd fought them off, Wan and I, with naught but our bare hands and a bottle of toilet cleaner.

Well, okay, Wan had a sword. And he killed most of them. But I'd done my fair share, although it was my own blood on my slippers.

Wan is a mouse. An ancient Chinese mouse, as far as I can figure. He hasn't been very forthcoming. He's been good company since he moved in about a month ago. He was teaching me tai chi, and I was teaching him football. I had to admit, it was nice to have someone around ... to have company. And yes, my social life does suck that bad.

He talks. Did I mention that?

At any rate, a few hours ago, we'd been attacked by people ... animals ... who also talked and who clearly knew more about Wan than I did. One of the rats had bitten through my finger, hence the visit to the ER.

Slamming the door had not been the best idea, since Itty and Bitty, my poor little white dogs, had been cowering under the seats in the back. They scrabbled up, put their feet on the window, and howled for attention.

My cowardly fat white Westies, who tend to fart when under stress. I opened the rear passenger door and petted and cooed over them for a minute, paying attention to the slash on Itty's nose. The possum had gotten her at one point in the fight, but it was only a slight scratch. I got them calmed back down, shut the door, and headed around to mine.

Wan was standing on my purse when I heaved my weary body into the driver's seat. He stood at the summit, his sword over his back, his arms crossed over his chest. "We should stay and talk with the learned doctor, Kate."

The doctor also seemed to know more about what was going on than I did. I sighed, looking at the ambulances. "Wan, he's going to be busy for quite some time. I want to go home and take a shower."

"He possesses knowledge that we do not have," Wan argued. "Why do we leave a potential ally behind us?"

"Because my hand hurts," I snapped. "Because I'm filthy and tired and the dogs are scared." I struggled with my seat belt using my bandaged hand. "Because that nurse said that the doctor would be working on those accident victims for hours. Because I'm not drinking that hideous coffee, and because ..." I snapped the belt in place and turned to glare at Mr. Holier-Than-Thou Talking Mouse. "Because I don't know who is friend or foe until you tell me what the hell is going on!"

Wan glared right back, and I promised myself that if he told me to be one with my pain, I was going to pitch him right out the window and drive off.

The damn mouse looked away. "You hold the keys, honorable lady."

I jammed them in the ignition and started the van.

What a surprise. There isn't a lot of traffic on the expressway at four in the morning on a Saturday.

Who'd a thunk it?

I pulled out of the hospital grounds and headed up Monroe Street toward Douglas. I'd take the expressway home. Wan sat silent, which was fine with me. I needed to think.

It had taken me aback when the ER doctor told me he knew my injury was from a ninja rat bite. Believe me when I say that I hadn't put that down on any forms. He'd taken pains to make sure the nurse didn't hear him, too, come to think of it. I narrowed my eyes as I pulled onto Douglas. His steel gray eyes had been sharp, sharp enough that he had probably known about Wan hiding in my purse.

But did that mean that I could trust him?

I turned onto the entrance ramp to the expressway, chewing my lower lip. Well, hell, I was trusting a talking mouse, wasn't I? And I hadn't exactly asked him for ID, had I?

My front window was fogging up, so I reached for the blower dial. Cold air flowed over my feet before I could get it set on defrost. We'd be almost home before it warmed up. I shivered and set the cruise control at sixty-two. The last thing I needed was a ticket.

My hand throbbed as I tilted the rearview mirror to look at the dogs. They were sound asleep on the back seat, exhausted, poor babies. I adjusted the mirror back with a wince. There were lights in the distance behind us. Far back enough not to worry about just yet.

I pulled my injured hand back and rested it on my chest, steering with my left hand.

"We should not return to the house," Wan stated firmly. "They will be waiting for us."

I sighed. He had a point, but I didn't really want to hear it. "All right. I'm too tired to argue. A hotel, then, but we will have to smuggle in the dogs." I sighed and checked the rearview mirror. If a hotel would let us in. I looked like hell. The lights behind us were getting closer. They were coming fast. Looked like motorcycles out for an evening cruise.

"Perhaps we could shelter in the home of a friend?" Wan asked carefully.

I stiffened. This was a sore point, and he damn well knew it. When I'd given up on my dreams, my fantasy writing, I'd walked away from friends who shared those dreams. Gamers, writers, dreamers, and geeks, I'd cut them out of my life. "Oh sure," I snapped. "I'll just show up with bloody slippers, dogs, a talking mouse, and they'll be glad to—"

The rumble of a gunned Harley cut me off. I glanced at the rearview mirror. The motorcycles had caught up with us, about twelve from the looks of things. They'd surround us, then pass as they—

Movement caused me to glance out my side window. A big Harley, a Fat Boy, had pulled up even with the van. I glanced at the tank first, seeing the logo, then noticed the rider's leg looked . . . odd. I looked up and gasped.

"KATE!" Wan shouted beside me.

The rider was a rat, a giant rat, riding a Harley and glaring at me through its ninja mask. With a big white ugly possum perched on its shoulder. The possum caught my gaze and gave me an open mouth hiss, waving its walking stick.

I swerved wildly.

The bikes all swerved with me, moving as if we'd rehearsed it. The rumble strip complained as my tires hit and I jerked the wheel back, frantic to stay on the road.

The dogs started barking, not sure what was happening but sure they could scare it away. The bike in front of me put on its brake light, and I hit the brake as well, instinctively.

"No, Kate," Wan urged. "Do not stop."

"But . . ." I said.

"It will put us at their mercy, of which there is little."
Wan's voice cut like a knife. "Go!"

Wan may be small, but that command made me jam
my foot on the gas. The van leaped forward, and the
biker swerved to the side, then gunned it to stay in front
of me. The ninja rat driver turned his head to look at me,
his eyes dark, beady, and vicious.

I swallowed hard. "How did they get so big?" I asked
in a whisper.

"Magic," Wan said.

Duh. I risked a quick glare in his direction, but the little snit was back down on the seat, digging in my purse,
pulling out my cell phone and the doctor's card. "Call
911," I said.

"And what do I say?" Wan asked as he opened the
phone.

He had a point. I gripped the steering wheel with two
hands and focused on the road. The bikes kept weaving
around me, trying to drive me off the road, but I hung
on grimly.

Then the one in front apparently decided to clip me,
and I saw my chance. Big mistake on his part. No amount
of magic was going to stop me. He swerved in front, and
I gunned the van.

She did me proud, surging forward just enough to clip
his rear fender. The rat wiped out, barely avoiding my
front tire as he and his bike hit the pavement and slid
off. Metal screamed and sparks flew as the bike and the
rat slid away.

Bet that ninja outfit was a whole lot of protection.

But even as I gloated, the one by my window moved
closer. I had a brief glimpse of the possum hefting up its
walking staff and—

THWACK

Tiny cracks blossomed in my side window.

That started the dogs howling, dancing in the back seat, and farting for all they were worth. I swore and swerved again, pressing on the accelerator, but the rats stayed right next to the van.

I glanced down at the speedometer. Sweet mother of—Where were the police? Normally I'd have a small army of Toledo PD on my ass waiting to write me six tickets for going this fast. But noooo—never one when ya—

The possum jumped on the hood.

One little claw grabbed the windshield wiper, and the other held that damn staff. He was grinning that toothy grin again, chanting something muffled by the glass. The staff started to glow. Not good, not good. I panicked. I wanted him off the glass, off the—

I hit the washer.

Blue fluid squirted up under his chin. WHAMP went the wipers, and the possum went flying off to the side, with any luck possum pie by the road.

One of the ninja rats lunged and caught him by the tail just before he hit the ground.

My heart was pounding in my throat. For an instant, the possum was swinging from his tail, spitting out washer fluid and pointing at me. Then with a flip, he landed on the back of the rat, and they fell away from the van, moving over a lane. They all did.

"Wan," I said nervously. "Wan, I think . . ."

Wan was talking into my phone excitedly in what sounded like Chinese.

"English, Wan!" I shouted. The possum was gesturing at the front of the van, and pointing at the—

BHAM.

The front tire blew.

The dogs were howling, Wan was howling, hell, I was probably howling, but I didn't care. My only focus was to control the van, and my teeth rattled with the effort.

The nosie was terrific, the rubber from the tire flying in every direction. Sparks fountained up from the rim, and my poor old minivan was steering like a dead cow. With metal screaming, and the hot smell of rubber and dog farts, the van went off the side, over the brim, and down to rest at an angle off the road.

The air bag exploded, punching me in the face. The silence was eerie as it deflated, and I unwrapped my hands from the wheel. "Is everyone—"

CRACK

The possum shattered my window.

I covered my head instinctively as bits of safely glass exploded into the van. I could barely hear Wan over the howling of the dogs, because I was completely focused on the rat snarls as they reached for me. Their claws sank into the arm of my bathrobe and my flesh as they tried to pull me out through the window.

Sorry boys, my fat middle-aged butt wasn't budging. They could tug and pull all they wanted—

One of them reached in and opened the van door. A sharp blade appeared and sliced through my seat belt.

I fell out onto the ground. The rats grabbed my robe and dragged me away from the van through the wet grass. The dogs howled, and I had just enough time to pray they stayed in the van when I was dropped to the ground.

I looked up to find myself surrounded by man-sized ninja rats. The possum perched on one's shoulder, glaring down at me. I took a deep breath, then wished I hadn't. That possum wasn't man-sized but he still stunk to high heaven. Ugh.

"You have offended, fat one. Now you die."

The rats all pulled daggers.

Er. I blinked up at him, confused. What about threats, rantings, that kind of thing? I mean, really . . .

"She dies, you die."

We all looked to see Wan standing on the seat of the car, backlit by the dome light of the minivan. Wisps of fog were gathered around his feet. He had his sword out and pointed at the ninjas. "Move away from her if you value your lives."

It would have been very impressive had he been more than a few inches tall.

The rats chuckled, and even I smiled. Wan looked so earnest, standing there with his sword in his hand.

"She dies," the possum laughed. "And then we beat the information out of you, traitor."

Okay, not so funny now.

I leaped up, dodged one of the rats and hit the possum right on the snoot. Impressed?

The only problem is it didn't happen that way. My middle-aged fat body wouldn't leap up for nothing. So I did the best I could. I kicked one of the rats right on the shins. Smartly.

He dropped his knife and clutched his leg. Some ninja.

All eyes were focused back on me. "Kill her," the possum snarled.

Wan squeaked his battle cry and darted forward, but that whole man-sized rat thing was working against him. I tried desperately to crawl away, my robe catching under my knees. The rats laughed, my cowardly dogs howled from the van, and I was sure I was dead.

One rat grabbed my shoulder and flipped me over, his teeth and knife gleaming. He was bringing the knife up to plunge into my stomach. I watched in horror as the gleaming blade arched over me.

There was a crackling flash, a stench of sulfur, and one dead rat falling down on top of me. The lightning caught him right in the chest.

I scrabbled back, trying to get out from under the smoldering, twitching corpse without throwing up. As my legs slipped clear, more bolts shivered over my head, seeming to almost hang in the air before striking the rats. I pressed myself flat to the grass and risked a glimpse.

It was the doctor from the ER.

He looked taller somehow, his white lab coat glowing and his stethoscope swinging wildly around his neck. The street lights reflected off his high forehead, and his long gray ponytail swung behind him.

He looked damn fine, to my way of thinking.

The fact that he was standing with both feet firmly braced as he flung lightning at the rats with ease also worked for me.

The rats were diving for cover, throwing themselves to the ground to hide behind the motorcycles they'd left scattered around.

The possum went for my van.

I felt the pressure of tiny paws on my shoulder and a whisper in my ear. "Stay down, Kate. I will protect you."

"The dogs," I screamed, trying to climb to my feet. My slippers slipped on the grass.

The doctor heard me. With a flip of his wrist, he sent a bright blue ball our way, floating, zeroing in on us like a missile. It zipped past my shoulder, and for a brief moment light flared around me. When it faded, I was pinned under the weight of a man-sized mouse, standing on my back.

Needless to say, the rats were focused on the doctor, their tails lashing, hissing, regrouping to attack him. I'd be okay. "Wan, please." With what little breath I had, I begged. "Save my babies."

Wan hesitated, then to my utter relief charged the van, sword in hand, his battle cry more impressive now. The possum had climbed in the driver's seat, but his head turned to look at the angry man-sized mouse charging his way.

I took a few deep breaths, certain that there'd be more help coming. But the expressway was empty, and there were no flashing cop cars. No, just a lovely brightly colored macaw flying at the rats, slashing with its beak and claws. And the lightning bolts being slung from the doctor's fingers at the rats.

Lightning. I felt oddly calm about the whole thing. Of course, lightning. What else ...

The possum was charging toward me.

Uh-oh. It occurred to me that just lying there was not a good idea. I needed to be running, or at least trotting, away from this madness.

Wan was chasing the possum, as were Itty and Bitty, barking madly. I struggled to my feet just as the possum threw something at me. A globe of light again, sparkly white and lovely. I threw up my hands to ward it off, even as Wan chopped at the possum.

The globe of light splattered over me, soft and warm, like a blanket. Just like a blanket, in fact, it was expanding, clinging, covering me quickly, my chest, mouth, and nose.

I couldn't breathe.

The stuff wrapped tight and started to constrict, forcing what air I had out of my chest. I struggled, pushed at it, but while I could move it, I couldn't break it. I had a brief moment to be thankful that there was no one around. I probably looked like a bag lady fighting a garbage bag.

Arms surrounded me. The doctor. I could see those gray eyes, feel his arms around me. Was that the macaw on his shoulder?

There was no air left. Interestingly enough, I actually felt my eyes roll back into my head as I lost consciousness.

I woke up and smelled the coffee.

Floating just on the edge of sleep, I took a deep breath, trying to get the caffeine into my system through my lungs. Deep and rich and dark. I could almost taste it on the back of my tongue. Clearly I was dead, and heaven smelled like French roast.

Warm. I was warm as well, lying wrapped in a blanket on what felt like a sofa. There was weight on my feet, which could only be Itty and Bitty. Poor things, they were probably exhausted from their . . .

From something. I couldn't remember exactly. I was wrapped in a soft blanket, on a couch. Did I fall asleep watching a game?

As much as I wanted coffee, I also wanted to float off again, just drift off for a while. But now sounds started to invade my private, perfect world. Voices, soft and persistent, with the clink of a spoon against a cup and the sound of coffee being poured.

"You shouldn't have approached her at all. You've put her in danger."

"Such was not my intent." Wan was speaking, but he sounded louder than normal. Sleep would have to wait, it seemed.

"But after so long," Wan continued. "I'd been alone for so long . . . she is a friend. A good person."

"And a mundane. With no knowledge, no skills. She's not going to be—"

Hell, that was the doctor. It came back then. The attack, the rats . . . the doctor throwing lightning bolts. I opened my eyes, blinking at the sun pouring into a strange living room. My dogs were asleep on my feet.

Crap. I was naked under the blanket.

"How long have you been with her?"

"A little more than a month." Wan answered. He sounded apologetic. "Can you make her forget this? Forget me?"

What? I started to struggle with the blanket at that point, clutching it close while trying to sit up. Itty and Bitty snorted and shifted, but they didn't even raise their heads.

"Kate?" Wan's voice came from behind the sofa.

I freed my arms and tried to push myself up, which jarred my wounded hand. I muffled my curse as I managed to sit up. "No one's mucking about in my head." I growled, trying to clear my throat and talk at the same time.

Wan came around the end of the sofa, still man sized, a pleased look on his face. "You are well?"

"I am naked." I snarled, lifting a hand to smooth my hair back. I pulled it back to find my hand smeared with dirt and white sticky stuff. "Oh, ick."

"No one is going to muck around in your head. After this long, I couldn't make you forget, even if I wanted to." The doctor came around the other corner of the sofa, a white mug in each hand. Steam rose from the cups, taunting me.

"Coffee." I wiped my hand on the blanket and reached out like a babe for a bottle.

The doctor wisely surrendered one of the mugs. He sat on the coffee table, opposite me.

I ignored him, taking my first sip, eyes closed with pleasure. It tasted as good as it smelled. I sighed and sank deeper into the cushions.

The doctor ... hell if I could remember his name ... studied me with those sharp steel gray eyes. "Your clothes were ruined, filthy and soaking wet. We," he emphasizing the word, "stripped them off you and wrapped you in the blanket."

Wan still hovered, his sword slung over his shoulder. It felt funny to have to look up at him. When I did, his tail flicked up and he clutched it with both paws. "Are you well, Kate?"

"I am not." I scowled at both of them. "What happened?"

"What do you remember?" The doctor leaned forward as he asked the question and laid two fingers on the inside of my wrist. His skin tingled against mine.

I pulled my hand back and rubbed my eyes. "Not being able to breathe."

"You collapsed, Kate." Wan drew a deep breath, his ears twitching. "You fell, lifeless—"

"She's fine, Wan." The doctor said. "You lost consciousness, but we got the stuff off you quickly."

I frowned, looking at the sunlight pouring through the windows. "How long was I out?"

Wan darted a glance at the doctor. "Doctor McDougall saw fit to cast—"

"I bespelled you. We needed to move fast, and I didn't have time for arguments. More coffee?" Doctor McDougall rose, supreme in his overblown confidence, and disappeared behind the couch.

Wan stood there, clutching his tail.

I relented and patted the cushion next to me.

Wan removed his sword and set it on the coffee table.

He sat next to me, his tail reaching out to wrap around my wrist. I was never going to get used to that. But he'd spent a thousand years practicing.

"I feared for you, honorable lady." Wan's warm fur rubbed against my arm. "This man removed the spell on you, then scooped you up in his arms, demanding I follow."

"What about the possum?" I asked. "Did you get him?"

Wan shook his head. "He escaped, along with the remaining rats." He leaned closer, his ear twitching. "Can we trust this man?"

"Do you have a choice?" Doctor McDougall stood over us, coffee pot in hand. I opened my mouth, but he shook his head as he poured. "Drink first. Argue later."

I glared at him over the rim of my mug. "Shower first. I can drink and argue at the same time."

"I'm not surprised," the doctor replied mildly.

"I will assist you, Kate." Wan sprang up, taking his sword and pulling the strap over his head.

I let him help me up, still clutching my precious caffeine and the blanket. The doctor preceded us, turning on lights and getting towels. What a surprise—the bathroom was huge, with a walk-in shower and spa tub. I leaned against the sink for a minute, just taking in the glory of the room, trying not to drool.

"I'll leave you to it," MacDougall said as he left.

"Kate," Wan said softly.

I turned, setting the mug down by the sink, the blanket twisting around my legs. I smiled at him. "It seems so odd, to look you in the eye."

"The spell will not last much longer, or so he said." Wan hesitated, then gave me a deep bow. "I wish to offer my humble apologies. I have brought danger upon you, honorable lady, and I am deeply shamed."

"Wan," I reached out and touched his shoulder. "I don't know what MacDougall said to you, but this is not your fault."

He straightened, shaking his head to negate my words. I could see the pain in his eyes, beady though they might be. On impulse, I reached out and hugged him, sliding my hands under the sheath of his sword.

Wan hesitated for a moment, then wrapped his paws . . . arms . . . around me and buried his face in my hair. His fur was warm and soft, and I could feel the strength in his arms. Paws. Whatever.

"I will defend you with my life," he whispered.

I tightened my arms around him, then released, making sure my blanket stayed up. "Go eat. I'll be quick, and maybe then we will get answers."

"Take your time, Kate." Wan said. "We are safe within this home."

I closed the door behind him and turned to look at myself in the mirror. Lord, I looked like hell. I started the shower and sank down on the toilet to let it warm.

Could we trust McDougall? Hell if I knew. I mean, points for saving my life and all, but . . .

On the other hand, we didn't have a lot of alternatives. Seems the public library was a tad short on information about "possums, the use of magic by." We had to get some information from somewhere. McDougall was a place to start.

But as I shed my blanket and stepped into the shower, I reminded myself of one thing. Wan had some explaining to do of his own. He hadn't come clean, and apologies aside, he damn well better.

To hell with it. For the next few minutes all I was going to think about was soap and hot water. I poured half a bottle of shampoo in my hand and started scrubbing.

I was enjoying the second rinse when the door of the bathroom opened.

I froze, as the cold air swirled around the hot steam and made me shiver. "Wan?"

"The spell wore off," McDougall said quietly. His voice echoed in the tiled room. "I found some clothes for you."

I couldn't see him through the shower wall, but I knew he was there. I covered myself, feeling very naked and vulnerable, suddenly convinced that he had x-ray vision. It occurred to me that I was naked in a stranger's house, a stranger who threw lightning and had talked about mucking with my head. With only a mouse-sized mouse as a protector.

"How do you like your eggs?"

Er . . . it took a moment to wrap my head around that question. "Scrambled."

"Cheese?"

Okay, it was hard to be suspicious of a man offering to cook for me. "Sure." I paused for a minute, but he didn't move. "Thank you, Doctor McDougall."

There was a longer pause. "My name is Sean. But I go by 'Mac'."

That seemed to require a response. "Thank you, Mac."

The door closed, and the steam started to build back up again. I turned off the water and stood there dripping for a moment, feeling as though I'd somehow missed an important part of that conversation.

*   *   *

"Magic exists." Mac said.

My fork full of eggs paused in midair as I glared at him. "That's it? That's all you're going to tell us?"

"Yes. More toast?"

I stuffed the eggs in my mouth and glared at him. They were perfect, light and fluffy with just the right amount of cheese. I can't cook an egg to save my life.

"That seems unfair." Wan was sitting on a small chair in the center of the table, sipping tea from a tiny cup. His sword hung on the back of the chair. "We need to know—"

"You don't need to know," Mac said. "Kate is mundane. Normally I'd be telling her that she'd had a fever dream or was hallucinating—"

"Lovely," I muttered through my eggs.

"I need to know more," Mac replied. "And consult with my colleagues. I will take you home and ward the house. That will keep you safe for now."

I rolled my eyes and slipped Itty and Bitty each a piece of toast. They were at my feet, taking anything they could get and begging for more.

"But first," Mac said, "I need to know what you protect."

"I don't know what you are talking—"

"Not you," Mac said, staring down at Wan.

Wan tilted his head to the side and set his cup down. "How is it that I must speak when you remain silent?"

"I came when you called." Mac said.

Wan studied him for a moment, then gave him a nod. "So be it." He stood and pulled a white paper napkin from the holder. He spread it out on the table and then turned to retrieve his sword.

Mac and I reached out to clear away the butter, jam, and other items, leaving the table clear. Wan walked to the middle of the napkin and knelt down. He set the sword down in front of him and then bowed, knocking his head three times three, moving with great dignity.

He lifted the sword then and removed the red tassel at the base of the hilt. He set that to one side and rapped the sword down three times on the table.

The hilt sprung open.

Mac and I leaned forward to watch, almost bumping heads.

Wan removed a small bundle wrapped in white silk from the hilt and set the sword aside. He placed the bundle before him and again prostrated himself before it. Normally I would have been impatient, but I was caught up in his approach to that bundle. To Wan, it was worth his life.

Wan raised his head, reached out, and pulled the cloth back. There, on the white silk, lay a necklace. Putting his hands under the silk, he arranged it in an oval.

It was lovely, with heavy jade pieces, bright green against the white. The pendant that hung from the necklace was almost circular and an odd color. It looked rough, like the inside of an oyster, yet it seemed to sparkle with all colors in its depths.

For just a moment, I seemed to feel the necklace around my neck, resting cool against my collarbones, then warming against my skin. The pendant would lay upon my breast, heavy yet light, with . . .

"It's lovely, Wan." I whispered.

"You look upon—"

I could barely hear him. The necklace seemed to call to me, and on impulse I reached out and brushed the pendant with my finger, just wanting to feel—

"Kate, NO!" Wan shouted.

My finger touched the jade, and the world went white.

I was floating, suspended between earth and the heavens, hanging freely as if underwater, clouds all around me.

I gasped at the change, then gasped again when cool air rushed into my lungs, with a taste of rain and spring in the air. I breathed again, filling my body with energy and light, lost in the sensation.

The clouds eddied around me, heavy with mist, white and intangible. I started to try to tread the air, to see if I could turn, but my hands passed through the clouds, collecting the heavy drops within. I couldn't move.

Something else could, though. I caught the movement out of the corner of my eye. There was a rumble, as of far distant thunder on a sunny day. I saw a huge form moving in and out of the clouds, flowing like a snake. I had a quick glimpse of scales that glittered all colors of the spectrum. Then a huge head reared up before me.

I'd seen enough to know a dragon. No wings, just a fierce, lovely face and huge teeth and claws. A museum print come to life, the only source of color in the white billowing clouds.

It saw me. Not just me, it saw through me somehow, right down to my soul, and I shook as I hung there, pierced by its gaze. Then it threw its head back, shook its mane, and laughed.

The heavens resounded, and the earth trembled with the sound, as if all of creation shared the joy of this being. For it did not mock, nor was it threatening. It was a joyful sound, and my heart shared in its delight.

It coiled around me, massive and powerful. It's . . . no . . . his eyes were warm and bright, considering me as if part of a series of endless possibilities. The laugh came again, and I felt it in my chest, as if it delighted in this strange happening.

"Let it be so," a voice thundered, and I was thrown back, pitched into a body of flesh and muscle.

"Kate, Kate, speak to me." Wan's voice sounded odd in my ear. He was on my shoulder, tugging at my earlobe.

Mac kneeled by my chair, one hand at my wrist, the other on my chest. I blinked at him and took a breath, feeling so very odd.

"What happened?" Mac demanded.

"I don't—" I licked my lips and swallowed. How the hell did you explain . . . ?

"Oh, Kate." Wan's voice was sorrowful. "You should not have done that."

What had I done?

Itty and Bitty raced ahead of us into the house as we walked in. Mac went first. Wan was on my shoulder, alert and ready for trouble.

Nothing had been touched. Even the computer room and Wan's library were intact.

"I'll go out and cast the wards. You'll be safe within the house." Mac said.

"The dogs," I started.

Mac nodded. "I'll do the backyard as well." He slipped out the sliding door.

I turned to the kitchen, determined to make a pot of coffee. Wan stayed silent as I worked. He'd been babbling in the car, about sacred guardians and destiny, until I had a headache and Mac's eyebrows had climbed into his hairline. I'd told Wan to shut up in no uncertain terms.

Yes, I knew he had things to tell me, but it could damn well wait until I'd had more coffee. About a gallon should do it.

Wan seemed to think that I'd offended the gods by my actions, but I remembered the joy in the dragon's laugh. I might have upset the balance of things, but I don't think he minded that much. In fact, I rather thought he'd delighted in it, truth be told.

I offered Mac some coffee when he came back inside, but he just shook his head. "I need to contact people. Don't leave this house until you hear from me. The possum is still out there."

Swell.

Mac turned to Wan. "Guard her with your life. Whatever has happened, Kate is extraordinary now. See to her safety."

Wan bowed. Mac gave me a nod and left.

I sighed, taking a long sip of my coffee. Hell of a few days. I dreaded checking e-mail and messages, but that could wait. Poor Wan was about to burst with talk, and I needed to hear it. "All right, Wan. Tell me what this all means."

I figure he'd burst right out, but he just jumped down to the counter and stood looking at me, his sword over his shoulder. "Kate, I thought you were extraordinary before you touched the sacred necklace."

I hid a smile in the rim of my mug. "So what did I do, exactly?"

Wan drew himself up and took a deep breath—

Someone knocked on the front door. Itty and Bitty raced for the entryway, farting like crazy and barking their fool heads off.

I sighed. Wan leaped for my arm and climbed up. "Careful, Kate. The doctor's wards are strong but we should have a care."

"It's probably the mailman." I put the cup down and headed for the door, only to find a small army of guys with tattoos and leathers on the other side, staring at me grimly.

"Uh..."

"Lady, your van was found with our stolen hogs alongside I-75. WHAT THE HELL HAPPENED?"

Uh-oh.

The End—or is it?

BATS IN THE BAYOU

By Steven H Silver

Steven H Silver is a science fiction writer, reviewer, and editor who has written several articles for fanzines, as well as publishing his own annual fanzine *Argentus*, and the monthly APA-zine *Plata*. In 2003, he edited three anthologies, *Wondrous Beginnings*, *Magical Beginnings*, and *Horrible Beginnings*, which reprinted the first published stories of authors in the science fiction, fantasy, and horror genres. In addition to his writing and editing activities, Silver is involved in running science fiction conventions. He has chaired Windycon twice, founded Midfan and chaired the first Midwest Construction, and ran programming for Chicon 2000, the World Science Fiction Convention. Since 1998, he has sat on the board of Illinois Science Fiction in Chicago and is also the publisher of ISFiC Press. In 1995, he founded the Sidewise Award for Alternate History and has served as a judge ever since. He has been nominated for the

Hugo Award in the Best Fan Writer category
nine times.

The swamp was filled with the alluring buzz of mosquitoes. N'ctath swooped through the teeming swarms, the thick, humid air providing an updraft beneath her wings, as she scooped up the succulent morsels. The taste of the insects was unlike anything N'ctath had experienced before her arrival on Earth, five years earlier.

Earth, especially the part she had settled in, which the natives called Thebayou, was a paradise. The air was warm and thick, the smells were reminiscent of her home planet, Tseekah, and even the plants resembled the trees back home. It was the animals that lived in Thebayou, however, that really made Earth worth the travel. And the fact that the sentient natives rarely encroached on N'ctath's hunting ground.

She swooped through another swarm of mosquitoes, relishing the way blood filled her mouth as the insects exploded with each bite. The tiny bodies provided a satisfying snap, but they didn't have any real taste of their own. In many ways, they were the greatest thing N'ctath had ever tasted.

A strange purple light caught her attention, and she glided over to see a strange glowing tube encased in a fine mesh hanging from a tree. N'ctath knew instantly that it meant the humans had come into the swamps.

Originally, the Tseekahn had planned a traditional invasion of the Earth, but shortly before the first landing, the final reconnaissance of the planet revealed that an alternative might be possible. In light of the new information, the Tseekahn launched what might be the strangest invasion in the known universe.

A junior member of the intelligence team had come to the admiral with his observations. The primary species on Earth lived in great manufactured concrete habitats, which were not entirely suitable for the Tseekahn. The Tseekahn preferred caves, swamps, and forests, which were often either free of the humans or only lightly populated. Even more important, the junior intelligence officer pointed out, although many of the areas the Tseekahn preferred were already populated by animals, they were populated by animals who bore an uncanny resemblance to the Tseekahn.

Plans were immediately made for the Tseekahn to invade only those areas where their terrestrial cousins, creatures called "bats," already lived. Five years later, aside from a few notes about strange bats, the humans still had no idea that their planet had been invaded by the Tseekahn.

Moonlight glistened off the scales on her broad wings, one of the differences between bats and Tseekahn. As she neared the glowing rod, she noticed a swarm of mosquitoes around the device. One of the mosquitoes got too close, and the air was filled with a loud buzz, a flash of light, and a burning smell as the mosquito was annihilated.

N'ctath saw a small house, its sides and roof made of a shiny fabric. It didn't look like the wood and metal structures the humans usually lived in. N'ctath flew closer to get a better look just as one of the humans emerged from the house.

"A bat!" the creature cried out as it ducked back into its shelter. A moment later, the human emerged clutching a shovel. When it saw N'ctath, it swung at her. She easily dodged the blow and flew up into the trees to keep an eye on the human without being within range of its weapon.

A few moments later, another human emerged from the tent. The two spoke quickly, and it was clear they were looking for N'ctath in the trees. She waited until both of their backs were turned and then flew off.

We had just gotten the tent pitched and hung a bug zapper from a tree. Jack was in the tent, and I went out to start a fire when I saw a large bat flying around the clearing. I was shocked and leaped back into the tent. Schooner started barking up a storm.

"Gimme a shovel!"

"Why're you gonna use a shovel to make a fire?"

"There's a ginormous bat out there. I'm gonna take a whack at it, chase it off."

Jack reached for one of the guns, but I waved him off, "Any fool knows you don't hunt bats with a gun. Just pass me the shovel."

I took the shovel and swung at the flying rat, which managed to avoid the blow, almost as if it saw what I was doing. Must be that bat radar stuff they have. By the time Jack came out of the tent, the bat seemed to be long gone, although Schooner stayed alert, growling every now and then at the trees.

"If we put skeeter netting up around the campsite, it should keep out the bats," Jack said.

"Do we have enough to cover the whole clearing?"

"We can do once around, if we hang it at the right height." Jack pointed at the trees and turned in a slow circle.

I thought I heard the bat's wings flapping in the air; nothing more than my imagination, I knew.

"You wanna get started on that while I build the fire?"

"Be easier if we both do it together. I'll probably have

to shimmy up the trees to get the right height. You can then pass the netting on up."

I nodded. Jack was right. "Let's do the netting first. It'll be dark soon, and you won't want to be climbing once the sun goes down."

We unpacked the nets, and Jack climbed up the cypress trees. I duct-taped the netting to one end of a boat oar and passed it up to him. It took about an hour, with Jack climbing up and down various trees, but eventually we had the netting in place. With the nets to protect us from the bats and the zapper to handle the mosquitoes, all we had to worry about were the snakes, and we quickly laid a coarse rope around the campsite to keep them away.

Once the camp was set up, we'd have two uninterrupted weeks of camping and hunting. It was always good to get away from the plant, but I always do miss fiddling around in my workshop when we get back to nature.

There was a small colony of Tseekahn nearby where N'ctath made her home. She flew back with the news of the human incursion.

"It is only two of the beasts," H'ckess said. "And it sounds like they aren't staying here if their house is only made of plastic."

"Not plastic, fabric," N'ctath corrected.

"Fabric? Plastic? Neither demonstrates that they'll be staying. There is no cause to worry," H'ckess said.

"We can, and should, keep watch over them. Make sure they move on or that we know if more come," Khakreet, the ranking member of the invasion force with this particular band, said.

"It makes sense," N'ctath said.

"I wouldn't worry about it. In fact, I won't," H'ckess said. "In fact, what I'll do is go off and hunt mosquitoes." He flew off before anyone else could respond.

"However, if the humans are moving into Thebayou," N'ctath said, "it might be time for us to move out. We can live here because we look a lot like their bats, but if they get too close, they'll learn we're different."

"I'll contact the colony at Cashone and see if it might make sense for us to move to their colony," Khakreet said. "If that's decided, H'ckess actually did have a good idea for once. I'm off to hunt."

N'ctath watched Khakreet fly off into the trees. She felt very alone, even knowing that at least three claws of Tseekahn were nearby. They were a space-faring race, a race that had successfully invaded this world only five years before, and now all of them were focused entirely on hunting the local animals. With a moment of reflection, N'ctath had to admit that even she was caught up in the desire to hunt, otherwise she would never have been where she was when she found the humans.

For four days, the Tseekahn colony in Thebayou kept watch on the humans. They seemed to have planted themselves, and, although they roamed through the region, they appeared to have no intention of leaving. Khakreet had sent a messenger to the Cashone colony, and late on the fourth day she returned.

"Our visitors are nothing compared to theirs," the messenger said. "While we have a simple *tent,* the human's word for the soft-sided house, in Thebayou, over in Cashone they have actual buildings. Several wood structures, with more going up. The humans use boats to navigate the bayous and get from one building to another."

"Those humans are far from here and nothing to worry about," H'ckess said.

"But we have humans right here," N'ctath responded. "If they have a tent today, they may have something more permanent tomorrow."

"I don't think it likely. Besides that, what do you think we should do?"

N'ctath thought about that. She hadn't really considered the best way to deal with the humans, just saw them as an obstacle, a danger to the Tseekahn colony.

A swarm of mosquitoes appeared near them, and N'ctath watched as H'ckess, Khakreet, and the messenger caught their aroma. It was a swarm that hadn't feasted recently, and without their prey's blood in them, mosquitoes were merely empty and tasteless calories. Nevertheless, N'ctath noted their reaction to the smell of the insects. It was all too similar to the way keers addicts responded when they tasted their drug of choice.

If mosquitoes were as addicting as keers, it meant the Tseekahn had much greater worries than humans on Earth. Later, when they were alone, N'ctath brought her concerns up to Khakreet.

"Interesting," he said. "Although I haven't noticed any negative behavior."

"Tseekahn are dropping everything up and down to hunt mosquitoes and you say there is no negative behavior? What would you . . ."

"No. I wouldn't. The jobs that need to be done are still getting done, perhaps a little slower than you or I might like, but there is really no urgency. We're living under primitive conditions here since we have decided to keep the invasion secret from the aborigines. Mosquito hunting is about the only real leisure activity we have. I don't think it is anything to be concerned about."

Before N'ctath could reply, another Tseekahn flew over and perched on the tree next to them. "The humans have captured H'ckess."

"Call a meeting of the colony," Khakreet said, immediately reverting to his military role. While Khakreet flew up to where a meetingnest had been fashioned in the upper branches of the trees, N'ctath and the other Tseekahn flew throughout the colonized region to gather as many Tseekahn as possible.

The meetingnest was full by the time N'ctath arrived. At least one hundred fifty Tseekahn, more than half the colony, were gathered, hanging from the fine mesh of branches. N'ctath was glad to see that when something important happened the Tseekahn of Thebayou could come together with the same determination that allowed them to conquer several planets using more traditional methods.

After a brief introduction of the news of H'ckess's disappearance, Khakreet allowed Th'kart, the Tseekahn who had first brought the news, to give details.

"H'ckess and I were flying through Thebayou, hunting mosquitoes," Th'kart began.

Damn, there are those mosquitoes again, N'ctath thought.

"We were over where the two gullies come together, and H'ckess seemed to see something and took off to look at it. I ignored him until I heard him shrieking and a strange noise. When I went to look, I saw two of the humans standing in a small clearing near a small house. They had put up nets around the clearing, and H'ckess had gotten tangled in the nets. The humans were beneath the net, trying to reach it with long sticks.

"When I flew back, H'ckess was still trapped in the net, but he was still alive. I called to let him know I was going for help and flew to find Khakreet as quickly as I could."

"A small group should be able to free H'ckess," Khakreet said. "Th'kart and N'ctath, you've both seen this human camp, assuming it *is* the same one. I'll go, and perhaps two more. Volunteers?"

Two more Tseekahn volunteered, and the group flew off toward the humans. As they flew, N'ctath found herself thinking about mosquitoes. Not focusing on their flavor or texture, but rather on the way they seemed to be at the basis of so many problems. Were they as addictive as keers, or was that just a false speculation on her part? Why did the humans set up their small killing device to slaughter any mosquitoes that got close to them? Everyone knew raw mosquitoes were so much tastier than cooked ones.

N'ctath was pulled from her reverie by the sounds of H'ckess screaming in anguish. It was a sound N'ctath had never heard on Earth and only rarely on Tseekah, a high-pitched, undulating shriek. Only a few moments later, the clearing came into view. The two humans seemed to be completely unaffected by H'ckess's pain, although their four-legged animal was making its own noise, clearly showing discomfort at the pain of another living creature.

As N'ctath watched, she saw one of the humans swing its axe at H'ckess. She couldn't tell if the human's blow struck home, but it did tear the netting beneath where the Tseekahn was trapped. For a moment, it looked as if H'ckess would fly free from the net, but instead, his body fell until it was caught by the net. The human started to take another swing with his axe, and N'ctath swooped down on him.

At the moment N'ctath launched her attack, she let

out a shrill scream. The humans' animal yipped and fled. Th'kart and the other two Tseekahn joined N'ctath in her attack. While they distracted the humans, Khakreet worked to free H'ckess from the netting.

A glancing blow from the shovel caught N'ctath's wing. She fell to the ground, and one of the humans started to run toward her. She launched herself into the air and just managed to avoid another blow from the shovel. A glance skyward showed her that Khakreet had managed to rescue H'ckess and get him away.

N'ctath called out to the other Tseekahn. They broke off their attack on the humans, and the four flew back toward the meetingnest.

Along the way, one of the volunteers left them to hunt a swarm of mosquitoes he saw in the distance.

Getting out of the factory and into the bayou was always the high point of my year. The factory paid well, which was about all I could say for it. If I could get a better-paying job somewhere else, especially somewhere that let me see the sky more often, I'd be off like a shot.

Bill was cleaning his gun again, and I could practically see him trying to figure out a way to muck about with it to improve its action. I was tending the fire when the screaming started. I looked up to see a giant bat caught in the mosquito netting we had set up on our first day. There was a second bat, fluttering around the first, but as I moved toward the netting, it flew off, leaving the trapped bat behind.

Bill ran up and handed me an axe, while he wielded a shovel. We swung at the bat a few times, but it was too high for us to reach, shrieking for all it was worth. Bill's worthless hunting dog, Schooner, came out of the tent and added its own yipping to the noise. Although I'd just as soon have swung the axe at Schooner, I focused on the bat we had caught.

Just as the creature dropped lower in the netting, we were attacked by a swarm of other bats that had flown over the nets and dropped on us. I swung the axe one more time and felt something tear, but I also felt a solid connection before I had to ignore the bat in the net and focus on the bats attacking me. Fortunately, Bill and I were far enough apart that I didn't have to worry about opening his skull with the axe.

Suddenly, the bats all up and flew off. I looked over at the torn netting and saw that the trapped bat had managed to get away.

"We can fix that with the duct tape," I told Bill. He seemed to be in his own little world, kneeling on the ground looking at something.

"You want to climb the trees, or you want to work from the bottom?" I asked him.

Instead of replying, Bill said, "What kind of bat has scales?"

I gave him a pitying look. "Bats are mammals. They don't have scales."

"The bat I just hit had scales." He held something up and I took a look at it. It was a brownish-black scale.

"Bill, snakes have scales. One must have gotten over the rope, or it was here before."

"Nope, I knocked this offa that bat," he insisted. "'Sides, does that look like a snake scale to you?"

He dropped it into my hand, and I took a closer look. The scale was a strange triangular shape, coming almost to a point before rounding out. It didn't look like a scale from any of the snakes that lived in the bayou.

"I don't know. So not a snake, a lizard, or a croc or something. But bats don't have scales."

Bill nodded, but his mind was off in another world. A world where bats had scales.

When they arrived in the meetingnest, Khakreet was hanging from a branch, but there was no sign of H'ckess. N'ctath asked about him.

"He didn't live," Khakreet spat.

N'ctath glanced over at the medicalnest. She was too far away to see anything, but she knew what would be happening. The doctors would be performing an autopsy on H'ckess, no longer an annoying, self-centered person but now merely a lump of meat, killed over his addiction to mosquitoes.

An addiction to mosquitoes, and N'ctath had to admit that she was as addicted to them as anyone else. Or was she, or they? Were mosquitoes really the addiction that she though they might be? As H'ckess lay dead in the medicalnest, N'ctath vowed to find out if mosquitoes really were addictive.

H'ckess was not the most loved, or even liked, of the Tseekahn in Thebayou. Nevertheless, with a colony as small as theirs, everyone turned out for his funeral. Khakreet said a few solemn words as the military leader of the colony, and Ghart, a woman N'ctath barely knew, spoke about H'ckess. It quickly became apparent that the two had been lovers, and N'ctath filed away a low opinion of the woman.

At the end of the funeral, N'ctath took only the smallest of nibbles from H'ckess's corpse. Despite what Khakreet and Ghart had said about H'ckess, she couldn't think of any of his qualities she wanted to carry with her. In fact, she didn't even want to carry any memories of H'ckess with her; however, she had to take some of him, for propriety's sake if nothing else.

Following H'ckess's funeral, Ghart and several of her friends went off on a mosquito hunt. It was clear that this was their way of mourning their loss. H'ckess had enjoyed the hunt, and if N'ctath felt there were things of greater importance that needed to be done, well, she wasn't exactly one of H'ckess's intimates. She could easily pursue her own agenda without infringing on the inanities of others.

N'ctath quickly learned how alone she would be. Khakreet brushed off her concern about mosquitoes.

"We've been on Earth for five years," he pointed out. "One of us was bound to be killed by humans eventually. Had we actually fought in a war to invade, doubtless many more would have died."

And he was right. Since their arrival, N'ctath had begun to feel less and less like a warrior of Tseekahn and more like a civilian. Her training had gone by the wayside as she worked to build a colony that had, surprisingly, grown up in peace alongside the natives. Some strife was bound to happen.

But the issue wasn't H'ckess's death, it was the potentially destructive influence of mosquitoes.

N'ctath tried to remember the last day she hadn't eaten a mosquito and failed. The Tseekahn had discovered them within days of their colonization and as word of their flavor spread, they became a staple of all the colonies.

She smelled a large swarm of blood-filled mosquitoes and felt herself drawn in their direction. But no, she wouldn't allow her basest yearnings to dictate her actions. Instead of swooping down on the morsels, she turned and flew off into the evening. She wondered how widespread mosquito addiction, if it was an addiction, was in the other colonies.

Five years. What had they accomplished? They had

found good hunting on Earth, and not just mosquitoes. They had successfully established several colonies without a shot being fired. Their ships were in orbit, undetected, around the Earth, using the human's own space debris as camouflage. But as far as N'ctath knew, all of the colonies were essentially living at a primitive, almost subsistence level. She wondered if she could get Khakreet to call some sort of confab where the various colonies could actually work together to figure out their next steps. Earth was nowhere near ready for an influx of Tseekahn, which was what the colonies should be striving for at this point.

She flew up to Khakreet's nest, but the old officer was not about. Instead, she got to talk to Chaaloth, who acted as Khakreet's aide-de-camp. Rather than just leave a message for Khakreet, she decided to outline her concerns, in detail, to Chaaloth.

"Things are happening," Chaaloth responded. "Khakreet just doesn't announce all of them to the colony. It is a holdover from his active military days. Perhaps not a holdover, since he still sees this as an invasion and occupying force, no matter the reality. In any event, he has been holding planning sessions with the leaders of the other colonies every twenty days."

"When is the next meeting?"

"Two days from now. They'll be meeting in Cashone. Khakreet will be leaving tonight."

Although the Tseekahn were diurnal, they tended to make longer trips at night to coincide with the sleep cycle of the Earth bats and not to draw attention to themselves.

"Is there any chance I'll be able to join him?"

"Have you discussed your concerns with him?" Chaaloth asked.

N'ctath flapped her wings in a way that indicated she had and that he had rejected them.

"Unless you can convince him, I doubt he'll want to take you along. Having you present your concerns without agreeing with you will make him seem weak, unable to control his colonists."

"Thanks, anyway."

N'ctath flew off to the edge of Thebayou, away from the colony. Along the way, she flew high over the camp of the humans. Although the tent and netting were still in place, the fire was dead and the humans seemed to have deserted it, at least for the time being.

That scale didn't come from a crocodile or lizard. It came from that bat. I saw it fall to the ground when I hit the bat with my shovel. And sure, bats are mammals and have fur instead of scales, but *this* bat had scales on its wings.

The bats also seemed to work together when they freed the trapped bats. I've seen bats swarm before, and there is a randomness to it. But this time, two bats came straight for me, and two attacked Jack at almost the same time. It was as if the bats could coordinate.

I've been camping in the bayou my entire life, and I've never seen anything like this. I'd love to take a closer look at these bats. I suggested to Jack that we try to trap another one, but he just looked at me as if I were crazy. I sort of think bats give him the willies.

The moon rose over Thebayou, and N'ctath allowed her eyes to adjust to the illumination. She listened carefully and sniffed every few moments until she eventually caught Khakreet's aroma. She kept still, hanging upside down from the cypress tree, waiting for him to pass, and then launched herself into the air behind him.

One of the best aspects of Earth was that with the denser atmosphere, it made flying and gliding easier. While normally a Tseekahn would be able to fly the distance from Thebayou to Cashone in two nights, on Earth it could be done without any heavy effort, and, in fact, Khakreet and N'ctath could take the time to rest and hunt while flying. While Khakreet hunted mosquitoes, N'ctath searched for sweet, edible fruits. Berries were plentiful, and all offered themselves up, without N'ctath wondering if the berries were filled with blood or were just the empty calories of an unsated mosquito.

In two nights of travel, they arrived at the conclave in Cashone, Khakreet still unaware of his shadow. The conclave itself was not what N'ctath expected. The idea of all the colonial governors meeting had a certain amount of ceremony associated with it. In fact, the gathering looked little different from H'ckess's funeral, although N'ctath knew fewer of the participants. A few she recognized. Khakreet, of course, but also Harleth, Dhaafren, and Sharsheth, the supreme commander of the Tseekahn Invasionary Force.

N'ctath listened as the talk revolved around the incursions the humans seemed to be making into Tseekahn-held territory. Most of the governors were of the opinion that if the humans were left alone, they would leave Tseekahn territory, but a few very vocal governors, including, N'ctath was reasonably pleased to hear, Khakreet, argued for more direct action.

"We came to Earth to fight a war," he said, "That we haven't is entirely due to sheer chance. We cannot let ourselves become complacent. This is the humans' home planet. Just as we spread across the face of Tseekah before venturing into space, so, too, will they fill their world if allowed. We have but two choices. We can fight the humans as we came here to do, or we can flee back to Tseekah, our wings clipped and unworthy of the name Tseekahn."

A swarm of mosquitoes buzzed nearby, their bloated bodies saturating the air with the scent of blood. N'cath realized that she didn't crave them. Whether that was because she had gone for two days and broken an addiction or because they weren't actually addictive, she didn't know. And then she did.

The governors were ignoring the mosquitoes, continuing to wrangle among themselves. A few agreed with Khakreet, but most didn't. Hardly any supported the idea of going back to Tseekah, and only slightly more wanted to get involved in a battle against the humans.

Harleth pointed out, "When we came here five years ago, we had only a limited understanding of what the humans were and their capabilities. Even with our technology, technology that many of us have turned our backs on since landing here, we would have been hard pressed to hold our own in a frontal assault. The humans really do have all the advantages here."

N'ctath had seen some of the governors hunting mosquitoes and assumed they were as addicted as anyone else. Now she saw that they didn't have to hunt the creatures, didn't even notice them if they were working on something important. Between her own actions and those of the governors, N'ctath was convinced that mosquitoes were harmless delicacies as quickly as she had been concerned that they were addictive. Her own fault, she realized, for basing her conclusion on H'ckess's idiocies.

"Who's there!"

It wasn't a question, but rather an order, and N'ctath

hopped along the branch on which she was perched until she was visible to the governors.

"N'ctath, is that you?" Khakreet asked.

She waved her wings in acknowledgement and tried to think of something to say. Her concern over mosquitoes was no longer something she felt the need to discuss with the governors, and even when she thought it was important, she realized now that it paled in comparison to the conversation they were having.

"Khakreet is wrong," she blurted out. The governors, and especially Khakreet, stared in her direction.

"How am I wrong?" he asked.

"There are more than just two options, flee or fight. There is the option of coexistence." N'ctath was trying to figure out what she was going to say next when one of the governors she didn't know spoke up.

"Isn't that what we've been doing? Living beside the humans?"

"No. We've been hiding from the humans." As she said this, she realized it was true. The plan for invasion that seemed so clever five years earlier was nothing more than hiding in secluded areas. Had bats not existed on Earth, so similar and familiar in appearance to Tseekahn, they would never have even attempted to live in the swamps apart from the humans.

"If we talk to the humans, let them know we are here, perhaps we can come to an arrangement."

Jack and I were packing up the tent when the weirdest thing happened. We hadn't seen any more bats since the attack had happened. And we didn't see any bats then, either. Instead we heard a voice. A very odd voice, sort of like what I imagine a pixie would sounds like, except, of course, pixies don't exist.

"Us would . . . I would talk with you to." the squeaky voice said from somewhere in the cypresses that surrounded our campsite.

"Okay, come on out," I called, waiting for a kid to come out. Instead I was surprised to see a bat fly, slowly, into the clearing. I was even more surprised to see a small chain around its neck from which hung some sort of pendant.

"My name is N'ctath. I am a Tseekahn," the bat said.

Jack's mouth was hanging open like he was trying to catch flies. I can't say as I blamed him. Bats aren't supposed to talk. Or wear jewelry.

"Let me guess," I said, "You're from Mars and I should take you to my leader, only I'm not exactly on a talking basis with the President."

"I'm not from Mars," the bat said. "We've been living here for five years and thought it was time to talk to you. You've proven yourselves less primitive than we expected, and we would like to open trade negotiations with you."

"Trade negotiations?" Jack had recovered his voice. "I'm not sure . . ."

I cut him off before he could say something stupid. Here we were, dealing with an alien space bat, and he was going to blow the entire deal simply because we knew that we were only second-shift laborers and the alien space bat thought we had something we could negotiate with.

"We can offer you some of our technology," the bat said, "Starting with these translators." The bat dipped its wing to indicate the charm around its neck. As it did, I noticed that each time it spoke, a ring on the pendant spun around. I'd need at least two of them, one to take apart and one to keep in working condition..

"And what do you want in return?" I asked, knowing I could promise anything but probably not deliver on it.

"We've colonized some of the areas of this world that aren't being used by you humans. We'd like humans to avoid them."

Our talks went on, a study in absurdism. I was talking to a bat, promising it things I'd never be able to give. More importantly, *I was talking to a bat.*

After the bat left, Jack commented, "We're going to be famous! We're going to be rich! We'll be on the cover of every newspaper!"

"Every newspaper you can buy in better supermarket checkout lines." I said, looking into the trees to see if the bat, or any other bats, had stuck around.

"We can sell our story. The newspapers'll pay us, and we can quit working in the factory! We'll be rich!"

"No, we won't. Nobody is going to believe us. They'll lock us up," I said. "And if someone does believe us, they'll take anything we get from the bats and turn the devices over to the government."

Jack shrugged into his backpack and began to walk to the edge of the clearing. I hoisted my backpack. Jack paused, and I picked up my rifle. We left the clearing to head back to civilization. I knew I'd have to convince him that keeping quiet would serve us best in the long run, and I knew that there was no way that two people could keep a secret, especially not when one of them was Jack.

N'ctath returned to where Khakreet was waiting near the humans' camp. Her negotiations had gone much more smoothly than she anticipated. In addition to getting promises that the colonies would be left alone and that trade deputations between the humans and the Tseekahn would be established, she also got a concession of her own, at least from the humans. Now she would have to convince Khakreet and the governors to support her.

N'ctath, however, was sure they would agree and award her a monopoly on the Earth mosquito-export business. She could already picture finer restaurants throughout the civilized universe battling to include N'ctath's Earth Mosquitoes on their menus.

TWILIGHT ANIMALS

By Nina Kiriki Hoffman

Over the past twenty-some years, Nina Kiriki
Hoffman has sold novels, juvenile and media
tie-in books, short story collections, and more
than two hundred fifty short stories. Her works
have been finalists for the Nebula, World Fantasy, Mythopoeic, Sturgeon, Philip K. Dick, and
Endeavour awards. Her first novel, *The Thread
That Binds the Bones*, won a Stoker Award.
Nina has also recently published a young adult
novel, *Spirits That Walk in Shadow*, and a short
science fiction novel, *Catalyst*. Nina does production work for the *Magazine of Fantasy &
Science Fiction* and teaches short story writing
through her local community college. She also
works with teen writers. She lives in Eugene,
Oregon, with several cats, a mannequin, and
many strange toys.

Milo had the run of his yuppie older brother Tad's
house for the month Tad and his wife and three
kids were traveling in Europe. Tad needed someone to

take care of his big, dumb, goofy dog, Paladin, and water the garden. Having the house occupied also meant it was less likely to be robbed, Tad said. Milo was doing him a favor by staying there, Tad said.

Tad was good at looking at the bright side. His wife, Sherry, was more realistic. "Yeah, freeloader, get it while the getting's good," Sherry muttered to Milo as he carried her suitcases out to the car the day Tad's family was leaving. "I'm going to hold you accountable for every missing or broken thing in the house when we get back. Don't think I won't. I took a video of everything and stashed it in the safety deposit box. Don't even think about throwing a party and inviting your college-age drug-addict buddies over here. I don't want to find their stink on my upholstery. I know you're a worthless bum, but I'll find a way to take it out of your hide if you break anything."

"Thanks, sis," Milo said. "I love you, too." So that canceled a few of his plans, because he knew Sherry well enough to know she would sell his organs if she couldn't get money out of him any other way. Not that his buddies were actually addicts, but they were relaxed about things in a way Sherry wasn't.

Milo sat in the back of the van as they drove to the airport, with his two nephews beside him and his niece behind him. Sherry glared at him from the front seat the whole trip, even though he carried her suitcases over to the skycap for check-in before driving the van home. It just didn't pay to be nice to some people.

Anyway, her threats didn't matter. His biggest plan was still greenlit. He was going to get away from dorm life and study a suburban community. Collect data. Write a paper that would make his sociology professor proud. "Daytime Ghost Town, Nighttime Party Town" was his thesis. Or maybe he would call it "A Slice of Summer Suburb Life."

After three days of sleeping really late and watching tons of satellite TV, he went out to test his theory.

He made his first foray around two in the afternoon. He'd read enough detective novels to know a person needed an apparent reason for wandering a neighborhood if he didn't want to get arrested, so Milo carried a clipboard and wore a brown uniform that looked vaguely UPS.

As he walked, he drew a plan of the three blocks nearest his brother's, sketching in six houses on the long sides and three houses on the short sides of Blocks One and Two. Block Three had a different layout, bigger houses, larger lots. Milo noted addresses and names, if he could discover them from mailboxes. He cataloged the types of fences everyone had or marked "nix" where there were no fences and noted whether there were bikes or trikes abandoned in the driveway, barking dogs in back yards, lawn gnomes out front.

As he had suspected, there was not a lot of daytime activity in the neighborhood. Mostly sprinklers. Automated. Some kids were around—he heard shouts from backyards—but hardly any grownups. He observed three young women pushing babies in strollers or leading toddlers to the park on Block Four, beyond the range of his area of study. He wasn't sure if the women were mothers or nannies.

He made his second round at dusk. This time he wore a more relaxed outfit, jeans and a university T-shirt, but he still carried the clipboard. Again confirming his suspicions, life had entered the houses. In the twilight summer heat, many people had their doors propped open, their curtains wide. Some shared their musical preferences with passersby and their neighbors. Milo heard the edges of conversations, saw phantom people on large-screen TVs through living room windows, smelled meat grilling. Other people strolled the street, some of them being dragged along by dogs. There were many cats out in the evening, perching on fences and watching him, darting across the street, rolling in the grass.

And there were possums.

Where he had grown up, out in the country, possums were night visitors, not active when the sky was still half full of light, and you never saw more than one at a time unless it was a mother carrying babies on her back.

When he saw the first possum crossing the street, he almost mistook it for a cat, but it carried its ratlike tail low to the ground, and with its short legs, its movement was more a trundle than a stroll or a lope. Once he recognized the first animal, he started noticing them everywhere.

Almost every house in Block Two and most of the houses on Block Three had a possum lurking near it. Some of the possums snuck up and ate from pet food dishes on people's porches. Others crouched in shadowed parts of the yards, almost catlike in their silhouettes, but not quite.

"What is with this plethora of possums?" Milo muttered. He had photocopied his first map earlier in the afternoon so he'd have a copy for each round he made and could note populations on it, people and things and animals. He used M for man, W for woman, C for child, D for dog, and K for cat (since C was already taken). There were little red Ps for possum all over.

"It's weird, isn't it?" said someone beside him.

He jumped so hard his teeth knocked when he landed. "What—who are you?" he asked.

"Bethany," said the girl. She wore a pale sundress that showed her nice breasts and good legs. Her black hair was bunched into a curly ponytail. Her skin was tan or naturally dark; she looked like caramel given a sultry shape. She had dark eyes that looked wise beyond her years, whatever they were—he wasn't sure if she was a teenager or a grownup. "I've been following you for two blocks."

"What?"

"What are you doing here?"

"Didn't your mother tell you not to talk to strangers?"

"You're not a stranger. Aren't you staying in Tad and Sherry's house? You're Milo, right?"

Milo's shoulders sagged. His clipboard hand lowered to his side. "How'd you know?"

"Sherry, she's not the type to trust people, you know?"

"I know."

"Well, she asked everybody to keep an eye on you and make sure you didn't do anything subversive, like, say, have fun while you're here. I live next door, and I've been watching you. Not that I'd rat on you to Sherry. I'm not a squealer. I'm just bored."

Milo looked at his clipboard, with its neat stack of maps, three for each day of the rest of his stay. He had planned to do one round in the morning (provided he woke up on time), one in the afternoon, one at twilight. He had even thought that he'd go up and knock on doors midway through the process, maybe pretend he was conducting a survey or something, and ask what people did with their days, how many of them were home and why. He wasn't sure anybody would talk to him, but he thought it was worth a try.

Not if everybody knew who he was. That would contaminate his data. He sighed a sigh that started in his toes and worked its way up.

Maybe he could start over, pick some blocks farther from Tad and Sherry's. He was getting into this data collection thing.

"So what *are* you doing?" Bethany asked.

Milo started walking again, and she walked beside him. "Just watching stuff," he said, lifting his clipboard to mark two children playing basketball on a concrete driveway.

"Sounds lonely," said Bethany. "Want some company?"

"How old are you, anyway?"

"Sixteen."

"Somebody's going to accuse me of a crime if I hang out with you."

"Oh? So how old are *you*? Eighteen?"

"Twenty," said Milo.

"We're just walking where anybody can see us. I can tell everybody I'm making sure you don't have any fun."

"Which would be the truth," he muttered. He marked another P on his map. This time the possum was under a hedge. Its eyes glowed red in the dusk. Milo glanced behind him to see if there were any lights shining that might have bounced off the back walls of the possum's eyeballs, but no.

Bethany tagged along as he finished his round of his three chosen blocks. He continued to make notes, including adding in another six possums, four with red eyes turned in his direction, spooky in the fading light.

Milo decided he would pick new blocks tomorrow, but in the meantime, he put his first two maps on the front step of Tad and Sherry's house and studied them side by side by porch light, with Bethany peering over his shoulder.

"That's the Nasser house," Bethany said, touching a house on the daytime map, which had more blank space for writing. "And that's where the Dylans live. This is where Rachel and David Saleh live with their kids, Jennifer and Alison."

Milo stared at her, then wrote down what she said. She filled in names on all the houses on his diagram. It was useless, he thought, to make these notes, since he was going to pick another route tomorrow, but what the heck, he might as well know more about the people he'd be living among for the next three weeks. Maybe he could shift the focus of his study, or maybe, if he kept the data dry enough, he could use what he had. Refocus the study somehow.

"Did you really see all these possums?" Bethany asked, touching red Ps on his second diagram.

"What do you think, I'm going to mark something down that's not true? It's not even relevant data. I don't care about possums. I'm interested in people."

"I knew I'd been seeing more possums than I used to, but I didn't realize there were this many," she said. She lifted the map and studied it, then looked across the front lawn. "Gimme your red pen." She held out a hand.

He gave her his red pen, and she wrote a P on the square in front of Tad and Sherry's house. He lifted his gaze and saw the red-eyed stare from a hunched shadow under the hydrangeas.

"They're freaking me out," Milo said. He stood, watching the possum, and went to the hose coiled against the side of the house. He shook loose a few coils, stuck his thumb over the end of the hose, turned it on, and then sprayed a stream of water toward the possum.

It gave a grunting snarl and turned tail, leaving behind a puff of smoke and a smell of burned wires. Milo shut off the hose.

"What?" Bethany said.

Paladin woofed from the back yard where Milo had left him. "Dumb dog," Milo said. "Can't even bark at an animal when it would matter. He waits till it's over before he adds his two cents."

"How come that thing smelled like electricity?" Bethany asked. "Sometimes they're rank, but that isn't right." She headed for the bush.

"Wait a sec," Milo said. He followed her. "Anybody ever tell you you're an idiot? If something's strange, that doesn't mean you rush toward it."

"You are *so* much more boring than Sherry said you'd be!" Bethany said. She stooped and peered under the bush. "It's gone anyway. Except for—ouch!" She snatched her hand back and stared at reddening fingers.

"What happened?" Milo grabbed her hand and saw the red was a rash, not blood. He peered at the dirt under the bush and saw a twisted piece of what looked like white metal.

"Ow ow ow," Bethany said.

"Let's wash that off." Michael kept a grip on her arm and dragged her into the house, where he thrust her hand under the kitchen faucet. She did some shrieking. He gently washed her hand with antibacterial liquid soap and warm water. The red stopped spreading, but it didn't fade. He held her hand under the light. The skin of her fingers was peppered with tiny blisters. He got out a kitchen towel and wrapped her hand in it, wondering if he should make her an ice pack. By this point she was sitting on a chair, crying.

"I'm sorry," he said. Maybe he should have listened to her when she told him to let go all those times.

"No," she said, and hiccupped, "it's all right. I feel better." Tears ran down her cheeks.

"I should probably take you to a hospital," he said.

"Get that piece of metal first."

"Okay." He opened the tool drawer and got out a pair of pliers, then fished a glass canning jar from Sherry's neatly arranged supplies. He headed toward the front yard, only to be stopped by a Hawaiian-shirted semi-man-shaped mountain.

"What did you do to my little girl?" roared the mountain, shoving Milo back into the kitchen. Seeing Bethany's tears, the mountain took a swing at Milo, who ducked the fist but lost his feet.

"Daddy!" Bethany shrieked. "He didn't do anything! I hurt myself, and he was just trying to take care of it!" She waved her towel-wrapped hand.

By the time Milo and Daddy and Bethany had straightened things out, the piece of mystery metal was gone.

Milo slept in the next morning. The previous night, while he and Bethany and Dad were sitting in the waiting room of the hospital emergency room, Bethany had told Milo which kids were headed to summer camp, what jobs the dads and moms were going off to, who stayed home (only two grownups in his three sample blocks), which houses had nannies and/or maids, and who the neighborhood housekeepers and gardeners were. He had written it all down, numbering each house on his map and then organizing a page of data for each house. Bethany's dad hadn't said anything to confirm or deny Bethany's intel; mainly he flipped through car magazines from the hospital's battered collection of reading material.

Collecting all his data from one informant whose veracity he had not yet had a chance to check wasn't an ideal situation, Milo thought, although he hadn't really talked to his professor about field studies and how they were conducted. Still, he'd lost his taste for making his rounds. If, while he was wearing his little brown pseudo-UPS outfit yesterday, everybody already knew who he was—he cringed, then overslept.

Paladin woofed him awake, finally, around eleven AM. The dog slept at the foot of the bed, all the manners Milo could get out of him, considering Milo was living in Tad's oldest kid's room, and that apparently was the kid the dog liked best. The first couple of nights the dog had actually tried to sleep on top of Milo. Since Paladin weighed more than a hundred pounds, Milo had protested, wondering how his nephew survived the crush of the dog at night. Locking the dog out of the room didn't serve; the dog whined at the crack under the door all night. Leaving him in the back yard was marginally better, until one of the neighbors woke Milo up at three AM. to complain about the howling. Finally they compromised. Paladin slept across Milo's feet, and Milo was happy the rest of him remained uncrushed.

Paladin woofed again. Milo struggled to his feet and pulled on a pair of boxers, then wandered out to the kitchen to get Paladin some kibble. It was only after he'd dished out two scoops that he realized someone was pounding on the front door.

He went to the door and peeped out. Bethany and her father stood on the welcome mat. He opened the door.

"Nice," said Bethany, looking at his boxers. He looked down, too, and realized these were the Valentine ones, covered in hearts with little arrows through them. Bethany's dad grunted something Milo couldn't understand, though he caught the gist of it. He closed the door, dressed, and returned.

"So I was telling Dad about the possums on your map," Bethany said when they were all in the kitchen. Milo fired up the yuppie coffeemaker, fetched his clipboard, and joined the other two at the breakfast nook table. He flipped to the map of last night's walk and showed it to Bethany's dad. Who, surprise, grunted.

"I know," Bethany said. "It's a lot. Hard to believe, except I was there when he was doing this part—" She traced her finger along half the route—"and I saw them, too."

Bethany's dad grunted.

"Yep," Bethany said. She turned to Milo. "We're both going with you tonight." She glanced at the top of his map, saw that he'd written start and end times for his evening observation. "Seven PM. We'll be here."

Milo transferred basic data to one of his empty maps (names and numbers of residents in each house, with the residents' ages, where known), went to Kinko's to make new copies, and then stopped off at Toys R Us to gear up. He dressed as himself for his afternoon route and stopped pretending he wasn't interested in everything he passed. Most of the houses were empty again. He had to get up early one of these days and see the houses before all the kids took off for their summer prisons of day camp, summer school, or planned activities. He hadn't repurposed his study yet. Maybe he should collect the data and then design his paper around what he actually found out.

Maybe he should just spend his summer the way he had when he was a kid, doing nothing but fun things, and come up with some other project a week before school started again.

He should at least give it two days before he gave up. He didn't anticipate showing Sherry any of his data, but he could imagine her sneering at him for again not finishing something he had started. Not that he cared what Sherry thought.

Bethany and her dad showed up at seven on the dot.

Milo issued them each a fully loaded Super Soaker Flash Flood.

"Thanks," said Bethany's dad. He tested the action by nailing an innocent hydrangea bush. "Nice."

As they strolled along the sidewalk, with frequent stops for Bethany to fill Milo in on local unwildlife and for Milo to make notes, they were greeted by neighbors this time. Milo often had to endure introductions. Bethany told everyone Milo was practicing to be a census taker in 2010. He was glad he had his Super Soaker on a shoulder strap. There was a lot of handshaking involved, and people told him more than he could write down.

"How come you didn't use the dog as a spy tool?" Bethany asked. They had stopped on a corner and studied the different directions they could go.

"Paladin is not a calm dog," Milo said. "He'd be pulling my arm out of the socket every time I stopped to take notes." So far they hadn't seen any possums, and Milo was feeling let down.

"Daddy, what's that black van doing?" Bethany pointed down Elm Street toward a block that was not part of Milo's route. A tall, shiny black van was parked in front of a fire hydrant.

"Good question," said Bethany's dad. He glanced at his Super Soaker, then at the van. In a cage match, Milo guessed the van would crush the Super Soaker.

"Hey, there's a possum," said Milo. It was under a snowball bush in the Salehs' front yard. And yes, its eyes glowed red for no apparent reason.

"Do we just shoot it to see what happens?" Bethany asked.

Milo marked a P on his map. "Let's look around some more first."

"What if it's the only one we see?"

"It's not," said Milo. He pointed his pen toward the Ford house. Another small animal shape hunched beside the stone pedestal the mailbox sat on. It turned red eyes toward them.

"Why are they watching us?" asked Bethany's dad.

"We're big potential threats in their environment," Milo said. "Although I'm not sure that's why. But if I were an animal, I'd be watching people, too. Let's find one more, and then we can zap it." He wasn't sure why he thought they should wait for three. Something about leaving a breeding population? Not that he could tell gender in distant possums. Who knew if the first two were boy and girl? But he was giving a nod to ecological correctness. Besides, what could water do to a possum? Get it wet.

"There's one over there," said Bethany. She pointed down the block away from the black van. "Hi, Alanis."

They paused while Bethany talked to a girl about her age for a few minutes. Milo made more marks on his map: the girl (not a woman, not a child; he settled on G), two dogs, and three more lurking possums. Bethany's dad, whom Milo had learned was named Razi, though Milo didn't dare call him that, lurked like a possum, a silent presence behind the three of them.

"What's with all the guns?" the girl asked.

"We're going to shoot a possum," said Bethany. "Have you noticed them?"

"The last three nights," said Alanis. "First time I saw one was after I babysat the Ford kids. Walking home afterward, those red eyes, oh, my God, I was ready to scream!"

"Can we do it now, Milo?" Bethany asked.

"Sure," he said.

"Let's pick one." Bethany pointed to a possum under a hedge in front of the Bliss house. "Ready? Aim—"

"Don't cross the streams," said Bethany's dad as Milo put down the clipboard and swung his Super Soaker into position.

Was that a *Ghostbusters* joke? Milo wondered as Bethany yelled, "Fire!" and they all let loose on the poor unsuspecting possum. It screamed and smoked and waddled away. They all dashed to where it had been. No twisted metal this time, only scorched leaves in the hedge.

"That is not a natural animal," said Bethany's dad.

"Let's shoot another one," Alanis said.

Milo retrieved his clipboard. They turned a corner, located another possum, and fired. This one shrieked as well. It sounded more like a *Star Wars* robot than an animal. Bethany's dad kept shooting it until he'd expended all his ammo, and this time they found a little piece of something in the smoking spot the possum left behind. "Nobody touch it," said Milo. He pulled gardening gloves, pliers, and a glass baby food jar out of his back pocket and put the piece carefully into the jar. It was hissing still. "Now we just have to figure out where to get it analyzed."

"My company has a lab," said Razi. Milo handed him the sealed glass jar.

They searched in vain for more possums, even consulting Milo's map from the night before. All of them had vanished.

Paladin barked his way into Milo's dream about alien possums, and this time he was serious. Before Milo opened his eyes, Paladin gave one last yelp and shut up.

His weight shifted off Milo's feet. Milo knew someone else was in the room.

His bedside light switched on. He sighed and opened his eyes. Two men with short hair and dark business suits were there, the black one with his hand around Paladin's muzzle, and the white one beside the bedside light. They both struck Milo as armed, though their clothing didn't bulge visibly.

"To what do I owe the honor?" Milo said.

The white guy sat in Milo's nephew's desk chair, seemingly unperturbed that it was shaped like a captain's chair on a TV starship. "We've got a bill for you."

"Huh?"

"Destroying government property. You know how much those surveillance devices cost?"

"No," said Milo.

"They're prototypes. This is a pilot project. They each cost more than you could make in a year if you were actually employed, and you damaged three of them."

"I don't have any money," he said, though he suspected poverty was no defense.

"It's all right. You can work it off." The man lifted Milo's clipboard, with its stack of marked and unmarked maps. "We've been observing you, and even though you're really raw at information gathering, we think you have potential. All you need is training."

"But I—"

"Think about it, kid." The man set an invoice down in front of Milo, who gasped when he saw the total. Way too many zeros. "You'd be working for the Department of Homeland Protection, so you know you're guaranteed a lifetime of work. You can get this money somehow—though with your student loan situation, we're not sure how—or you can make this all go away by signing up to work for us. We'll give you training and real good benefits. You have until tomorrow to decide."

Milo helped Tad unload the van of suitcases and progeny. Sherry had griped, griped, griped all the way home from the airport. Europe was full of people who didn't speak English and didn't shave *anything* and smelled bad. The Cokes tasted different. Everything was dirty and small and old. And the house better be in good shape, or Milo was going to learn all about pain.

Milo just smiled as Tad and the kids rushed forward to greet Paladin. He decided he'd wait a while to tell Sherry he had a new job, a new underage girlfriend, and a sociology paper that was going to raise his GPA. Let her stew while he savored.

"What happened to my hydrangea bush?" she screamed.

He'd forgotten to clip off the burned parts. The rest of it looked fine. Oh, well. If it wasn't the hydrangea, it would have been something else. That's what Razi and his wife said. As did most of the other people he'd met around here. Sherry was always complaining about something, and the neighbors knew better than to take her seriously.

Oh, yeah. She'd find out pretty soon she'd lost her neighbor cred.

Milo smiled.

THE RIDGES

By Larry D. Sweazy

Larry D. Sweazy (www.larrydsweazy.com) won the WWA (Western Writers of America) Spur award for Best Short Fiction in 2005 and was nominated for a Derringer award in 2007. His other short stories have appeared in, or will appear in, *The Adventure of the Missing Detective: And 25 of the Year's Finest Crime and Mystery Stories, Boy's Life* magazine, *Ellery Queen's Mystery Magazine*, Amazon Shorts, and other publications and anthologies. His first novel, *The Rattlesnake Season*, was published in the fall of 2009. Larry lives in Noblesville, Indiana, with his wife, Rose, two dogs, and a cat.

1.

The red fox stopped, suddenly, when a rusty floodlight flipped on automatically, illuminating a limestone pillar. Twilight was setting in, and the predator had been pursuing a rabbit that was proving to be more athletic than it should be. The rabbit's scent was overpowering, but the bright light caused the fox to stop and freeze. After a brief pause, she didn't see or smell any immediate danger, and she decided to resume the hunt.

Before moving on, the fox squatted and left her mark at the base of the roughly carved pillar that was wrapped in out-of-control ivy and bind weed. If she could read English, or understand the language of man, the fox would know that she had just crossed a boundary and entered a gathering of human homes known as The Ridges.

The fox was uninterested in the boundaries and languages of man. At the moment, she was only interested in finding enough to eat to last through the night at hand.

Like all foxes, this one knew no boundaries other than her own—but this was no ordinary fox. She had no fear of man—and she *did* understand their language.

All too well.

2.

Kyle Ludlow had been given the unlikely nickname of Kravitz by his ex-girlfriend, Ramona, not long after they moved in together. For the most part, Kyle didn't mind the nickname even though it implied that he was a busybody, or as Ramona was quick point out, after his many quirks had gone from cute to tiresome, he was *more* than a busybody—he was a class-A nib-shit.

As far as Kyle was concerned, you can't argue with the truth. He had accepted his inner nib-shittyness long before Ramona Withers came into the picture.

What Kyle had minded, though, was Ramona's constant nagging and judgmental attitude about everything, from the color of the living room curtains in their furnished apartment to the two "allowed" sexual positions in their brief romantic relationship. She had an opinion about everything, and no one else was allowed to have an opinion that was opposed to hers. Period.

Like *he* was the only one with issues.

Ramona hit the road after a couple of months of living together, and he went back to his nib-shit single life, living in the suburbs, in the basement of the house he grew up in, writing C++ programs at night and caring for his ailing father during the day.

It was an okay life, even though it could be a little monotonous and monastic. He'd sworn off the Internet dating life after meeting Ramona on a website that was supposed to cater to geeks only. She was a geek all right. A control geek. There were worse things than being on a female diet, or fast, as Kyle liked to think of it, but he did get lonely sometimes.

His dad, referred to affectionately as Baba since Kyle could remember, was getting worse by the day, and he needed Kyle more than Kyle needed to find another relationship to destroy—so the fast was okay. Life as a C++ monk could stay just the way it was at the moment.

The nickname Kravitz, however, caught on with his friends (three that you could actually touch, the rest could only be reached by keyboard), family (four cousins on his father's side who lived within a three-mile radius), and neighbors (everyone on Kyle's street knew he was a class-A nib-shit whether they liked it or not), even though most people were unaware of the genus.

Even Kyle would forget, from time to time, that the name had originated from his ill-fated relationship with Ramona.

Kyle was constantly explaining to new people that he

was not related to the pop singer Lenny Kravitz. To start with, they looked nothing alike, and singing was not a talent that Kyle even remotely possessed.

It would've been cool to have Roxie Roker (Helen from *The Jeffersons*) as a mom, though.

He looked like a typical thirty-year-old slacker, a little too hip (in his mind) to be classified as a computer nerd—but he was forever dressed in cargo shorts, T-shirts with stupid quotes like the classic "I'm With Stupid," and sandals, in the summer—so he essentially *was* a classic computer nerd, minus the taped-together glasses and proverbial pocket protector.

His winter wardrobe consisted of flannel shirts, jeans, and hiking boots. His black hair hit the middle of his back and was usually tied back in a ponytail, the only outward sign of Asian ancestry. His Anglo ancestry was more apparent, overwhelmingly so—he was the spitting image of his father, whose family had immigrated to America from England in the twentieth century, save the color of his hair. Baba had a royal profile but lacked the British accent, manners, and bloodline to act as if he were anything other than a commoner.

Kyle's pale skin was void of piercings and tattoos, but neither were entirely out of the question. The right moment had not presented itself, and Kyle's aversion to needles was legendary—he'd screamed endlessly during all of his vaccines—so it was almost a certainty that he'd only submit to a needle if it was absolutely necessary.

His eyes were as blue as a perfect day at the beach, and his skin was quick to burn, which was one of the reasons he rarely ventured out into the sunlight for any length of time.

One of the great things about being a freelance computer programmer, about working from home, was he could work when it was best for him.

Nighttime was when Kyle Ludlow felt most alive, when he was in tune with his own true nature. He had always been more active at night, even when he was a baby, according to his father. His mother, a beautiful girl from Japan whom Baba had met when he was stationed in Okinawa after the fall of Saigon, had died two days after Kyle was born, so Kyle had no memory of her, but he had apparently kicked all through the night, every night, during the pregnancy, right up to the time he popped out, feet first.

People had gotten so comfortable calling Kyle Kravitz that he didn't hesitate before answering.

The Lenny Kravitz thing was annoying, but Kyle rarely had to explain that his nickname was actually a nod to Gladys Kravitz, a character on the old TV show *Bewitched*, which ran from 1964 to 1972. Most people had forgotten about the TV show.

He preferred the first Gladys, portrayed by the actress Alice Pearce. She died after two seasons and was replaced by Sandra Gould, but the show was never the same for Kyle.

He was a trivia junkie, which was one of the few matches on his Internet dating profile he actually shared with Ramona Withers. An addiction to trivia games was one of his many admitted quirks that Ramona quickly grew tired of.

He collected information. It was a great asset for C++ writers.

Bewitched, of course, had two Darrins, and that always made Kyle wonder what was really going on behind the scenes. Something in the water on the set? Or real witchcraft? That would've been a hoot.

Gladys Kravitz was his favorite character because she was always frustrated by her husband, Abner, who failed to notice the odd behavior that came from the home across the street that was occupied by Darrin and Samantha Stephens—who was really a witch. Alice Pearce had great comic timing. Something Kyle felt he, himself, lacked.

Kyle's constant peering out the apartment window every time a car door opened or closed had proven too much for Ramona, who could not have cared less about what was going on five feet outside the circle of her physical being.

"You're worse than Gladys Kravitz," Ramona had said three days into their new living arrangement. She proceeded to call him Kravitz in front of his friends, family, and neighbors, trying her best to embarrass Kyle and change his behavior. Which, of course, proved how little she had paid attention to her new boyfriend and lover. She could no more change Kyle's behavior than she could convince Kyle that the color of the curtains really mattered.

All of this had no bearing in Kyle Ludlow's mind on the day the moving van pulled up in front of the vacant house next door to his father's house, not so long after the not-so-painful break up with Ramona Withers.

But it should have. Especially when Baba went missing shortly thereafter.

3.

Kyle had never known anyone who owned three refrigerators. Two were reasonably normal; one for the kitchen, one for the garage to hold an overflow of beer, soda, and winter meat in the freezer. Baba had always had two refrigerators. Just about everybody on the street did. But three? That was curious.

Why would anyone need three refrigerators? Kyle wondered.

From his vantage point, peeking from behind the closed blinds in the living room, Kyle could see only the big yellow moving van and the two men unloading it. They didn't look like the stereotypical moving men—muscular, tattooed, wearing T-shirts and jeans; instead they were both nearly identical in build, which could only be described as thin and slight, and both had similar toned red hair. Not carrot-top red, but a deep, sunset red, that Kyle found oddly comforting and familiar.

One man wore his hair spiked, and the other, a shorter man by about a half inch, had his hair parted down the middle. Otherwise they looked like twins right down to the uniforms they wore—white Oxford shirts, black cuffed trousers, and tasseled slip-on loafers. There was no logo on the truck or on the movers' clothes.

Neither man was sweating, which may have not been an issue since it was mid-October and the sky was gray, threatening a chilly rain, but Kyle noticed anyway.

Just as he noticed the ease with which both men moved heavy appliances such as the three refrigerators, the three freezers that followed (and looked big enough to hold two sides of beef each), and the two stoves that came after that, without any strain or real effort at all.

Obviously, Mrs. Shirkline, across the street, had noticed the odd assortment of appliances being moved into the vacant house, too. She had walked her dog, Dippy, a thirteen-year-old Welsh corgi, around the block four times since the moving van had started to unload.

Dippy looked as if he was ready to expire as soon as

he stepped out on the front porch for the first go around, but Mrs. Shirkline persisted.

Kyle figured Dippy would be dead before the evening if the moving van wasn't empty by then. That would suit Kyle just fine. He didn't like Dippy. The dog was mean, baring its teeth every time Kyle came around.

For the most part, Kyle didn't like dogs at all. One of his first memories as a child was being bitten by a stray dog when he was playing out on the patio by himself. But Kyle liked Mrs. Shirkline well enough ... she was a cohort, a fellow nib-shit, who would trade bits of news with him when the chance arose and keep an eye on Baba when Kyle had to run occasional errands. He was not as fond of all his neighbors as he was Mrs. Shirkline, and after nearly a lifetime in the neighborhood, not all of his neighbors were as fond of him, either.

It was not often that a new person moved into The Ridges. The houses were well established, over thirty years old—older than Kyle by a year or two, and he'd lived there alone with Baba, who had never remarried, since he was born.

The houses were mostly all brick ranches with double-car garages attached and sat atop cinder-block basements. In all, there were nearly two hundred houses in The Ridges.

The name for the development was derived from the hills that encircled the houses. All of the houses sat in a shallow valley, with the town and all of its services—hospital, grocery stores, gas stations, schools, and restaurants—less than two miles away. It was an ideal suburban location, accessible to every necessity in just minutes.

Most of the houses had yards with several towering oaks or elms in them. Massive juniper bushes covered the fronts of most of the houses, and the sidewalks were uneven, broken by the maze of roots of the giant trees that had popped up out of the ground.

Autumn brought the smells of decay and the laborious job of raking leaves to the forefront of everyone's life in The Ridges. In the days before burning leaves was outlawed, the sky would be so thick with gray smoke that a driver would have to flip on his bright lights to drive through the neighborhood in the middle of the day.

The houses in The Ridges were a little weary, but the neighborhood couldn't really be called run-down. Everybody mowed their yards, planted flowers in the spring, and kept their driveways free of old cars (only because of a local ordinance)—but there was an energy lacking that could be seen in the newer housing developments springing up south of town. The will to keep up with the Joneses had pretty much worked its way out of everybody's system around the time Kyle graduated from high school twelve or thirteen years ago—including Baba, who never really had that inclination in the first place.

So everyone on the street had been on alert since the sold sign went on the Fergusons' old house. Every time an unfamiliar car drove down the street, people stopped and stared, wondering if it was the "new" person. Members of the Welcome Wagon were gathering for the first time in years, putting together a basket of food and coupons from the local restaurants.

The curious neighbors reminded Kyle of a town of prairie dogs, popping up and down at every new noise. The only thing missing was a squeal or two to alert everyone when to dive underground. He knew he could be categorized as a prairie dog, too, but he didn't care. He'd liked the Fergusons, and having someone new next door made him nervous now that he had fully readjusted to life in The Ridges, since his brief foray with Ramona.

The Fergusons' house had sat empty for nearly three years after Lloyd Ferguson died of a stroke. The house went to probate court because he and his wife, Matlida, who had died a year earlier, had no children and no apparent heirs other than some distant relatives in Texas who obviously weren't interested in keeping the property.

From what Kyle could gather, no one on his street could recall seeing a Realtor or the buyers ever looking at the house. One day a red sold sign appeared, and not long after that the moving van showed up.

The identity of the buyer was still a mystery.

And the bets were still on whether the new neighbor would take sides in neighborhood battles that always seemed to be raging about one thing or another—who was mowing over whose property lines, barking dogs, or just plain, flat-out annoyance with each others' existence. Kyle wondered that too. No neighborhood with houses that sat ten feet apart was without its conflicts.

After seeing the three refrigerators and three freezers moved easily into the garage, he hoped they wouldn't join forces with the people who lived on the other side of the Fergusons' old house.

The Pinters were Kyle's archenemies, keepers of more dogs than should be legally allowed by anyone living within the city limits, and they were not amused by his nib-shit ways.

Kyle had called animal control on them more than once, but the Pinters, Lena, Lou, and their three sons whose names all started with L's (and who looked like bulldogs: heavy jowls and a constant stupid look in their eyes), weren't breaking any ordinances. Kyle had checked.

Desperate to get some sleep during the day, but unable to because the dogs barked constantly, Kyle called the police. But they couldn't do anything unless somebody else complained—and all the other somebody else's were at work during the day, so the dogs didn't bother them. That, and Kyle was sure that the Pinters had a police scanner—or were psychic—because every time he called the police, after the first time, all the dogs were quiet and mysteriously absent when they arrived.

He had given up the fight, had quit calling the police, but the Pinters hated him, and depending on the day and how much sleep he'd been deprived of, he felt the same way about them. He avoided them if they were out in their yard, went the other way if he saw them coming. They did the same.

The last thing Kyle needed at the moment, considering Baba's condition, was an enemy next door.

4.

"Hey, Kravitz, what's up?"

Kyle turned to see his cousin Randy standing next to him. "Not much, just getting some groceries."

"How's your dad?" Unlike his nickname, which was available to the world, Baba was Kyle's own special name for his father. Randy was one of Baba's sister's sons that also lived in The Ridges. Five streets over, about half a mile away. Two other cousins and another aunt lived on the outskirts of the neighborhood. It was nice having family nearby, but they weren't particularly close. No family reunions or cookouts in the summer. But they did manage to get together once a year at Christmas time.

"He's about the same," Kyle answered.

It was two o'clock in the afternoon, and the grocery store wasn't very busy. An instrumental version of "Hungry Heart," the Bruce Springsteen song, was playing in the background.

Kyle had been standing just inside the entrance, staring at the bulletin board, when Randy had sauntered up—he hadn't moved.

"Man, that's a bad gig your dad's playing. I hope my mind never goes," Randy said.

There was no mistaking that Randy had Ludlow blood in him. All of the Ludlows that Kyle had ever met were on the short side, less than five foot five inches tall, but none of them had a Napoleon complex. They were agile, almost spry, and all of them, including Kyle, excelled at athletics.

Randy shared the same blue eyes as Kyle, and his facial features were similar. They all had slanted noses and lips that were hardly lips at all, making it hard for any of the Ludlows to smile. It was almost as though they didn't have muscles in their faces that allowed them to bare their teeth. Kyle and Baba had the same problem, and everyone usually mistook their expressions, interpreting them as stoic and angry instead of focused and reasonably playful, which was a truer depiction of their attitudes, expressions, and approach to life.

Kyle was still staring at all of the handmade posters plastered on the bulletin board, barely paying any attention to Randy. He liked Randy well enough, though they rarely saw each other, but something had caught his eye that wasn't making any sense.

"Huh?"

"Your dad. The Alzheimer's. You all right, Kravitz?"

Kyle finally turned away from the posters. "Yeah. I'm

sorry. You're right, it's a bad gig. But Baba still has his good days."

Alzheimer's was a bad word that Kyle refused to speak. He wasn't in denial. There was no mistaking what was happening to his father, but he believed in the power of words, of self-fulfilling prophecies, so he chose not to name the illness that was stealing his father away from him.

Kyle could not imagine being alone in the world. Even though he was thirty and had family in the neighborhood, the thought of living in an empty house terrified him.

A nurse had told Kyle, right after they diagnosed Baba, that Alzheimer's wasn't forgetting where your keys were, it was forgetting that a key was a key, what it was for. One of these days Baba would forget that he had a son and what he was for. The medicines were helping, but even they had an expiration date, and Kyle knew it.

"That's weird," Kyle said, after a long pause.

"What?"

"All of those." He pointed to the posters on the bulletin board. Almost all of them were pictures of missing cats. Muffy. Fluffy. Charlie. All of them had been lost or vanished in the last couple of weeks. There were twelve posters, all told. Most offering a reward, with little tabs offering a phone number. None of the tabs had been pulled.

Randy shrugged. "Fox probably got 'em."

"There are foxes around here?"

"Yeah, I've seen three in the last week. A buddy of mine down the street says one's got a den under his shed. I've never seen so many before. Once, when I was a little kid, I saw one trot through our backyard.

I think you were still a baby. It was a gray one, too. A big male carrying a squirrel. I'll never forget it. The fox stopped and stared at me. I swear I thought it was going to say something. But it just shook its head, flipping the squirrel back and forth like it was proud of its kill, then trotted on. Scared the crap out of me. I never saw it, or another fox, again, until lately. These were red though, not gray like that one."

"Really, a fox could do all of that?"

"Yeah, a fox has got to eat."

"They eat cats?"

"Makes sense doesn't it? People leave their cats all the time, don't they? Little dogs, too. I think a fox will eat just about anything, especially if they have young ones to feed. It's getting to be that time of year." Randy smiled, or tried to smile. His nose crinkled up just like Baba's, and Kyle looked instinctively at his watch. He had told Mrs. Shirkline he would only be gone half an hour.

"I guess it makes sense. I just never considered there were foxes around."

"You don't have a cat, do you?"

"We've never had pets."

"Us, either. Must be a family thing."

"Yeah," Kyle said. He made a mental note to tell Mrs. Shirkline about the foxes. It wouldn't be the end of the world if Dippy went missing, but Mrs. Shirkline would be terribly upset if she thought her beloved corgi had been torn apart by a wild animal—and she might not be able to watch Baba when Kyle had things to do.

"Well," Randy said with a nod, "I need to get a move on. I'll swing by soon and see your dad."

"He'd like that."

"See ya, Kravitz." Randy hustled off toward the beer

aisle, and Kyle glanced back at the missing cat posters, trying to remember if he had ever seen a fox in The Ridges.

5.

Rain pelted the windshield of Kyle's car. The back seat of the VW Beetle was loaded with brown grocery sacks. Kyle had read somewhere that fish helped Alzheimer's patients, so he had a couple of packages of wild salmon that Baba seemed to like, but there wasn't too much other seafood that he would eat aggressively. Fruits and vegetables, especially apples and berries, didn't last long in the house. There was a time when Baba wasn't so picky and would eat just about anything—just like Kyle—but lately he seemed to want only things that were wild, even raw, like salmon. Kyle wasn't opposed to eating sushi, since that was his heritage too, on his mother's side of the family, whom he had never ever met, but Baba wanted his meat raw all the time now.

He made a mental note to talk to the doctor and see if it was normal behavior for eating habits to change so drastically.

It wasn't a long drive from the store to the house, but long enough to dwell on Baba, so he tried to think of something else.

The first thing to pop into his mind was the wall of lost cats. For some reason, even though he'd never owned a pet, the thought of all of those cats gone missing bothered him.

He knew nothing about foxes. Biology bored him. He was more interested in old TV shows than he was about the wildlife that lived in The Ridges—even *Wild King-*

dom with Marlin Perkins hadn't piqued his interest in animals.

Birds. Squirrels. Rabbits. They were just there to annoy the Pinters' dogs and make them bark. He'd just never had reason to pay attention before. Not that he did now. He just thought it was weird about the cats. And . . . the timing.

Maybe there was a reason why the next door neighbor had three refrigerators.

He'd only caught a glimpse of the new neighbor once since she'd moved in, and that was as she pulled her little sports car into the garage one morning, right before he'd gone to bed after creating an application to track stock performance. His eyes had been more than a little blurry—but not too blurry to know a beautiful woman when he saw one.

The top was up on the car, a little European two seater, but the windows were down, and even though it was just the break of dawn, the woman had on dark sunglasses. Her hair was pulled into a ponytail, and she was wearing a skintight running suit—all red, which was starting to bother him a little.

His mind was collecting information and sorting it. Unconsciously, he had created a new application database and titled it RED. All of the colors related to the new neighbor were a subtle shade of red, crimson. Not bright, eye-catching red, but elegant, subdued, if that were possible for red.

The woman moved lightly, athletically, getting out of the car to check the mail, then hurrying back to deposit the car in the garage.

Kyle could not take his eyes off her. Something rumbled to life inside of him that he wasn't sure still existed after his tryst with Ramona—flat-out hunger and desire.

He had an unintended erection before the garage door closed.

Other than that one time, he'd never seen the neighbor again, and it had been nearly two months since the moving van had been emptied and had pulled away into the dark of night. He watched, though, and jumped at every noise he heard, hoping to catch more than a glimpse.

Mrs. Shirkline had said she'd heard from another one of the neighbors (not the Pinters—Mrs. Shirkline didn't like them, either) that the woman was an airline stewardess and wasn't home much. Her name, according to the newly printed name on the mailbox, was V. Volman. The V. stood for Vivian.

There were never any lights on in the house at night, and Kyle couldn't begin to think why a sexy redheaded stewardess would need three refrigerators and be involved in the disappearance of so many cats—but his gut told him that they were all somehow connected.

As Kyle turned into the neighborhood, past the pillars with THE RIDGES carved in them, the rain began to fall harder. Thunder boomed in the distance. The defroster in the VW was about to croak, so the windows were steaming up, but Kyle saw something in the road ahead of him. Maybe twenty yards. A faint outline. A dog. Small. He had time to slam on the brakes and swerve and miss it.

The dog froze and stared into the headlights—past the headlights, really, as if it were looking right at Kyle, trying to make eye contact.

It only took Kyle a second to realize that it was not a dog at all but a fox, a gray fox. It was old, mangy, and wet. He could see the fox's rib cage, see it struggling to keep its breath.

Lightning flashed, and the fox turned its attention

to the sky, looked briefly back into the headlights, then limped off and disappeared out of view.

"Whoa," Kyle said out loud to himself. "That was weird. Randy must have conjured you."

He took a deep breath, still in awe of the sighting, and shifted the car into gear. He let the clutch out slower than usual, crept forward, and had no choice but to slam on the brakes again.

This time, a red fox leaped from the right side of the road, out of nowhere, sped across the road, paying Kyle no mind at all, and disappeared on the left side in just about the same spot as the gray fox. It looked as though the red fox was pursuing the gray fox . . . which seemed odd. It was frothing at the mouth.

Did foxes hunt foxes? Kyle wondered. He shook his head. Of all the things he didn't know about foxes, he didn't think cannibalism was a pattern of behavior.

But, then, what did he know? He wrote computer programs for a living. Maybe he should have paid more attention to Marlin Perkins after all.

He inched home, the windshield wipers furiously waving away the torrential downpour. He could see barely three feet in front of the car.

The garage door was moody, working only half the time, and usually not when Kyle needed it the most, like in a rainstorm or a blizzard. It was nearly an antique, and time and lack of maintenance had taken its toll. Luckily, though, the garage door popped right up when Kyle hit the button.

He was still thinking about the foxes when he got out of the car, but that quickly changed when he noticed the back door standing wide open. Rain bounced off the cement floor, and a cold wind wrapped around Kyle, making him shiver.

"Baba!"

A loud clap of thunder was the only answer he received.

Kyle didn't even think about the raw salmon in the car. He ran through the house screaming for his father . . . but Baba was nowhere to found. The house was empty.

6.

Baba had wandered off before. The first thing Kyle did was call Mrs. Shirkline. The phone rang ten times before he hung up. Her answering machine was obviously turned off.

He looked out the window, and it didn't look as though Mrs. Shirkline was home.

The storm was directly overhead, and the thought of Baba lost somewhere in the neighborhood, not sure where he was, what he was doing, or even who he was, enraged Kyle. Alzheimer's was an evil disease. Sometimes, Kyle wished Baba would have a heart attack and die in the blink of an eye, instead of wasting away day by day, little by little.

He threw a jacket over his head and ran outside, calling after Baba, hoping beyond hope that his father would hear him.

The Pinters' dogs were howling as if it were a full moon, even though it was midafternoon. The clouds were dark. The rain was cold. The heat of the sun was blanketed, hidden, almost like an eclipse, but it wasn't.

It's just a storm, Kyle kept telling himself. It's just a storm, and Baba is safe.

He skirted the Pinters' yard, eyeing two dogs in the backyard that were barking at him furiously. He circled the block quickly, coming up behind Vivian Volman's house.

Lightning flashed overhead, sending tentacles of electricity reaching out into the black sky. Thunder boomed, and it was so close it scared Kyle, made him jump. He was afraid he was going to get struck by lightning.

What would happen to Baba then?

So he ran under the eave of the garage and stopped. His heartbeat matched the downpour of the rain. He was soaked to the bone, and he couldn't tell if it was rain or tears that ran down his face.

The rain started to let up, and Kyle decided to make a run for his house. He'd call Randy. Get the cousins out looking for Baba. They'd helped before.

Something caught his eye as he started to run toward home. The door to Vivian Volman's side-entry garage door was ajar. He couldn't help himself and eased back, stopping just outside the door. All he could hear was three refrigerators running simultaneously. It was not out of the question that Baba had wandered into the garage seeking shelter from the storm. Baba might not know what a garage was any more, but Kyle was certain that his father still had enough sense to avoid danger. At least he hoped so.

Kyle pushed the door open slowly. It didn't creak—it was freshly greased.

The garage was not completely dark; it was lit from the remaining daylight outside, but the storm made it look like it was dusk instead of midafternoon.

An odd metallic smell accosted his nose as soon as he stepped inside. The smell was familiar, evoking a memory he could barely grasp, but somehow, somewhere, deep in his early childhood, there was an incident that involved a lot of blood.

All Kyle could really remember about the incident was screaming, and then screaming more, and then screaming until nothing came out of his mouth until Baba appeared out of nowhere and promised that he was safe.

There was no such comfort now. But the smell was definitely blood, and the memory was strong. It was his turn to save Baba. Times sure had changed.

For a moment Kyle thought about turning on a light, but he realized that he was trespassing. Vivian Volman might even think he was a burglar, shoot first and ask questions later, if she was the kind of woman who kept a gun in the house. Since she appeared to live in the house alone, Kyle assumed Vivian Volman *was* the kind of woman who kept a gun in the house, so he decided against turning on the light.

He could see a little way in front of him, from the light coming through the door.

The refrigerators were to his left a few feet, lined up against the back wall. One of them kicked off. A whirling fan blade sounded like something was dripping on it. Plop. Whirl. Plop. Splatter. Splatter.

"Baba, are you in here?"

Silence. No answer.

"It's me, Kyle. Please be here."

He took a deep breath, thought about running home when no answer came again. But his curiosity easily won him over, and he didn't budge Even he couldn't argue that Gladys Kravitz would not have opened the doors to all three refrigerators in Samantha Stephens' garage, given half the chance.

So . . . reluctantly, looking over his shoulder first . . . Kyle opened the first refrigerator. It was empty and smelled brand new, as if it had never been used.

The second refrigerator was new and empty, too.

He was starting to feel relieved. There had been no question in his mind that the refrigerators were being used to house all of those missing cats ... That's exactly what he had expected to find. Of course, three refrigerators full of dead cats would have only confirmed his suspicions. Then he would have been compelled to find out what the reasoning was, why Vivian Volman was collecting cats in the first place. He was really, really, glad that he was wrong. Vivian Volman didn't look like a cat killer.

The third refrigerator was at least thirty years old. It was olive green, not white like the other two, and it was dented and scratched up. The drip, drip, drip on the fan blades was coming from this refrigerator. A little voice in the back of Kyle's mind urged him to run home, but he couldn't ... he just couldn't leave without seeing what was inside the old refrigerator. So he opened the door, and a scream froze deep inside his chest.

Kyle could not move.

Time stopped.

He wasn't even sure if he was breathing.

He was awash in the light emanating from inside the refrigerator. Thunder boomed overhead. Flashes of lightning reached across the floor, hurting Kyle's eyes even more than they already were. The inside of the garage was filled with strobe light effects. Nothing seemed real or reachable.

The refrigerator was not stuffed with dead cats as Kyle had expected.

It was stuffed with dead foxes.

Partial foxes. Fox heads. No bodies. Cleanly sheered at the neck. All staring at him as if they expected him to help them ... but it was too late. Rivulets of blood ran down the back of the refrigerator.

Each shelf was lined with exactly six fox heads, with the exception of the top shelf . . . there were five there . . . room for one more.

All of the heads were facing forward, all placed equal distances apart. And all of them were red. Red foxes. Like the one he had seen as he pulled into The Ridges, chasing the gray fox.

Nothing made sense at the moment. Kyle shook his head and slammed the door shut.

"Help me."

It was a whisper.

Baba's voice.

But Kyle couldn't see anything, couldn't begin to process that he had somehow missed Baba when he came into the garage.

He cracked opened the refrigerator door, ignoring the severed fox heads as best he could, to give himself a bit more light. His stomach lurched at the sight.

This time he saw Baba.

His father was balled up in the corner of the garage, naked, holding his throat as tight as he could, keeping blood from pumping out. It looked as though the carotid artery had been cut clean open.

Baba's eyes were filled with terror, and Kyle had the distinct feeling that something, or somebody, was standing directly behind him.

7.

A million questions ran through Kyle's mind, but there wasn't time to do anything but try to save Baba—he wasn't thinking, wasn't afraid, wasn't anything but focused on helping his injured father.

If there was something behind him . . . it could just

bring it on. Baba was hurt, and he'd tear through cement walls to get to him if he had to.

Kyle took a step forward, but he didn't move. A strong hand appeared out of nowhere and held him back. He cocked his head and came face to face with the most beautiful woman he had ever seen.

Vivian Volman was staring back at him, holding him with more strength than he thought a woman could possess.

"He won't recognize you yet. Wait."

"But . . . he's hurt," Kyle said.

"I am here to make sure nothing happens to him."

Confused, but oddly comforted, Kyle submitted even though he was afraid and could not even begin to forget the fox heads in the refrigerator. "You're too late."

"Maybe."

Vivian had soft, thick, red hair—the most beautiful hair he had ever seen, though the sheen seemed to be fading, becoming less lustrous by the second. Her eyes were almost golden with distinct vertical slits, almost like a cat's eye.

When she blinked, the pupil was normal, black and round . . . he must have been seeing things . . . and the color was more green than golden. The light in the garage was playing tricks on his eyes.

He pulled to get to Baba again.

"Wait."

Kyle watched his father struggle, watched the wound on his throat close up and heal itself as though it had never been there in the first place.

There were also wounds on Baba's legs . . . it was a wonder he could walk, they looked so deep. At the very least, Baba had limped into the garage. In another blink, those wounds vanished, just like the slit on Baba's throat.

Vivian Volman relaxed her grip. "We haven't much time."

Kyle rushed to his father, ignoring his confusion.

Baba reached up to him. "I'm sorry."

There was a lucidity to Baba's voice, to his eyes, that Kyle had not seen or heard in a long time.

"Are you all right?" He took his father's hands and allowed himself to be pulled down so they were face to face.

"I'm dying."

"No."

"Yes. I should have prepared you, but I didn't expect to be sought out."

Vivian Volman was suddenly standing next to Kyle. Her fists were clenched. "You were hunted," she said to Baba.

"I was foolish to believe no one would notice us now," Baba said. He looked up at Vivian. "He does not know what we are."

Vivian nodded, started to say something, but another loud thunderclap exploded overhead. Fingers of lightning reached in through the side-entry garage door. Her words stopped in her throat. After the thunder subsided, all Kyle could hear was a low, gurgling growl.

Mrs. Shirkline was standing in the doorway with Dippy stuffed in one arm, a butcher knife dangling from the other hand. She was not alone.

The Pinters, with all of their growling, snarling dogs, stood behind her ... armed with picks, axes, and shovels. They were trapped. But Kyle didn't know why or by what.

8.

Kyle stood up, but Vivian pushed him back down. "Leave this to me," she said.

There was no mistaking that she was a warrior. Her muscles were flexed, her eyes focused like those of the most highly trained martial artists he had ever seen.

Vivian cocked her head up and yipped three times as loud as she could.

Mrs. Shirkline laughed. Her face looked mangled, all twisted up with hate, scratched down the side, caked with blood, as if she had already seen battle. In one swift motion, the old corgi, Dippy, jumped from Mrs. Shirkline's arm and came running at Vivian with its teeth bared, snapping wildly.

Kyle cowered, protecting Baba as best he could.

Vivian kicked out to the side, and the dog went flying with a loud yelp, falling to the ground with a whine. It was a powerful kick. The dog wasn't getting up any time soon.

Rage crossed Mrs. Shirkline's face. Kyle wanted to; call out to her, tell her to stop, ask what she was doing, she was supposed to be his friend. Well, maybe she wasn't his friend after all. Something told him she had hurt Baba, tried to kill him.

Mrs. Shirkline rushed toward Vivian, swinging the knife. The Pinters followed. They let their dogs loose as soon as they broke through the door.

The storm continued to clap and boom outside.

Mrs. Shirkline and Vivian were engaged in serious hand-to-hand combat. They looked equally matched. Mrs. Shirkline was surprisingly agile for such an old woman.

The dogs charged Kyle and Baba, surrounding them

immediately. They snapped and barked. Kyle could smell the dogs' breath. It smelled like blood. The Pinters and all their sons laughed.

Kyle was not only afraid for Baba, but he was certain he was going to die . . . and he wasn't sure why. The neighborhood had gone nuts.

Vivian yipped again. This time louder, more desperate, as Mrs. Shirkline punched her square in the nose, sending her flying against the same wall as Dippy. The dog attacked Vivian's ankle, and she screamed as if she had just stepped into a vat of acid.

Kyle was trapped, cornered. He heard Baba say something . . . but he couldn't quite make it out right away.

"It's time. It's time."

The big double-bay garage door flung open, letting in the rain, the wind. The movers Kyle had seen cart in the refrigerators, still dressed in white Oxford shirts, black cuffed trousers, and tasseled slip-on loafers, rushed into the fight.

The two movers immediately attacked the Pinter boys. Randy and all of Kyle's cousins rushed into the fight. But not soon enough to get at the dogs that surrounded Kyle and Baba. One of the dogs, a German shepherd mix, had Baba by the throat. Baba did not fight or struggle. He did not fight back. It was almost as though he wanted to die.

Kyle reached out to Baba, tried to stop the dog, but it bit him, drawing blood, stirring something deep inside of him that he had not known existed. He was changing, transforming, becoming his one true self.

But he was too late to save Baba. He heard his father yelp, then saw the life go out of him, saw him fall limply to the ground and transform into the wet, mangy, old gray fox who had jumped across the road in front of Kyle only an hour before.

Kyle fought with an enthusiasm that suddenly came easily to him. It was kill or be killed. The melee continued for what seemed like an eternity but in reality was probably only a few minutes. Time for a fox was much different than it was for a human.

When the last bite had been taken and the last drop of blood had fallen to the ground, Mrs. Shirkline lay on the floor dead. Baba was dead. Kyle had a few scrapes and bruises as he stood up on two feet, transforming back into a human.

His legs fell out from underneath him, and he collapsed to the floor.

Vivian was alive, her injuries not life threatening, but she would be out of commission for the foreseeable future. She was on the floor next to Baba, sobbing.

The Pinters were nowhere to be found. A few of their dogs lay dead.

Randy helped Kyle up. "Come on, let's get you home."

The two movers were unhurt. They set about cleaning up the mess as quickly as possible.

Kyle had a million more questions, but now wasn't the time. His heart was broken. He had lost Baba. But at least he had been given the chance to stand and fight for him. Alzheimer's did not steal Baba away in the middle of the night.

9.

Vivian was sitting next to Kyle's bed when he awoke. "It wasn't a nightmare was it?" he asked.

"No."

"Baba's still dead, isn't he?"

"Yes."

Kyle hesitated. "If Baba is really dead . . . then what are you? What am I?"

Vivian had a scar under her eye, but other than that she looked unhurt. She was still the most beautiful woman Kyle had ever seen. "Do you know the legend of werewolves?"

Kyle nodded. Of course he knew the legend. He'd seen the movies as a kid. Lon Chaney, Jr. was his favorite Wolfman.

"They are our cousins," Vivian continued.

"Cousins?"

"We are werefoxes. Canines still. The strain does not just affect wolves."

"Baba was a . . . monster?"

"A werefox, yes. A monster, no. There was never a gentler creature than your father."

"And my mother?"

"No, she was human." Vivian said. "That is why she died at your birth and why you only showed varying signs and talents but did not transform fully. Your father felt that guilt for many years. He hoped that you would be saved from the pain of knowing the truth. But now you know."

"When it was too late to save Baba. Why didn't he tell me sooner?"

Vivian shrugged heavily. "I failed you, failed your father. He was a fine leader for many years . . . he was protecting you, just as I was charged with protecting him, once we knew for sure that he was dying."

"Why did Mrs. Shirkline want to hurt him?"

Vivian stiffened. "She was a slayer. The Pinters worked for her. Your father was strong enough to keep them at bay for a very long time. Randy and your cousins were his strength. There are more slayers out there. More that want to wipe us from the world. This will not be the last battle."

"I don't want any of this," Kyle said. "I want to live my life like I was living it before, writing C++ programs in the basement, loving Baba as much as I could. I don't want this."

Vivian stood up, leaned over, and kissed Kyle on the forehead. "None of us do."

She headed for the door but stopped when Kyle asked, "Why are there heads in the refrigerator? How do I know you're telling me the truth?"

"Because you walked in the skin of the fox. You became. You are one of us. You can smell me now. Just like I can smell you." She hesitated. "If a slayer takes one of us, they take our power. They cannot take anything if they don't have the entire body. We will bury our dead now that your father's power is safe within you. We will be safe from the slayers for now."

10.

Kyle stood at the window watching the two fox kittens playing in the back yard. He and Vivian had built a den under the shed, and he had been given a son and a daughter. Baba would have been proud.

Loving Vivian was not difficult. She was gorgeous. She knew his one true self and accepted him for what he was—unlike Ramona Withers.

Kyle did not know he could be so happy. He only wished Baba were around to see it—and he worried, now that he had children, about Mrs. Shirkline's old house across the street, which was for sale. He was more than a little concerned the new neighbors would have dogs, would be slayers looking to strike the werefoxes from the world.

As Kyle listened to his children laugh and watched them romp with their mother, he took a deep breath and knew all was well in The Ridges.

For the moment.

ABOUT THE EDITORS

Martin H. Greenberg is the CEP of Tekno Books and its predecessor companies, now the largest book developer of commercial fiction and nonfiction in the world, with over 2,100 published books that have been translated into thirty-three languages. He is the recipient of an unprecedented three Lifetime Achievement Awards in the science fiction, mystery, and supernatural horror genres—the Milford Award in Science Fiction, the Bram Stoker Award in Horror, and the Ellery Queen Award in Mystery—the only person in publishing history to have received all three awards.

Kerrie Hughes lives in Wisconsin after traveling throughout the states and seeing a bit of the world, but she has a list of more travels to accomplish. She has a marvelous husband in John Helfers, four perfect cats, and a grown son who is beginning to suspect that his main purpose in life is to watch said cats and house while his parental units waste his inheritance on travel. Thank you, Justin. She has written seven short stories: "Judgment" in *Haunted Holidays*, "Geiko" in *Women of*

War, "Doorways" in *Furry Fantastic,* and "A Traveler's Guide to Valdemar" in *The Valdemar Companion.* And with John Helfers: "Between a Bank and a Hard Place" in *Texas Rangers,* "The Last Ride of the Colton Gang" in *Boot Hill,* and "The Tombstone Run" in *Lost Trails.* She has also written nonfiction, including the article "Bog Bodies" in *Haunted Museums,* and has edited two concordances for *The Vorkosigan Companion* and *The Valdemar Companion. Gamer Fantastic* is her seventh coedited anthology, along with *Maiden, Matron, Crone, Children of Magic, Fellowship Fantastic, The Dimension Next Door,* and *Zombie Raccoons and Killer Bunnies.* She hopes to finish the novel she's been writing forever in between getting her master's degree in counseling and working full time for an evil corporation.

There is an old story...

...you might have heard it—about a
young mermaid, the daughter of a king, who
saved the life of a human prince
and fell in love.

So innocent was her love, so pure her
devotion, that she would pay any price for the
chance to be with her prince. She gave up her
voice, her family, and the sea, and became
human. But the prince had fallen in love with
another woman.

The tales say the little mermaid sacrificed her
own life so that her beloved prince could find
happiness with his bride.

The tales lie.

Danielle, Talia, and Snow return in

The Mermaid's Madness
by Jim C. Hines

"Do we *look* like we need to be rescued?"

DAW 109

Jim Hines

The **Jig the Goblin** series

"Clever satire… Reminiscent of Terry Pratchett
and Robert Asprin at their best."
—*Romantic Times*

"If you've always kinda rooted for the little guy,
even maybe had a bit of a place in your heart for
Gollum, rather than the Boromirs and Gandalfs
of the world, pick up *Goblin Quest*."
—*The SF Site*

"This exciting adult fairy tale is filled with
adventure and action, but the keys to the fantasy
are Jig and the belief that the mythological creatures are real in the realm of Jim C. Hines."
—*Midwest Book Review*

"A rollicking ride, enjoyable from beginning to
end… Jim Hines has just become one of my
must-read authors." -—Julie E. Czerneda

GOBLIN QUEST	978-07564-0400-0
GOBLIN HERO	978-07564-0442-0
GOBLIN WAR	978-07564-0493-2

To Order Call: 1-800-788-6262
www.dawbooks.com

DAW 100

Tanya Huff

Tony Foster—familiar to Tanya Huff fans from her
Blood series—has relocated to Vancouver with Henry
Fitzroy, vampire son of Henry VIII. Tony landed a
job as a production assistant at CB Productions, iron-
ically working on a syndicated TV series, "Darkest
Night," about a vampire detective. Tony was pretty
content with his new life—until wizards, demons, and
haunted houses became more than just episodes on
his TV series...

"An exciting, creepy adventure"—*Booklist*

SMOKE AND SHADOWS
0-7564-0263-8 $7.99
SMOKE AND MIRRORS
0-7564-0348-0 $7.99
SMOKE AND ASHES
0-7564-0415-4 $7.99

To Order Call: 1-800-788-6262
www.dawbooks.com